Awake Under the Night Sky

Vanya Sharma

For my lovely daughters, Ayra and Alyosha, who mean the world to me

ACKNOWLEDGMENTS

'Awake Under the Night sky', though written by me, is a result of contributions from so many people. I cannot express how thankful I am for having such wonderful people, and their constant support, in my life.

Thanks to my parents who have made me confident enough to be able to pursue my dreams. If it was not for the self-belief which was nurtured in me as a child, I would have never been able to write this book. Thanks to all my family and friends, who were the first ones to read drafts of the book. They not only gave me valuable feedback but also a lot of encouragement. It is because of all of you that my story came to life. Special mention of Esha Tyagi, who has pretty much read every draft of my book, from the very first to the last. She has been my ultimate critic and beta-reader in the long journey of three and a half years.

Thanks to Reetuj Tyagi & Angie, for translating my ideas into a fabulous cover and being so patient with all the changes that I suggested.

Thanks to my husband, Rahul, for putting up with all my book talk for months and years.

Thanks to my editorial team for all the effort they put in. I am indebted to Purti Bhatia for the exceptional structural feedback. Special gratitude to my editor Michael Faulkner, for so thoroughly editing the book. To Thomas Mayo for proof reading and picking up all the mistakes which I was blind to. To Matthew for beautifully formatting the book.

Thanks to all my beta readers for their feedback and words of encouragement. It was what I held on to. There are so many more I want to name but the list would just go on!

Chapter One

2000

The cold water beneath his body felt brutal, washing him back and forth remorselessly, the cold piercing him, stabbing him at will. His aching body and the pounding in his chest told him that he was, at least, alive. Alive, but with a searing pain. His limbs refused to respond to the demands of his dulled and weary brain; he had no option but to clutch the thin raft on which half his body lay. Where was he and how did he get here? He had no answers, no recollection. Beneath the gloomy sky he lay, hopelessly, not knowing what would come next.

Even in this condition, he refused to let the sea intimidate him – after all, he had grown up swimming in these waters. The darkness around him had to be explored, if only he could get his eyes to stay open. He had to gather himself, but the jolts of pain at the back of his head and neck were taking over, and he felt himself on the edge of an abyss. His scream for help was not audible to his ears; it was frozen in his throat.

A childhood memory of he and his mother laughing, running across the green fields, flashed through his mind. The memory woke him with a start and left a familiar emptiness in his heart. He didn't know if any of the salty water that lapped at the raft belonged to him. Surely not; although tears rose from the depths of his heart, no longer was his grief allowed to run over.

His eyes flickered open in another vain attempt at wakefulness, but all he saw was a flash of lightning before they closed again. At least he was still above the water – cold air, mixed with rainwater, filled his mouth. Thoughts were playing in his brain like clips from a motion picture. The image of his father, extending his hand to grab hold of him, added to his misery. He could not do this to his father, not now, not after what had happened almost a year ago, in the cruel winter of despair. He had to force himself to wake, to resist the water, to rise up and breathe the air above.

A few distant voices started to filter through, into his consciousness. He thought he heard his name. Was he imagining it or was someone actually looking for him? The sea was harsh, and the waves had begun to splash madly onto the thin wooden raft to which he clung. Fear that it might break apart sent a wave of panic through him, but his body still refused to react. Only his curled fingers seemed to move, gripping the edge more tightly. The splinters of the wooden raft rubbed at his numb skin as he desperately tried to move his arms. The voices meant that there were people around, his only hope in this vast ocean.

The voices got even louder – and then, a yell. 'Look! Over there … Over there, dammit … hurry!' There was commotion after that – broken sentences, yelling, and the roar of a motor boat. Andre regained some semblance of normal sensation. Someone was trying to check for signs of life, feeling his heartbeat, warm hands touching his forehead and the sides of his neck. Then the words became clearer.

'He's alive. Oh Lord, he's alive.' He recognised the choked voice to be his father's. It almost sounded like a whimper, and a rush of warm air, tinged with the faint smell of wine, caressed his cheek. He imagined his father tracing the form of the cross, his hands moving by habit, echoing the sacred shape. Other, less familiar voices rose above the noise of the rain splattering on the thin wooden raft.

He felt himself being lifted, firm hands around his shoulders, legs and back. His body was being moved from the raft to a surface that felt like rubber. The raindrops had become fiercer and were wildly dancing on his face; the wind echoed in his ears and he was aware of another flash of light, followed by a roll of thunder. But it was the sound of human voices, infused with concern, which gave him much needed hope. Again, strong hands were lifting him, and this time he was lowered onto a harder, more unyielding surface.

The voices faded away and the cold water was no longer beneath him. Instead it was the damp wooden deck of a boat; he recognised the pungent smell of salt-laden timber.

He knew now that he would live. Live to restore everything to the way it had been, to the way it should be.

He had to get a hold of himself. He could not remember how he had ended up on the raft; his tired brain flashed images of a few of his friends, but all else was shrouded in darkness. He could sort that out later, but for now he allowed his senses to submit to the sweet embrace of slumber.

The barrier between day and night remained blurred for what seemed like weeks. He tried to remember what had happened, but only fleeting and broken images came to his mind, nothing from which he could make any sense.

When he woke, the sun was piercing his eyes from a chink in the curtained window and he could smell pasta sauce, a familiar aroma mixed with that of red wine.

Wine ... That's it, I was drinking with the usual group, we were definitely drinking, but that can't be what hit me. I don't remember having more than a few glasses. It had to be something else.

His father came in with a plate of pasta.

'It smells delicious.'

His papà responded with a faint smile.

After eating in silence for a few minutes, Andre asked,

'How is the factory, Papà?'

'It's the same.' As much as Andre did not want to let the conversation end, he knew it was painful for his father – the sadness which came over his face at the word 'factory' spoke volumes. He switched topic and returned to his own broken and distracted thoughts, desperately hoping that he would remember something as he talked.

'I don't know what happened that evening. I'd just had a few drinks, not too much …'

His father was listening to him, staring over the top of his bifocals, his eyebrows raised and his breathing becoming deeper. He continued to listen as Andre related the broken fragments of a reality which was wiped from his memory.

When he got to the last piece of penne, Andre said, 'I want to speak to Giovanni. We were together – he will know.'

'It does not matter, Andre. You are fine and that's what matters.' His voice was firm, in complete contrast to the way he looked. 'Talking about it is meaningless. What happened is in the past – it's the future you need to embrace.' He took the plate from Andre and let him slip back under the sheets. Andre had a feeling his papà was not merely talking about the incident. His words meant more than that.

Andre looked up at the ceiling and said, 'Same holds true for you, Papà.' He closed his eyes, immediately regretting his words.

He heard his father shift in the leather chair as he replied, 'I am trying, son ... I'm trying.'

Andre felt the pain in those words, and when he turned his bandaged head towards his papà, what he saw made him feel worse. Here was a father standing helpless and broken, trying to come to terms with reality and worried for his twenty-year-old son. Andre wanted to soothe those lines on his forehead, see his lips curve into a smile again and brighten his face as they used to. He extended his bruised hand to meet his father's, told him that it would all be fine; then the sedatives started to kick in and he was floating again, into a state of delirium.

Chapter Two

Sergio Paolo left the room thanking the Lord for saving his son. The damage done by the fall could have been a lot worse; it had been a long way down but Andre's jacket had caught a jagged rock and that had not only slowed his fall but reduced the impact. Even when he had been close to succumbing, Andre must have forced himself to swim and then to cling to the thin wooden raft on which they had found him. That's what made Andre different from him – the boy was strong, with an even stronger willpower.

Giovanni had come running to Sergio in a state of hysteria, telling him that Andre had fallen into the sea and that others were there, trying to find him. 'Trying' was the word that almost stopped Sergio's heart. The waves had been particularly strong that day, and the wind high. Sergio had run as never before, shouting curt instructions to Giovanni to find a few others. The run to the boat had taken a lifetime; even now there was sweat clinging to his skin at the mere thought of Andre lying helpless in the sea.

He gulped wine from the glass he still held in his hand, as the dryness in his throat spread like a desert.

Andre got out of bed the next day – or the one after, he couldn't be sure – and went to the window to take in some fresh air. This small act took much of his energy. Exhaustion made him cling to the armchair by the window, and after a few minutes he climbed back into bed. It was late afternoon, and suddenly his bedroom door creaked. It was Giovanni – finally. Andre could not contain himself.

'Where the hell have you been? What the fuck happened? How did I end up out there, at sea?'

'Calm down. Just hear me out.' Giovanni looked worried, almost flustered as he went on, 'I came here many times, but there is a reason why Uncle Sergio did not let me see you. He thought you would get too agitated, and he was right – look at you! So first, just calm down.'

He sounded absolutely unlike Giovanni, he sounded in control and responsible; he was normally neither.

'Okay, fine. Tell me what happened.' Andre irritably adjusted the pillow stack behind him.

'We were all drinking, you remember that?'

Andre nodded and Giovanni continued,

'Drinking was all fine, but do you remember the damn cakes that Corrado pestered us to eat?'

Andre rubbed his aching forehead and nodded again.

'I do remember the cakes; what about them?'

'That *pezzo di merda* spiked them. He wanted to get even with you for sleeping with Rosetta.'

'What?! Rosetta? Are you fucking kidding me? It was just one night, and he's not even dating her. Is he a maniac?'

'Andre, you have got to calm down. The guy is a nut.'

Drawing a deep breath and, with a frown spread all over his angular face, Andre said, 'Fine. What happened after that?'

'Andre, you had too many – combined with the drinks, they played havoc with your system. The whole thing got out of hand. You got up and started walking – very unsteadily. Said you needed fresh air.'

Andre tried to think, then wondered at the absurdity. They'd been on top of a cliff already. How much more fresh air had he needed?

Giovanni read his thoughts. 'I know. It sounds bizarre. But you went on walking towards the edge and then everything … happened so fast. One minute you were standing there with us, and the next I was running after you. Your foot slipped and you hit your head on a rock before going over. God's grace your jacket got caught before you landed in the water.'

Giovanni's mention of God's grace was far from normal for him. He looked genuinely shaken by the whole incident and his voice was laden with horror as he spoke.

'I saw you fall, Andre. I saw you fall from the damn clifftop and I couldn't do a thing to save you. *Cazzo* … We were all there … No one could do

9

anything.' He ran his fingers through his hair and Andre felt his distress, his despair.

The memories started to come back. He remembered dangling for a moment, he remembered Giovanni's frantic voice shouting his name and he remembered the cold brutal contact when he hit the water.

Giovanni continued, 'Corrado didn't expect something as drastic as that to happen, and, knowing you as he does, he's scared to death. The bastard has fled somewhere. But don't worry, we can find him.'

Andre looked at Giovanni, collected his thoughts, and, after a pause, said, 'As much as thrashing Corrado would ideally be my first choice, it isn't going to help anyone.' He took a deep breath and continued, 'Rosetta and I, we wanted to have a good time and I didn't think any more of it. Had I known Corrado felt anything for her, I would have stayed away from this mess. There is no point wasting another minute of my life trying to get even. Sometimes, I guess, forgiveness is necessary.'

Giovanni looked shocked. 'Are you sure? I mean, we can definitely find him.'

'I'm sure you can, and then I can box him to the floor. But then what? It'd be a never-ending cycle. There is no point keeping grudges, sometimes it's better to let them go. What you've told me cannot be repeated. I need to think about Papà. You know how it is, I'm all he has left. If something happens to me, he won't be able to survive.'

Giovanni could not hide his shock, but he nevertheless agreed. 'I'll come and see you again. Rest, buddy.'

Silence descended as Giovanni left. But the silence was much more peaceful, for there was no scouring the roads of memory – he knew now what had happened. Sleep overtook him, but this time it was not a restless, broken sleep.

Over the next few days, his body recovered, and as the sedatives were reduced by the doctor, his alertness increased. He went out for short strolls, though typically just around the house. Within a few weeks of the incident, he had recovered dramatically, falling back into his usual routine. Since it was the summer break, he did not have to go to college, and outings were limited to meeting friends, running some errands and occasional visits to the factory.

Chapter Three

The day was warm. Usually, Andre would've gone for a walk along the shore. Today he hesitated for a split second, but then decided to go anyway.

Walking slowly, with measured steps, he arrived on the beach. It was usually just a five-minute walk from the house, but today it had taken twenty.

He could not let fear get the better of him. It was still the water he had grown up with. He stood there, watching the waves hit the shore with relentless rhythm, more determined than ever to get a hold of his life. The sun left the orange-purple sky and began to disappear below the horizon. The wind ruffled his hair and, beneath him, the cobbled stones started hurting his bare feet, but for some reason he did not slip into the old Skechers hanging by the crook of his index finger.

The wisps of scattered clouds which dotted the sky started to change colour, and the sun, giving itself to the sea, was now completely submerged. But still Andre stood there, expressionless despite the storm that swirled and clutched at his stomach, trying to create in him a mindless fear. Firmly, he pushed it aside. He forced himself to stand for a few more minutes to spite his fear, to still the panic.

After a while, when the dread within had subsided, he turned, slipped into the old and worn Skechers, and carried on walking the narrow stretch towards home, the sea on one side and a series of houses with identical fronts on the other. The wind from the sea struck harshly against the immovable concrete line as he walked towards an empty home.

Slamming a piece of ham between two slices of white bread, he watched the clock tick to seven. Since Andre's recovery, his father was spending much more time in the factory.

Still eating, Andre walked the narrow, cobbled path to the factory. Stopping in front of the iron gates, he looked at a building now dilapidated and small – the family had sold off most of the workshops and warehouses to pay for … The thoughts which had taken over his mind many times before did so again. He tried to brush them away but they were like a constant pain hanging over him.

What had happened back then had not only broken them emotionally but also financially. All that was left of the factory now was a tiny room where Papà sat in silence, papers cluttered around his desk, a pencil in his hand, and his face creased with worry. Andre had seen that expression many times before.

'New bills, Papà?'

His father's head jerked up. He looked at his son and, after a moment's silence, said simply,

'Yes.' He did not even say his regular, "I didn't realise it was so late." Instead, he covered his face with his hands and, sliding them up through his hair, he said in a voice even lower than normal, 'I think we will have to close all of it, Andre. It cannot continue.'

Those words burned like acid into Andre's heart. The factory and the house were all that they had left, and closing the factory was like drawing a curtain on all the beautiful childhood memories, all the things which he had cherished so dearly. But he also knew how hard it must have been for his father to take a decision like this.

Andre came and sat next to his papà, who slouched, forlorn and somehow diminished, on the wooden bench. He rested his hand on his father's shoulder and said,

'It's okay, Papà. We'll find something else. It will all be fine one day.'

Sergio looked at his son and the sorrow in his eyes was replaced with softness.

'Andre, you have an inherent quality of keeping hope even when things aren't going so great. Don't ever let that change.' Very softly he added, 'It reminds me of someone.' His shoulders dropped even further as he continued, 'I have been applying for jobs at various places.' There was a long sigh. 'Never spoke to you about it as you had enough to cope with already.' He fished a letter from his desk and handed it to Andre. It was an offer of a job in New Delhi, India. 'This is the only place from which I have been able to secure an offer, and unfortunately we don't have the luxury of waiting for others when there is no way of knowing if they will materialise.' His voice dipped still further. 'Getting just one offer took months.'

Andre took the paper from his father's hand. He looked at the salary first, and that part looked good; in fact in their current situation, it was great.

'They also pay for flights, rent and arrangements for college, for you – that is, if you want to come along ...' Sergio stood up. 'But how can I leave all of this? New Delhi is all ... new, dammit! At least in Murano we are where we belong.' He was talking to himself as much as he was talking to Andre, before he sat down again with his head in his hands.

Finally, Andre spoke. 'Papà, I know it is not your first choice, but sometimes life can give us compelling reasons to pick a path we never would have chosen. I guess it's impossible to foresee what destiny holds for us, and for all you know this might be the path to a new beginning.'

Silence engulfed the room, as if reality was sinking in and taking its time, forcing its way in like an uninvited guest. They both sat, father and son, each other's only hope and only support.

Sergio spoke with a voice clouded with sorrow. 'You are right. I think Delhi might be a good change – we both need to escape from the clutches of the past.' After a pause he added, 'You are an exceptional man, Andre, and I want you to go places, not be restricted to this small town. So as you say, it may just be for the better.'

Andre said, 'Just don't sell this little office. I'll come back one day and set up the factory the way it used to be. But for now, let's look ahead.'

Sergio gave him a little pat on the shoulder and nodded.

Within two months, they were all packed and on a flight to New Delhi.

It turned out they'd been right; it was a pleasant change – different, certainly, but nice. With new people and new work, both of them tried to adapt instead of dwelling on the past. Andre was admitted to Hinduja College of Delhi University, in year two of a three-year bachelor programme. His father travelled a lot, which kept him busy, and Andre stayed with a bunch of fellow students near the college. He tried to concentrate all his energies on finishing his Bachelor's and getting enrolled in a good Master's programme towards the end of his third and final year.

But all along, he knew he would go back one day and restore the factory to its former glory.

Chapter Four

Ghana 2002

On a misty morning in July, 2002, flying at thirty thousand feet above sea level, Vivian Capello sat looking at the speckles of sunlight filtering through the hazy window and dancing over her cold hands.

Her mind was wandering through the desert of the unknown, as she absently rubbed her thumb over the sides of her palm. Her life so far had been predictable, one of contentment. But four months after she'd turned eighteen, a storm had swept in from nowhere, crushing a good many things in her life. The most harrowing episode was the stroke suffered by her beloved grandmother, which had left the right side of her body paralysed. It was the first truly painful dose of reality she had had to endure, and to look at Nonna every day, coping with the limitations which paralysis had forced upon her, was heartbreaking.

So when Nonna had told her about her last wish, Vivian could not say no. Nonna had been a doctor with Red Trust Charities and all her life she had worked in the interior of Africa, with people who needed her help the most. And now, as the curtain seemed to be closing, all that Nonna wished for was to go back there, to Africa. Vivian had to do it for her, for the woman she idolised, adored and loved beyond words.

And as a result, here she was in a seat with no legroom, straightening the non-existent creases of her skirt for the third time in a row. The sweat clung to her palms no matter how many times she wiped them. The only reassuring factor for her was that Kristoff was travelling with them – he had been one of Nonna's colleagues but, more importantly, he was a true and loyal friend of the family.

It was at the very least a distraction from the other facets of her life, which had been driving her insane just a couple of weeks ago. One of them was that her father, due to work commitments, had bulldozed them into moving to New Delhi, leaving behind her cherished Barcelona, where she was born and had grown up. No matter how much she argued, it had been futile. Her father had flatly refused to leave her behind to study in Barcelona. It had angered her but she did understand his concerns, for she was still his little girl and he had always been fiercely protective of her. As a result of the decision, she had gained admittance to a university which was not exactly her first choice, in a city which was even less so, but she had no option other than to go with the flow and find out what life had in store.

The bumpy landing made Nonna open her eyes and a smile spread over her tired and wrinkled face like sunshine.

'Viv, don't look so upset, honey. Your smile is so infectious. You should never stop smiling – it is a gift, and with it you will always bring a smile to others.'

Vivian looked at her grandmother. She was peering out of the window like a curious child, utterly content. Vivian only wanted to make Nonna smile, and that was the single most important thing right now.

Her grandmother's tone was relaxed and easy as she said, 'Honey, it's like coming home. You'll love it. Have faith.'

Vivian nodded, trying to look calm, but her stomach was churning.

The din of the aircraft, once landed, was lost in the more immediate hum of chattering passengers as they pulled their bags from the overhead lockers. A flight attendant appeared with a wheelchair as the aircraft stopped, and then helped them move through the pandemonium of immigration and customs.

Outside the airport, Vivian was hit by a gush of hot air and a bout of nervousness. They made their way over to the area where a man stood, holding a sign with Nonna's name on it. The driver opened the car door and smiled, but Vivian was too preoccupied to notice.

Sitting in the car, she maintained the death grip on her shoulder bag, which contained the only money she had, her passport, and numbers to call in case of emergency. The ride was to a small town in the Sissala district in the Upper West region of north Ghana. The roads, barely more than muddy tracks, meandered through a barren landscape, where the car threw up clouds of dust and dirt. The sun was harsh, its rays penetrating the torn seats of the car and making them feel furnace-hot as they touched her exposed legs below her skirt. She kept shifting in her seat as she stared outside, at the passing countryside, which seemed devoid of life. Salty sweat clung to her forehead – from the heat, but also from senseless fear.

After more than a couple of hours' drive, scattered huts with thatched roofs began to punctuate the horizon. Women and children, barely clad, stopped along the roadside as their car passed. A lot more activity was evident now, and everyone had one thing in common: they all stared at the car as it went by. Not many cars would pass this way, thought Vivian. Why would they? Why come to this tiny, neglected, poverty-stricken region? Pity began to well up in her; then she caught her breath as the car came slowly to a standstill.

There was a horde coming towards them. The driver had no option but to stop as the crowd seemed to engulf them, surrounding the car from all directions. A jolt of fear shot up her spine as she saw people pushing each other to get closer to the car. Many of them had their hands cupped to the sides of their faces to get a better view of the inside. Fear turned to panic and a possibility of an attack was the first thing that came to her mind. She had read on the internet that the place was devastatingly poor, and that there had been a few incidents. Maybe, she thought, foreigners were targeted … Maybe they were next. She could not think clearly, suffocated by fear as she struggled for a way to escape. Even if they kept the doors locked, the crowd could break the windows.

But as she turned towards Nonna and saw her expression, the fear started to evaporate. It took her a couple of seconds to come to terms with the fact that Nonna was completely relaxed and that her soft green eyes were moist. Then she heard a click as, with her one working hand, Nonna opened her door and the people crowded in to meet her, the women crying, the men wearing massive smiles of affection and welcome. Someone lifted the wheelchair out and helped her into it, and as she sat there, people touched her paralysed hand and stroked her hair, while the younger children looked on, dazed but curious.

One after the other, tears trickled down Nonna's face as everyone tried to welcome her. Vivian looked at those faces again, which moments before had seemed so dreadful but now looked so gentle and so in need of help. This reminded her of the time when she was seven, and she had been frantically running through her garden because a crazy June bug was in her hair. Her mother had said, softly, 'Vivian, nothing is scary, it's the fear inside you that makes things scary; it is up to you, honey, whether you let them frighten you.' Even now, more than ten years on, she often thought of that incident and she knew that her mother had been right. It was the fear inside her which made her panic.

They carefully pushed Nonna to a tiny shack in a row of uneven houses and placed her on the bed with great tenderness, as if handling a piece of porcelain. Someone brought food and others drinks. Nonna happily nibbled the home-cooked food, served in tiny earthen pots, and spoke to all of them as she rested after the long journey, showing little sign of fatigue.

After a considerable amount of chit-chat, people began to leave. The sun was still orange in the sky and Vivian found the heat a bit much, compared to what she was used to. The sweat on her skin was mixed with the dust which hung in the evening air. But somehow, neither the heat nor the prickly sweat bothered her anymore. She came and sat next to Nonna, and said,

'Now I know why you wanted to come here. I have never seen so much love and so much gratitude. The people here adore you. We all love you, but, well, we're your family. These people have no connection by blood but look at the effort they made, the love they showered you with, the hope reflected in these tiny cards.' She pointed at the cards, made by the children on plain paper, which she thought must have been torn from school notebooks. Her favourite was a rough sketch of Nonna dancing, coloured in crayon and with the word 'Futre' written at the top. She assumed the little one had wanted to write 'Future'.

The food had been prepared for Nonna by people whose need was even greater than hers. In this tiny village, where poverty was a fact of life – as was greed – here were these people who had put together whatever each could get hold of and managed to create a meal just for Nonna. This was something Vivian had never seen; the selflessness left her speechless.

'How is this all lost in our world, Nonna?'

'I don't know the answer to that. What I do know is that it's up to us, what we make of ourselves. It's our choice, Viv; make yours carefully.'

She had barely finished when her eyes turned upwards and her eyelids began to tremble. Vivian immediately started shouting for help, all the while rubbing Nonna's back and watching her face. Nonna was blinking rapidly. Vivian had seen a similar expression the last time her grandmother had had a stroke. Kristoff ran outside after taking a quick look at Nonna and returned with one of the villagers. They lifted Nonna carefully onto the makeshift stretcher and headed towards a waiting jeep. Vivian was running alongside them, tears running down her cheeks. *Please God,* she said to herself, *let her be okay.*

The journey to the hospital took almost two hours. Nonna was rushed to the emergency ward and Vivian stood helpless, a mere spectator in all the chaos. They asked her to sit outside while one of the doctors examined Nonna. The minutes ticked slowly by as Vivian sat on a lurid green iron chair outside the ward, sobbing. Her father had been supposed to join them after two days – she so wished he could have come with them.

Her fingers twisted and curled continuously as she waited for the doctor to come out. Finally, he appeared, but instead of tension there was a calming smile on his face.

He looked down at her and said, 'It was fatigue, and not another stroke as we thought, so relax. She is absolutely fine. She's sleeping. It is best if you stay here today.'

Taking a deep breath, Vivian nodded, went into the ward, and lay down on the bed next to Nonna.

Vivian could not sleep – her heart was too full of emotion from the events of the day and her mind was preoccupied with thoughts of Nonna and the welcome she had received from the villagers. How could Vivian possibly help those people in return? Somewhere in all these thoughts, her eyes finally closed.

Chapter Five

Next day, when Nonna woke up, she was smiling as usual and ready to get on with her day. No matter how much anyone argued, she insisted that she would make a round of the hospital – after all, this was the place she had worked for years.

'Nonna, only this hospital please,' Vivian insisted, firmly. 'Yesterday you did too much and look how fatigued you got.'

Nonna gently stroked her hair and said, 'Honey, this is the only hospital in the area.' She shifted herself in the wheelchair.

Vivian was surprised – one hospital for such a big area? And one so basic? But she did not voice her thoughts; instead she followed in silence as Nonna and one of the doctors made their way through a maze of corridors.

As they moved through the wards, Vivian noticed a little boy lying with his head tilted to one side. Drips and tubes seemed to cascade around his bed, encircling him, while a thick bandage covered his remaining leg. When she asked the doctor, he told them that the boy's name was Eneka and he had severely injured his leg, along with losing his family, in the recent blast. As a result, his leg had had to be amputated a few months back. He'd struggled to cope in the recent months and had tried to commit suicide, but the neighbours found him and got him here. It was too overwhelming for Vivian, too much to absorb. With emotions welling inside her and her eyes becoming dewy, she looked at Eneka again and asked,

'Is there nothing that can be done to fix his leg?' She could sense he needed much more than a leg, but that could be a start.

'Of course. A prosthetic leg can be attached and he can walk, but everything costs money. It's complicated.' The doctor smiled, and turned to talk to Nonna. It was one of those smiles signifying polite dismissal.

He had to be British, she thought. So polite even when trying to ignore her; an old school Brit, she concluded. He had overlooked the presence of the boy so easily but she could not. She returned her gaze to Eneka and a determination started to take shape within her, a determination to bring something positive into the life of a boy who she could clearly see was surrounded by misery.

'How much will it cost?'

'The charity does not have that kind of money. We have to be extremely careful with everything we spend and anything life-threatening takes priority.' He turned to talk to her grandmother but Vivian persisted.

'Still, I want to know how much it actually costs.'

Narrowing his eyes, he thought for a moment and, without looking at Vivian, he said, 'It doesn't cost so much if we use the one produced in Ghana – about five hundred dollars. If we get the one from the U.S. it's about seven thousand dollars, but the point is we don't even have the money to spare for the five hundred one.'

Vivian did the math. Seven thousand was definitely out of her budget. Even five hundred dollars was a huge amount, but she had about three hundred euros in the kitty, which she had been saving to go backpacking with her friends. She looked at Eneka, and that holiday suddenly seemed trivial, easily ignored. She had to find the difference. *Nonna can help*, she thought. She smiled inwardly as the sum rose to five hundred dollars.

Nonna, Kristoff and the doctor seemed to be discussing a new operating theatre.

Vivian interrupted, 'I'll pay for Eneka's leg.' Her voice dipped a little. 'The five hundred dollar option. I would love to opt for the expensive one but that's way out of my budget.'

All three were stunned, the local doctor more than anybody. Looking at Nonna, Vivian said,

'I have three, three-fifty; I need to borrow a few dollars from you. I will save up and return it in a few months.'

Nonna looked at her granddaughter, pride filling every bit of the tired eyes that smiled behind the wrinkles, and very softly she said,

'Do you want to go tell the boy yourself? It will be nice for both of you.'

Vivian was unsure, but nodded nevertheless.

She walked to Eneka's bed and smiled. 'Hi, I'm Vivian. What's your name?' She tried to sound enthusiastic, although for some reason she felt a little uncomfortable.

'Eneka.' It was one word, nothing more. He looked at her and she felt his empty eyes reflect the agony in his heart, although when he spoke his voice had been devoid of emotion.

'Eneka, would you like to walk to school on two legs?'

He merely pointed to his leg before saying, 'I only have one leg and no money to buy another one. What are you talking about?'

She could hear mild irritation in his voice now, but continued, feeling a frisson of excitement, a smile playing on her lips.

'You are too small to talk about money; life is more than that.'

How those words came out even she did not know. Never had she spoken to anybody like that – that was the way Nonna spoke to people. But she wanted to talk, to see a glimmer of positivity, of hope, reflected on his face, so she continued,

'I spoke to the doctor and he said it is possible to fix your leg, to get you a prosthetic. You'll be practising walking soon.'

He stared at her as if she was demented, but then his gaze moved to the doctor and when he looked at her again, she could see he simply wasn't sure he could trust what he had just heard. He craned his neck forwards to see her more clearly. And she kept smiling.

'That can't be,' he said. His voice almost choked as he wiped his eyes and cheeks with his little palms.

Bending down and looking straight into those sad little eyes, Vivian said, 'You only need faith. Bad things happen so that good things can follow. Life is a circle. If you are at the bottom of the curve, one day you'll reach the top as well. Always remember that.' She stroked his head with a tenderness that needed no further reassurance, and with that walked on, leaving the little boy brimming with hope.

She had never felt this good, and when she saw Nonna smiling, she understood why she had asked her to go tell the news to the little boy.

Staying at the village for a few days gave Vivian a new perspective on life.

She went back to meet Eneka a couple of weeks after his new leg was attached. As she entered the cluttered ward, with its rows of beds so close together, she saw him doing a wobbly walk, holding onto a nurse, a smile spread across his face. It was the most beautiful thing she had ever seen; it was the smile of a child who had been given a tiny part of his life back, who had been given hope. As she walked towards him, Eneka looked at her, his face brimming with happiness, and asked her to stop where she was. Eneka released his grip on the nurse's arm and, with staggering steps, walked towards her. When he reached her, he threw his arms around her in a fierce hug, tears flowing uncontrollably as he mumbled,

'I can walk … I can walk.'

Vivian hugged him, stroking his head as she tried to control her tears. There was loud applause from all the patients and nurses who had witnessed the little scene, and for a moment Vivian felt embarrassed and delighted at the same time. Eneka was a proud little boy. He took her hand and walked to his bed, then said,

'Thank you. Thank you. I'm not sure if I can ever thank you enough.'

'It is my pleasure, Eneka, I'm glad I could help.'

They sat and spoke for some time. Eneka told her how he used to play in school, about his friends, and then the conversation turned to his family and Vivian heard the sorrow and pain in his voice. She recognised the expression in his eyes she had seen the very first time they'd met. Very gently, she took his hand again and said,

'Eneka, sometimes things happen beyond our control, but you never know where destiny will take you. Have faith and I'm sure one day it will all be alright. God has given us this life, treasure it. If you cannot give a life, you have no right to take it.'

He was looking into her eyes, as if knowing what she meant but, at the same time, as though willing it to be true.

She saw a flicker of hope flash across his face and felt something she had never felt before: the serenity of true contentment. She bid him goodbye and pressed a kiss on his forehead before saying, 'You are a very special boy and big things are meant for you. Never lose hope.'

Eneka was beaming at her when she left. She returned to the tiny shack tired from the day, and fell into a dreamless sleep.

The next day was their last in the village, and as Vivian got up, she asked Nonna if she was ready for coffee – strong coffee was her morning ritual. But there was no reply, just silence from the other side of the bed. Vivian slowly turned her head to look at Nonna's peaceful face. She was no more; Vivian could feel it. With slow steps, full of dread, she walked to her grandmother's side and stood there, frozen.

How long she stood there she did not know, but the silence was broken by Kristoff and her father entering the shack. Carlos looked at Vivian, then at Nonna, and stepped forward to take his daughter in his arms. Father and daughter stood there, very still, the silence of the room echoing in their hearts, a silence which was deafening.

Nonna was buried in the village. Carlos, Kristoff and Vivian left with all the notes and cards, the little mementos, and the satisfaction that Nonna left the world peaceful and content.

Chapter Six
New Delhi

Vivian and Carlos returned to New Delhi, but life was not the same without Nonna. Maria, Vivian's mother, was very supportive – Vivian knew her mother understood the bond she'd had with Nonna.

The Africa trip had made a deep impression on her. She was devastated but somehow all the more determined to carry Nonna's legacy forward. The poverty, the people, everything had moved her deeply. She had a clear goal now, a clear vision of what she wanted to do, and how, but achieving it would not be so easy. The medical colleges had an entrance exam which she was already late for; half the country wanted to be a doctor, so clearing that exam would be a herculean task. The best option was to enrol in graduate college and prepare for the examination there, then go on to medical college next year – and that was precisely what she decided to do.

On a day when fresh raindrops were clinging to the green leaves, Carlos left Vivian at Hinduja College. The new surroundings were still playing havoc with her sense of reality; everything was different and she felt somewhat overwhelmed, even a little scared. She stood there at the kerb and watched the car disappear, then turned to the huge iron gates which were, to her mind at least, a dark and foreboding entrance. Reluctantly, she dragged her feet along a concrete path overhung with trees.

The place was bustling with activity, way too many people, happy faces for the most part. Hers was the only one which looked, she feared, like a scared peach. Trying to lift her mood and reminding herself that she had promised her parents she would genuinely try to adjust to the place instead of complaining, she looked at the filtered sunlight dancing on the concrete path and breathed in the smell of wet leaves which filled the air.

A huge spiral staircase of white marble rose in front of her as she entered the building; climbing it, she could feel the coolness through her thin plimsolls. It was 8:35 a.m., and she made her way to room 25A, entered, and found a seat.

Groups of people came pouring in, and a loud and animated chatter slowly filled the classroom. A girl with a slightly frazzled look came and stared at her before dumping her bag on the adjacent seat. Vivian looked at her and raised her eyebrows.

'Is there anything I can help you with?'

'Chill, dude, it's just that you're sitting in my seat. It's okay.'

With that she popped some gum in her mouth and sat at the desk to the side, her head more or less colliding with the desk as she attempted to rest it on her beautifully tanned hands, which were adorned with a dozen pieces of jewellery. Vivian sat there not knowing how to react, cornered on a wooden bench next to a girl who was almost sleeping. She acknowledged the few smiles she got from students who were sitting close by. On hearing a moan of pain, she turned her head in the direction of the sleeping beauty.

The girl murmured, 'Damn late-night movies and drinking. Bloody hell, my head is splitting.'

Vivian did not know where to look or what to do with herself – the girl was talking to herself as much as to Vivian.

'Hi, by the way, I'm Devyani.'

Finally a sentence actually directed at her, and one she could make sense of.

'Hi, I'm Vivian.'

Devyani extended her arm, her eyes only half-open. She returned her head to the cocoon of her arms for a moment before forcing herself up and saying,

'Normally, I'm quite pleasant to talk to. Really bad hangover today.'

Vivian nodded in agreement. She rarely had alcohol but didn't want to look like a naïve fool who didn't drink. As a result she was nodding way more than required.

Heads which had been turned towards the duo looked to the front as the professor entered. A short guy, with grey, unkempt, frizzy hair, he looked at a note on his table and the wide eyes behind the glasses started a scan of the room. His eyes stopped when he spotted Vivian, and with a very brief smile he said,

'We have a new student – Vivian. Can everyone help her with whatever she needs,' and after a pause he added, 'as she is joining in the middle of term.' Vivian was sure she'd heard a few giggles when he said, 'Whatever she needs', but she tried, like the professor, to ignore it.

A few minutes into the lecture, she pretty much lost track of what was being taught and her thoughts drifted to Nonna and the village in Africa. The smile of Eneka when he had walked. She forced herself to concentrate – if she was going to get anywhere she needed to listen – but it was difficult, coming to a subject from the middle of nowhere.

After the longest forty minutes, the class ended. Vivian wondered how she would survive another four lectures. Devyani went vertical the moment the professor stepped out. She demanded coffee, looking at Vivian.

'I could definitely do with some.' Vivian didn't hesitate as there was a half-hour break before the second lecture. She put her notebook back in her multi-coloured tote.

She was walking the narrow path between benches when she heard someone say, 'Newbie!!' in an easy, sensual voice. Vivian turned and said,

'Hi, I'm Vivian.'

The girl who had spoken looked to be straight out of a salon, her hair falling in a perfect straight line and a figure as if from a fashion magazine. Her face was covered in makeup, finished to a level which Vivian was sure she could never achieve; the girl was looking at Vivian as if she was some kind of a circus clown.

'I don't have memory loss,' the girl said. 'The bore just introduced you before the damn class. Bye, *Hi-I'm-Vivian.*'

There was a burst of laughter as the others walked away. Vivian was thoroughly embarrassed and she felt a little flush of anger.

'What a pathetic attempt at humour. Looks sure can be deceptive,' she said.

'Don't worry about her, she's a sad little loser. Pure pain in the arse. Name's Lenny. Come on, let's get some coffee.' With that, Devyani stretched her arms and let out another big yawn.

Vivian walked with her but inside she was fuming. Damn dolled-up fool.

She heard a giggle beside her. 'Still fuming?' asked Devyani, the corners of her mouth twitching into a smile. 'I know, she can be very annoying – but ignore her, she's always like that and, with you, she had a solid reason.'

'A reason? I barely know her!'

'Honey, people like Lenny are jealous of anyone who is more attractive, or smart, or in any way better than them. Like you, for instance, in the looks department – look at all the attention from the men in the class. And honestly, you don't seem that dumb either.'

That was the weirdest compliment she had ever heard – if it even was a compliment.

'So you're telling me she behaved in that nonsensical way because I might be attractive and possibly not so dumb ...' The girls looked at each other and then burst out laughing.

'I'm afraid so.'

More laughter echoed in the corridor – the sound of a new friendship – as the two girls walked on, shafts of sunlight sending the shadows of pillars obliquely across the red sandstone flags, creating the illusion of a flight of stairs that disappeared and reformed as their own shadows moved in front of them.

The girls emerged onto a curving path which led to the canteen, between patches of grass and a few scattered trees. Vivian noticed one ancient, misshapen tree which was encircled by a fieldstone wall capped with redstone. It seemed to attract the greatest concentration of students.

They reached a room which was large and yet barely in need of artificial lighting. The huge windows seemed to extend the physical scope of the room so that it merged with the world outside.

Devyani took a deep breath. 'This is it. The canteen. And I can smell food and coffee! Should clear the head a bit …'

They settled themselves on a long bench at a corner table and Devyani went to the counter, returning with coffee and nibbles.

'So, have you seen much of Delhi?' she asked. 'You're clearly not from here.'

'I'm from Barcelona, and nope, just a few tourist spots, nothing much.'

'Ah, that means you've seen nothing – seeing tourist spots is like judging a book by its cover. It needs to be read, every single page of it.' Another quick opinion, and her black eyes reflected her conviction.

Vivian tilted her head and nodded; it made perfect sense. She had no real sense of the place in which she found herself. Devyani offered to show her around and Vivian jumped at the idea without stopping to think whether she might have asked out of politeness. Anyway, it was too late – she had accepted the offer and it was time for the next class.

One class led to another and finally the day ended, leaving her mentally exhausted. But that wasn't quite it for Vivian; she went straight to her evening class in preparation for the medical entrance exam.

Her room was pinned with cards and letters from the villagers in Africa as a constant reminder of how humanity needed to be. College was an interim arrangement till she was admitted to medical school. She thought she had it all planned out in black and white, no shades of grey permitted. In her perfectly planned life there was no room for dimensions beyond the ones that already existed.

Chapter Seven

As the days went by, slow and steady, thoughts of Nonna still clouded Vivian's mind, but she started to become more adjusted to college life, and to life in general in Delhi. She began to take in and appreciate the lectures instead of zoning out and looking at the guy sitting next to her, making cartoons with a deadpan expression. The annoyance of Lenny was a constant presence, but so was the bond of friendship with Devyani, which was getting stronger every day.

Devyani took time out to show her around. At Janpath, the local market, she was initially overwhelmed by the number of people who gawked at her, and after a few brushes she was annoyed enough to go home in disgust. But Devyani told her how to react, how to protect herself and be strong, to give back right then and there to anyone who tried to act smart. She did her best, but instead of looking at the trendy and colourful clothes in the market all she was aware of was anyone who walked closer than they should. It was not a pleasant experience for her.

Devyani, who was more accustomed to the place, tried to make her understand. 'You have to live with these things in Delhi. You have to decide if you want to let it get you down every time, ignore it, or fight back. You can't stop going out because there are a bunch of assholes looking for an opportunity. You need to be strong.' Her eyes reflected her annoyance as she said the word 'assholes'; it was not pleasant for her either but perhaps over the years she had learnt to handle it.

Vivian nodded. She knew Devyani was right; she did have to be strong. College was a secure shell, but a shell nevertheless. The outside world had to be treated with caution and Vivian had to learn the art. Slowly, as she got around more, she learned what to expect, how to react and what to avoid. She started enjoying the place, with its beauty as well as its limitations.

The attentions of the men in the class were generously showered upon her. She saw it and avoided it, preferring for the most part to hang out with Devyani. For her there was a very clear goal, something which had been born within her when she was a little girl, nurtured by Nonna's life and strengthened by Nonna's death. She wanted to concentrate only on that and nothing else, which was completely in contrast to what Devyani suggested most of the time.

She was getting snowed under with her studies, and by way of relief, or at least distraction, she decided to audition for a part in the college play after Devyani coaxed her enough. Acting was not one of her known talents, but the idea did appeal and, to her surprise, she was selected for the part. Her love of books had covered Shakespeare, but to act in a play written by him was a completely new and, to a great extent, rejuvenating experience. Networking, finding her feet, getting to know her surroundings and being more involved in college activities were all a part of campus life!

All the plays were in preparation for the upcoming festival season. Universities and colleges across the country held a three-to-five-day cultural festival, which encompassed everything from drama, music, and creative writing, to debates and much more. The only hiccup was that the festival for which they were preparing the play was in Nainital, supposedly a beautiful hill station nestled in the foothills of the Himalayas – but that would not help to convince her dad.

Vivian knew it would be a nightmare trying to talk him into allowing an outstation visit. He had always been protective of her but since they had moved to India that protective streak had increased at an alarming rate … Nevertheless, this trip to Nainital was Vivian's chance to see more of the country, to experience a city other than Delhi.

She put the proposal to her family over their evening cup of coffee at the table.

As soon as the discussion started, Vivian could hear the tension in her father's voice, a mounting annoyance reflected by the sudden attention being given to his coffee cup.

'Dad, the trip is through the faculty and is open to all the students from the college. Over there we'll stay on the college campus, so …'

Her father got up for the second time and went to the kitchen, supposedly to get sugar and biscuits. Vivian knew it was not going to be easy to convince him – but when she turned her attention towards her mother, who was looking at her with calm and supportive eyes, she thought it might not be that difficult either. Vivian waited patiently, hearing clattering noises in the kitchen. How long could it take to get biscuits and sugar? Dad was setting a new record. But she sat there, tapping her fingers on her knees.

He came back, sat down, and took a full minute to adjust himself on the sofa before he spoke.

'How safe is it? I hear all these things in the news and I can't help being worried.'

Finally, a question, thought Vivian, *instead of the frown and the tightening jawline.*

His round eyes were getting bigger and rounder behind his glasses with every passing minute.

Maria leaned forward with her hands resting firmly on the wooden table. She spoke in a clear, level tone.

'Darling, it's a college trip, she's not going backpacking on her own. She goes with a group of students who stay in hostel accommodation at another university; it sounds completely safe to me.'

'You don't know the country, Maria, and nor does Vivian. I watch the news; there are so many things about foreigners …' Carlos pushed his chair back and got up, and his voice faltered a little on the next sentence. 'Besides, she is still so young.'

Vivian thought she saw flashes of anger in her mother's beautiful emerald eyes, and rightly so. He was testing their patience and coming up with ludicrous arguments. Too young?

Refusing to be cowed, Maria too pushed her chair back and stood up.

'We need to draw a line somewhere. I don't think there is anything to be paranoid about. We will have to get to know the country, we can't sit at home all the time, scared to travel, to discover India. It was your decision to get us here and we cannot always remain in fear of the unknown. And Vivian is not a child, she knows how to handle herself. If she really wants to go, I don't see any reason to stop her. In fact, it's a good thing that her play has been selected. You should be proud!'

When she had finished, she took a deep breath and glanced at Vivian, who had been the mute spectator for the last five minutes. Vivian felt as if history was repeating itself; instead of convincing her dad about the trip to Africa, she was convincing him about Nainital.

Carlos had listened to the ladies of the house but looked unconvinced.

'Come on, Dad, it's not unsafe. It's fine, there are so many other students going.'

He was left with no option but to give his consent, which he duly, if half-heartedly, did. The decision brought an ear-to-ear smile to Vivian's face and the urge to start packing immediately. She walked around the table to give her father a warm hug, and winked at her mother. Carlos encircled her with his arms and whispered,

'Be careful.'

Chapter Eight

October had given way to November. Vivian waited for the bus along with a diverse group of students from various colleges. Some faces she recognised, some were complete strangers. Some languages she had heard before, some she couldn't guess at all.

Devyani had a natural way with people and made some introductions. Unfortunately, voluptuous Lenny and her group were also a part of this trip.

Damn her ... How can she look so perfect all the time?

Next to Lenny, Vivian felt like a wild goose. While Lenny's straight shiny hair always lay so perfectly, her unruly curls were all over the place. Moreover, Lenny's eyes had that lovely smoky effect which Vivian was sure she could never achieve even if she tried – she would have ended up blotching her eyes.

She tried to dismiss these thoughts of latent insecurity and concentrated on what Devyani was saying to the bloke standing next to them.

The clock ticked to 5:30 p.m. and still there was no sign of the bus. To top it all off, the rain gods were feeling generous; clear skies were replaced by dark, heavy clouds and thunder, as lightning lined the clouds, making them look even more dense and heavy. As the downpour started, the students huddled in the corridor, taking up almost its whole length. After just one fierce shower, the rain stopped and the skies cleared, once more friendly and soft, with only the raw fragrance of raindrops on dry mud left behind.

Tired of waiting, the students lit a bonfire, releasing showers of sparks to mingle with the clear evening air. As the twilight descended, one of the guys strummed 'Love is All Around' on his guitar, filling the place with music.

Andre was representing Hinduja College in a debate on 'Economic Development in the Context of Climate Change' for the festival in Nainital. Now two years in Delhi, he was used to the place, but what still annoyed him was the traffic – and right now he was stuck in traffic on his way to college from home.

He got out of the cab, and although he was almost sure he had missed the bus, he decided to make a run for it.

When he arrived, he was pleasantly surprised to find everyone waiting and music floating in the air. Trying to catch his breath, he scanned the place for his group of friends and sat next to them, dumping his navy blue rucksack on the bench beside him and exchanging a casual nod with a few other acquaintances. The evening breeze was slowly drying the sweat from his face from all the running, and he was pleased that his group was sitting a good way from the remnants of the bonfire. Shifting to lean on his rucksack, he stretched his legs, which had been curled up in the cab for two hours. He was handed a chilled beer by one of his friends and they all raised a counter-toast, cursing the city's traffic.

His gaze drifted from the bonfire to the short flight of stairs, where a brunette was emerging alongside Devyani, whom he vaguely knew. It was the brunette who caught his attention. She walked slightly hesitantly, with Devyani, to a little group of people and there were multiple nods and handshakes. The guys obviously liked what they saw, as they were all trying to appear charming. Andre knew those looks well, he was an expert, but what intrigued him was that the beauty he was observing so intently appeared very naïve in comparison to the crapbags around her.

One of the guys motioned to the two ladies to sit with them. The flames from the fire flickered on the brunette's face, making it glow, and the mass of curls tumbling down her shoulders started to shimmer. The purple of the night spread its wings behind her as she sat in silence. She was wearing a plain white dress – an angel gliding on the shadows of the fire. His beer can sat untouched in his hands; he could not take his eyes off her.

Ekta interrupted his thoughts. 'What are you watching so intently?'

'Oh, *niente*, nothing at all,' he said, like a thief caught in the act. He averted his eyes, but only momentarily.

Ekta gave an impish smile before adding, 'She is beautiful.'

'Indeed she is,' he said. 'Who is she?'

'Vivian, first year biology honours. She's Spanish. If you want more information, you need to take me out for coffee. You want me to introduce her, then it's lunch at the new Thai place.'

Andre looked at Ekta as she burst out in a fit of laughter, 'What, I need to wheedle out something for the hundred bucks I lost on the bet.'

'Done, lunch and coffee both. Take me now.' Andre stood up, almost pulling his friend by the arm.

As he walked across to the bonfire, his eyes remained fixed on Vivian while she was listening to something Devyani was saying. Ekta, in her ever-cheerful way, said,

'Hi, how are we all?'

There was the customary girly hugging and kissing routine. He knew that she noticed him, as he was standing right behind Ekta and staring over her shoulder.

Damn. Acting like an idiot. This was not how he normally behaved; he had surprised himself.

Ekta stepped back and said, 'By the way, this is Andre, a really good friend of mine.'

'Hi.' He extended his hand and, looking at her closely, he understood why all those guys were drooling.

His heart momentarily stopped as Vivian raised her long lashes and looked at him with warm eyes, extending her hand to meet his. He experienced a fuzzy feeling inside from just that one look, and the touch of her cold fingers as she placed her hand in his. He knew he had to say something before it became patently clear that he was oblivious to everything but her eyes and the clasp of her hand.

'The English would say *Andre*, but it's actually an Italian name and should be pronounced *Andréia*.'

She slightly nodded her head as he continued,

'Saying that, my parents decided to spell my name as Andre instead of Andrea which is really strange considering my Italian descent.

'Andre is just fine,' he added, lamely.

'Hmm,' was all she said.

Why the hell did I act like a Wikipedia on the name Andre? he thought.

The guy standing behind her was staring at Andre as if he was encroaching on his territory, but in all honesty he did not care one bit – nor, he thought, did Vivian.

Somehow he felt she was aware of the intensity with which he was looking at her. Ekta made some more small talk as Andre stood quietly, his gaze fixed upon Vivian. Her brown hair gently brushed her shoulders every time she moved her head in anticipation of seeing the bus; her face, even without a trace of makeup, was exquisite. Coupled with those eyes, it was a lethal combination. He felt foolish, behaving in such a way after meeting a girl for the first time. But there was something different about her; he did not know what, but there was a strange unspoken feeling welling up inside him.

She did not try asking him anything, standard things like where he was from, questions he was so used to. She was paying so much attention to Ekta that for a moment he felt invisible – but then for just a fraction of a second her eyes flickered from Ekta to him. It must have unnerved her as, immediately, she shifted her gaze back to Ekta.

At this first encounter they barely spoke, and Andre soon went back to his group of friends. Finally, the buses came and the excited group of students climbed aboard and settled themselves in for the journey.

The six-hour bus ride was a babble of conversation of varying intensity, which dipped as the journey progressed and then finally fell silent as, one by one, the students fell into the arms of slumber.

A chilly breeze, along with a slight drizzle, welcomed them to Nainital. At the university, they were shown the girls' and boys' hostels respectively, with a bed allocated to each of them. Andre and Vivian had exchanged no more than a casual glance or two during the journey.

The next day, he dropped by during Vivian's rehearsal.

'Hi,' he said, trying to sound indifferent and unaffected by the morning freshness of her face, to make his presence seem like a coincidence rather than a planned visit. 'I was just passing by. Nice play.'

'Thanks,' she said, in an even, almost indifferent tone, which disappointed him.

'We're going to visit the city – would you like to come along?' The words came out almost unbidden.

'I can, but I have a rehearsal to finish, so maybe it's better if you—'

'No hurry. You finish your rehearsal, I'll wait.'

'You'll wait? It could be a while.'

'Honestly, I'm in no hurry.'

She looked at him curiously, as if getting to grips with his authoritative tone. She seemed unsure of the whole scenario but thankfully didn't say any more. Instead, she climbed back onto the stage and he had the opportunity to observe her at length. Clad in jeans and t-shirt, her hair left loose, she looked somehow different than the others on stage. There was a serene, untouched innocence in her, and something magnetic. He thoroughly enjoyed the next few minutes.

As she got down from the stage, he said,

'Are you ready to go?'

'Yup.'

She stepped back up and told the others she was done for the day. Then, slinging her bag over her shoulder, she jumped off again, leaving a somewhat bemused group behind. Andre tried to look away, as most of the group seemed to be staring at the two of them. The director and Andre exchanged glances, and not happy ones. But before the director could say anything, quick as the wind, Vivian was gone.

They walked together down the concrete path leading to the main gate. His hands desperately wanted to hold her, but they were firmly tucked in his pockets. He walked slowly, making random conversation, enjoying her casual and carefree walk.

The rest were already at the gate with their bicycles.

'I didn't know we needed bikes,' she said. 'I haven't rented one. Where do I go?'

'The bike place is closed. You can sit with me.' Andre was beaming as he spoke, his legs on either side of the bike and his arms folded across his chest. An outright fib for no reason but he was enjoying himself. This chance that was too precious to pass up. Surprisingly, instead of debating what he had said, which he'd half-expected, she gave one of her captivating smiles and stepped over to his bike, slipping sideways onto the bar in front of the seat.

'Did you know you have the most enchanting smile I have ever seen?' he said, gazing dreamily at the back of her head as she sat on the iron bar in front of him.

Her eyes were full of surprise when she turned to look at him, and after a pause she simply said,

'Thanks.' She swiftly turned her head back and Andre smiled inwardly at this attempt to hide the array of emotions evident on her refreshingly transparent face.

The breeze brushed her hair and he leant forward unconsciously to take in the fragrance emanating from her. The tip of his nose lightly touched her cheek as he tried to listen to what she was saying. He almost felt her stiffen with that slight touch, and a smile wavered on his lips as he saw a little rush of colour on her cheekbones.

As his arms encircled her she tried hesitantly to hold the handlebars. Her futile efforts to talk were overwhelmed by her thoughts, her consciousness of their arms touching and the tingling of her every sense. Yesterday, when he had come over with Ekta, she had been acutely aware of the intensity with which he was looking at her. There was something so strong yet so soft in that look and today, when she'd first seen him, she had been unexpectedly delighted. The fact that he seemed equally eager to be with her was the cherry on top. She had tried to be her usual self, to say no, but the way he had asked her – or rather told her – made it impossible.

She smiled to herself as she thought about the expression on his face when she had come off the stage only to find him absorbed in staring at her. God, he looked charming, standing next to the pillar in the auditorium. When they had walked the concrete path to the main entrance, there had been some small talk. It should not have taken more than five minutes, but for a man who looked so fit, either he was awfully slow at walking or had deliberately spent more time with her. She sincerely hoped the latter.

She was so lost in thought that she hadn't spoken a word for a while. His rich voice broke in.

'Are you okay? Can't be very comfortable sitting on a steel bar.'

She could sit on it all day if he was with her.

'Yeah, I'm fine. I'm sure you're struggling more, dragging my weight up and down these hills.'

He laughed out loud and nudged the side of her head with his chin.

'I'm good.'

She was grateful that he could not see her, otherwise he would have caught the idiotic blush on her face at almost everything he was doing or saying. His arms made her feel strangely secure, almost as if she belonged. He had a unique, musky fragrance which she could smell every time he leant forward. She was acutely aware of their unspoken intimacy, but at the same time unwilling to admit it to herself.

It is nothing. We're just sitting on a bike! But then why was her heart galloping at every touch, every word? She knew instinctively that moments like this made memories; whether beautiful or painful, only time would tell – perhaps both – but memories nevertheless, which would last a lifetime.

She couldn't remember ever going 'out' with anyone after only meeting them twice, and yet she found herself being pulled by some strange, invisible force towards Andre. She had pretty much agreed to go with him as soon as he'd asked, and she barely knew him. There was a distinct difference between Andre and all the other guys who drooled over her. He had an undiluted charm about him, his beaming smile softening his face and his eyes captivating her just by looking.

As they reached the mall road where the bikes had to be parked, Vivian got down from the bike and hoped desperately that the separation she felt was matched by Andre. He stood against the backdrop of the glittering lake, around which the road circled. The sun glinted in his eyes as he parked the bike, and the wind lifted his hair as his fingers tried to deal with his stubborn locks. The scenery behind him looked serenely beautiful, but it was the foreground which was capturing all her attention.

Normally in a place like this she would have been entranced, but at this moment even the sound of the lapping water, the song of the birds, the bent tree branches stroking the surface of the water, left her unmoved. What did cause a stir was Andre extending his hand to hold hers in front of the whole group. She could feel their eyes upon her but clearly it did not bother him at all, and despite herself she slid her fingers into his palm, where he gently held them. His hands felt so warm and so comfortable; his thumb gently brushed her palm as they walked, and they stood in front of the lake to watch the sun going down behind the hills, leaving a golden glow which seemed to cup the landscape. How could just holding hands feel so wonderful?

They all stood there, taking in the immense beauty which surrounded them. She caught him staring at her a few times and each time it was she who got self-conscious – he was absolutely self-assured. At one point, he pulled her a little closer to hear what she was saying and she stammered like an idiot. She was sure she saw him grin before he gave her shoulders a slight squeeze and held onto her hand again.

The winding roads stretched uphill and a decision was taken by the rest of the students to walk to the temple of Naina Devi, a staple of the tourist trade. They walked beside the lake to the place of worship; it was supposed to give a sense of tranquillity and peace but all she felt was the warmth of his hand in hers. There were numerous bells hanging all along the path leading into the temple, and a procession, or *pooja*, was going on when they entered. The entire place was lit with *diyas* – oil lamps. Devyani came over and dragged Vivian off to where the bells were hanging. Vivian reluctantly followed her and, when she looked back, she saw a look of disappointment, tinged with annoyance, on Andre's face. Yes, she felt a little guilty for spending all her time with Andre, but then Devyani had been busy enough herself with a bloke they'd met while waiting for the bus, so the guilt passed.

The soft ringing of the bells and the chanting in praise of the Almighty raised her soul to another level. Rather than merely seeing the divinity, she felt it – it was a moment which could only be felt, one of those times when she knew someone was watching over her and everything would be fine.

The chirpy voice of Devyani brought her down to earth.

'What's going on?'

'Going on?' Vivian raised her eyebrows but the smile on her face was slowly spreading.

'Vivian, don't act smart with me, I know you too well. With Andre, of course. He's sooo—'

'Stop drooling, Devyani.'

'I'm not, honey.' She laughed. 'Can't believe you're already jealous.'

Was she jealous? No, but she did not like Devyani's expression, or the way she was about to describe Andre. Maybe just a tad jealous, she concluded, but she tried not to show it.

'No, I'm not, it's nothing, you're reading too much into things – now tell me, what's going on with you?' She was speaking too fast and, to calm herself down, she gently swung the bells, which tinkled at her touch.

Andre looked at her as she stood silhouetted against the light from the oil lamps, talking to

Devyani, who had literally dragged her away – but then it was a treat to even look at her. His senses were filled by the sight of her, her beauty plucked at strings unknown to him, its purity brought feelings which he'd never known existed. Never had such a silly thing as holding hands felt so wonderful. He was not the kind of guy to settle for holding hands – he'd passed that stage years back – but with her it was different. He grinned as he remembered her expression when he had given her shoulders a slight squeeze. Her eyes had widened and then she had looked as far away from him as possible.

'You don't let go of something so beautiful.' The voice came from somewhere behind him.

'I'm sorry … what?' said Andre, trying to return to reality, shifting his gaze from Vivian to the strange man now standing beside him.

'Something so beautiful. You should never let go of it.'

'Who are you?' As he spoke, his eyebrows knotted into a frown. He was genuinely concerned for Vivian, as he saw this man looking at her. Strangely, he felt a rush of jealousy, and a fierce will to protect her.

'Don't worry, my friend, I'm just a priest. I work here in the temple. I saw you looking at the girl. She has honesty in her eyes, and so do you. Hard to find in today's world. True love is next to God, you should embrace it when you find it.'

'I don't believe in God,' said Andre, trying not to sound rude. He was mildly irritated by this stranger giving unsolicited advice on his life, but the jealousy was subsiding along with his defensiveness.

The man standing in front of him continued, 'Do not worry. When you find true love, you will start believing in the Almighty. Have a good life. May God protect you.' And with that he walked up the steps, leaving behind a puzzled and somewhat disconcerted Andre.

Strange guy, thought Andre. *"True love." He has to be mad – although he does have a positive aura about him*. He said, 'Thank you' as politely as he could, and the priest turned back and smiled at him, raising his hand to bless him. Andre's eyes followed him as he walked up the steps, somehow so permanent and reassuring, to the temple, and disappeared into the dimly lit interior.

Andre came and stood next to Vivian, completely dismissing the priest from his thoughts, only to fill them with the present in which he found himself. Placing a firm hand under her elbow, he dragged her away from Devyani, as he could see she was somewhat struggling with the conversation.

Admiring the splendour of the place, they ascended the steps and entered the temple. He took a few pictures and then held the camera in front of him, taking some more with Vivian, their heads together, smiling. For some reason she did not question anything he said or did, which gave him a wonderful feeling, and he snapped some more photos with his arm around her.

The other students wanted to go boating but Andre said,

'We want to stay here a little longer.' He whispered in Vivian's ear, 'Can I say "we"?'

'Yes,' was all she could manage …

There was a big 'Oooh' from the rest of the group, and as they left the pair alone they were laughing.

'A date in a temple, is it?' she asked, trying to be her usual, confident self, but this time he was prepared.

'It is whatever you want it to be,' he said, placing his hand on her shoulder and looking straight into her eyes.

He felt as if all her self-assuredness had withered and the real Vivian stood there, without defences, shy and vulnerable. Andre loved every bit of that expression in her brown eyes, which told him he had some sort of unexplainable power over her.

They got to talking, sitting on the temple steps, and time passed as never before. He brushed her hand once in a while and she let him. It was a different feeling, strange and strong, compelling and shapeless. They talked endlessly about mundane things, nothing important; what was important was this time together. When the realisation of passing time set in, it was late enough for the mountain slope in front of them to be illuminated by the lights from the houses scattered across it. The mystical surroundings, the two of them together, the darkness of the night and the cool breeze gave Andre an indescribable feeling of delight, as if the time and the place belonged only to them.

'So beautiful,' said Vivian, looking at the mountain in front of them.

'Breathtaking, I'd say.'

Vivian turned her head at the change in tone. The glint of amusement in his eyes was enough to make her suddenly feel self-conscious. Shifting her gaze from his eyes, she decided to observe the mountain even more intently, and Andre found it endearing that she tried to keep a straight face, that she stared at the mountain when she wanted to look at him. That's what he dearly hoped – that she wanted to look only at him – and in his mind he decided that it was so. He wanted to pull her into his arms and kiss her but she was becoming so self-conscious with even holding hands that for a moment he wondered if it was all too quick for her. She needed more time, he thought, and felt annoyed with himself that he placed that discovery before his desire to kiss her. Never had that been the case before. All his affairs had one thing in common – they were driven by physical desire – but this Spanish girl with wild brown hair had touched a different chord and for the first time in his life he would not put himself first. He cursed himself for it, as he felt even closer to her in the gathering darkness. They both stood there, wide awake under the night sky.

They started back to the hostel on the bike and he could smell her hair, feel her cheek against his. His mind wandered in her intoxicating fragrance. As they spoke, the tip of his nose again brushed against her cheek and the new intimacy of whispering in her ear was as a drug …

As the hostel neared, an uncomfortable silence grew between them, an unspoken longing for more. The bicycle came to a halt in front of the girls' hostel, and she got down – a physical separation which made him ache. His arms longed to pull her back into their secret circle, where he could feel her belong to him. Then her words brought him back to reality with a jolt.

'Thank you for the ride. I know I'm not light to cart around.'

'I loved carting you. I'd cart you anytime.' He was amazed at his own directness, especially with the choice of words. Loved. He was not normally a fall-madly-in-love-guy, although he did appreciate beauty. The series of expressions reflected in her eyes told him that she was equally surprised – and equally happy. Her face lit up like a schoolgirl's and he felt she could have twirled and laughed at his words, but all she said was,

'Thanks.'

They were trying to find something to say, anything to stay together a little longer.

'Pleasure – no need to thank me, you can always pay me back.'

'How would that be, then?'

'By seeing me tomorrow?'

'Sure,' she laughed.

Hands deep in his pockets, standing with a leg on each side of the bike, Andre had a compelling, boyish charm about him. Just looking at him made Vivian smile. Those enigmatic eyes, she felt, could see through her soul.

'Goodnight, *cara*,' he said, softly, feeling her palm.

'*Cara*? What is *cara*?' she asked.

'*Cara* is Italian for dearest.' He smiled and said, 'I'll see you tomorrow.'

As he cycled away, she had a strong urge to stop him, but all the two of them did was keep looking at each other over their shoulders.

It had barely been a few hours and she was becoming caught in a web of attraction. Fiddling with one of her rings, she thought,

Is he as attracted to me as I am to him, or am I dreaming? He may be ... The way he said 'breathtaking'! A smile hovered on her lips as she remembered Andre's expressions. *Maybe it's just flirting; he does seem an expert at that.* She sighed deeply as she reached the dorm and sat on her bed, thinking about the wonderful moments they had spent together. He was a strange mix of authority and gentleness. Everything he did was with an authority, as if she belonged to him, whether it was holding hands or asking her to sit on the bike.

God I'm an idiot. I've just met the guy.

She buried her head in the pillow and closed her eyes, still feeling the sweetness of the day.

Andre could not sleep either. Thoughts of Vivian had enslaved his mind and, unusually, he felt a slight impact on his heart as well, though he was not yet ready to accept it. He lay staring at the ceiling in the dark, and all he could see was Vivian's face shining by the glow of the bonfire. He closed his eyes to relive every moment he had spent with her that day.

Then a thought came to him, and it filled him with dread. He would have to leave in five weeks.

Suddenly, Vivian began to feel like an unattainable dream. He needed to tell Vivian but he was reluctant – what if she just walked away, thought of him as the guy who was going to leave anyway? God, if only she could understand. But why the hell was he so desperate to make her understand? After all, she was just the girl he'd met by the bus – twenty-four hours ago! He was getting too involved, too early; Vivian was a dangerous distraction and he had too much at stake to be entangled in some spur of the moment emotional attachment. But Vivian did not look like the type who could continue without the involvement of her emotions – she looked like a diehard romantic.

No emotional attachments, he reminded himself, and turned his thoughts back to the glass factory. The money needed to revive the factory had finally been arranged in Murano, but a prerequisite was that it would be paid off within five years of signing the contract. He did not have an option; if he was to do anything with his dream of resurrecting the business he had to work his heart out to set up that factory and get some returns – and for that, he had to leave for Murano. His plan was to complete the rest of the programme through distance learning, which was all very well, but …

Images of a laughing Vivian flashed into his mind again, and he covered his head with the blanket as if protecting himself from thoughts of her, from letting her into his life so easily. It looked like a losing battle, and finally he gave up and allowed his mind to wander the tracks of the day he had spent with her once more. The softness of her hands was still alive in his fingers, and his senses were still full of her sweet fragrance.

Chapter Nine

The following morning, Andre received a note.

I'm waiting for you by the lake ... Felt like cycling around so went early. Hope you don't mind. See you soon. Vivian

Andre was perplexed. Ideally he would have expected her to wait for him instead of going all by herself to the city. *Damn fool, thinking about her all night and she's gone all by herself. It's too early to be thinking like this, way too early. I need to slow down.*

He cycled to the lake and went all the way round, but Vivian was nowhere to be seen. *She actually left without me? Left me a random note and now she's nowhere to be seen?*

His thoughts were broken when a girl stepped onto the path in front of him. She was wearing a low-cut scarlet dress.

'Hi. I'm Lenny. Are you here for the Enigma festival as well?'

'Yes. Andre. Nice to meet you.'

Andre was scanning the place for any trace of Vivian, his brows tightly knotted.

'Looks like you're waiting for somebody. So am I. It's so irritating when people don't turn up on time.'

Andre looked at her and nodded. She bent to flick a leaf from her shoe and the plunging neckline provided a view which Andre could scarcely ignore. He had seen this performance way too many times before, and at this moment all it stirred in him was disgust. On some other day he might have enjoyed the view, but today his mind was somewhere else. The girl he was dealing with was awfully persistent as, without any encouragement from him, she went on:

'I'm so glad I bumped into you. I was beginning to wonder if I was the only soul alive in the world. It's so tranquil ...'

His eyes again swept the area.

Lenny continued her one-way conversation, giving him information in which he was not the least bit interested – how much she enjoyed her course, how she looked forward to the plays, how strange it was that they had never met before even though they were in the same college ...

Then she said, 'Would you care to go for a cup of coffee?'

Thoroughly miffed at Vivian for standing him up, and at himself for acting like a teenage fool, he decided to take up the offer. They found a café which had tables overlooking the lake.

During coffee, she dropped her spoon once and her napkin three times. Andre wanted to go back to the hostel but what, he thought, if Vivian really was waiting and then went back because he didn't appear? Maybe she had been delayed. Surprisingly, even that thought softened him more than the continuous blabber from across the table. His mind drifted again to the time he had spent with Vivian yesterday …

The moment they finished coffee, Andre walked at speed to the water's edge to scan the path again. An hour and a half passed without any sign of Vivian and Andre's irritation turned to anger. He had never been stood up before and he had certainly never waited for a girl for hours next to a lake, sitting on concrete steps.

If she doesn't want to meet, fine. There's no need for this nonsense.

Lenny said, 'I think I'm going back. I've waited long enough and I can't do any more. Nobody's making a fool out of me like this. Nice to meet you – and thanks for the lovely company.' She smiled and started to walk away.

'I'll come along. I think I've waited long enough too.'

They walked to where the bikes were parked and, as they approached, Lenny said,

'Oh no! Look at this, it really isn't my lucky day. I have a flat tyre.' She looked at Andre and clasped her hands in front of her. 'I know it's a lot to ask but is it possible that you could give me a ride? I can leave the bike locked and come back for it later.'

Andre wasn't sure but he nodded. It would be unacceptable to leave a girl stranded out here alone, no matter how annoying she was.

Throughout the ride he had to deal with further nonsensical chatter from Lenny while he fumed at

Vivian for making a fool out of him. As they reached the university campus, he took her to the girls' hostel. He saw Vivian, talking to two guys; he was ready to explode. She'd stood him up and here she was chatting away, in the most charming manner, to these guys? And he'd actually thought she was falling for him. How could he be so idiotic?

With this kind of judgement about people, Andre, you're not going to make a go of the business, that's for sure.

He dropped Lenny and she was just planting a thank-you kiss on his cheek when Vivian saw him. They stared at each other and in that moment he thought he saw flames rising in those eyes.

Vivian was not just angry, she was outraged. *What the hell is this? Lenny? Really, I thought the guy had some taste, but all men are the same. Creeps.*

She had received a note in the morning which read: *I'll pick you up from the girls' hostel, wait for me there ... Andre.*

She had been delighted after reading the note and, like a fool, had been waiting for him. Three long hours while he was having a good time with Lenny. She had never waited for anyone that long. Nor had anyone ever stood her up.

I shouldn't bother. I barely know him. None of my business what he does or with whom. She realised she had been standing and staring for too long. Thoroughly disgusted with herself for being so vulnerable towards a guy she had only just met, she started to walk away. Her face was set but her stomach was churning at the sight of Andre and

Lenny talking, Lenny touching his arm and tilting her head. She foolishly felt like crying but instead she gave them a haughty glance over her shoulder and continued walking. *I don't need any of this nonsense. I'll go to the rehearsal, that'll clear my head.*

Man, look at her attitude. She stood me up and no apologies – and now she's giving me the looks. Fine. I'm not going to go crawling.

'Want a coffee? I would love one,' said Lenny.

He merely nodded, his gaze still fixed on Vivian walking away. Her face looked unaccountably sad to him, in spite of all the anger in her eyes.

The coffee sat in the clay mug in front of him but he couldn't enjoy it. His thoughts kept wandering to Vivian standing in front of the hostel. Abruptly, he asked Lenny to finish whatever she was drinking, as he had to do some work. The moment she did, he walked out and went looking for Vivian, thinking,

What a moron I am, she stood me up and I'm pandering to her. Not only that, I'm actually looking for her. All the mixed up thoughts were clouding his mind when he saw her.

She was at the hall, rehearsing her part. She looked so innocent and so sad that he almost relented, and all he wanted to do was hold her in his arms and comfort her. He stood there for a while observing her and, somehow, logic started to melt into his fuming mind, like snowflakes on a warm roof. She did not seem like the sort of girl who would do something like this. What he did next was on pure impulse.

He walked up onto the stage and stood in front of her. Her eyes sparked with anger as she looked away and said,

'I'm rehearsing, do you mind?'

'Yes, I do.' With that he took her hand and turned away. She was clearly furious but he did not let that bother him.

'What do you think you're doing?' She tried to pull her hand away.

'We need to talk,' he said, with clear and measured authority.

'Why? You have a free moment from your date? How about you cart Lenny around a bit more.'

He could see the effort it took her to say something like that, for she had wrapped her hands around her stomach and turned her face to hide the emotional turmoil she was going through. The tears which were stinging those mesmerising eyes started to shine, the little droplets forced to stay where they were by force of will. Seeing her so affected, he thought about that stupid kiss that Lenny had planted on his cheek, and all the anger from waiting for those hours melted away.

He softened his tone and, resting his hands on her shoulders, turned her towards him. Cupping her face, he asked her to look at him. When he looked into her eyes, he knew that she hadn't sent that note. She could not have. She was too sweet, too naïve, and right now a bit confused by what was happening as well.

'What do you think you're doing?' She placed her palms on his chest to push him away, but his hands slipped around her waist and tightened their grip.

He said quietly, 'I'm holding you.'

'I can see that …'

'Then why are you asking?' A smile lurked on his face while hers became haughtier.

'Leave me alone.'

'I will not.'

'What?!' she said, bewildered, but her palms were no longer pushing him, they were resting stationary on his chest.

He laughed out loud and then, softening his grip and checking his urge to kiss her, he said,

'Tell me something, *cara*, did you send me a note asking me to wait by the lake?'

'No. Hell no, you sent me a note asking me to wait in front of the hostel.' Her expression changed from surprise, to horror, to slow realisation, and then it softened as she asked, 'Were you waiting for me for all that time at the lake?'

'Yes.'

'Oh God, and you thought I stood you up? Oh dear God. Andre, I swear I didn't send the note; I was waiting here, I swear I was.' Their faces were inches apart, and he wanted to close that distance, taste her sweetness on his lips, but all he did was rub her cheeks with his knuckles and very softly say,

'I know that now.'

'So, who would do something as horrible as that?' She was talking to herself as much as to him. 'It has to be Lenny. No one else could act so silly.'

He ran his fingers through her hair and said, 'I'll straighten her out, don't you worry.' Then, changing tack completely, he said, 'Now, what do you want to do considering we've lost half the day? Stick with the original plan or—'

'Stick with the original plan.'

Andre smiled at her and hugged her closer.

Vivian was relieved – and bewildered that it had affected her so much. Andre's fingers were softly exploring her hair and playing with the tousles as she stood motionless, lost in his arms. The same musky fragrance was filling her senses. She had been on the verge of crying when he had come over to talk to her. Controlling those tears was the hardest thing; in a matter of minutes she had gone from being angry, to sad, to wildly happy. She was comfortably engulfed in his arms when she heard one of the guys from the stage say that the director was calling for her, and she thought she heard a whispered 'Damn' from Andre.

'I'll be back soon,' she said.

He smiled and nodded, looking at her with such intensity that she wanted to surrender herself into his arms for eternity, but the guy who had come to call her was still lingering like a parasite.

Andre patiently waited in the audience for her to complete her rehearsal. He did not mind at all, and was amused to find that every time she looked at him she faltered and blushed. After forgetting her lines twice, she deliberately avoided looking at him. It was hilarious to see her staring off into the distance when so much of her attention was clearly directed towards him. There was a flutter of laughter when Vivian said his name instead of 'Palmo'. She turned beautifully red after that; it was the purest pleasure to observe.

So much for no emotional attachment, he thought – he was being pulled towards her like iron to a magnet. Earlier he had been ready to explode when he saw her talking to the other guys; jealousy had flowed through every vein in his body, and when she told him that she had been waiting for him, relief had flowed in its place. He was bewildered that a day with her had had such a drastic impact on him.

After a disastrous round of rehearsals she came down and said with a sigh,

'Finally, it's over, let's go.'

Everyone seemed to be staring at them. He knew he was not helping by sliding his arm around her waist – speculative eyes must have narrowed – but somehow she looked comfortable. Shy, but comfortable.

Chapter Ten

They went to explore the city again. They had both fallen in love with the place and, with just the two of them, it looked even prettier.

It was almost noon when they parked the bike on the mall road. As they walked further to the north of the road, dozens of little peddler stalls lined the sides, selling everything from bubble toys to woollen scarves. The market was right opposite the Nainidevi temple and was called the Bhutia Market. It had the most beautiful collection of handmade candles Vivian had ever seen.

Walking down one of the alleyways, Vivian's attention was taken by a little girl with tattered clothes and straw-like hair who stood staring at the bubble maker, which was selling little transparent bottles with wands attached to the inside of the tops. Her nose was runny but her eyes had a brightness in them as she watched the bubble maker, although a little sadness too. She made no attempt to buy the little toy, and when she looked at the other kids blowing bubbles, it was more in wonder than envy.

Vivian, who was observing the scene intently, told Andre, 'Give me a minute.'

He did not quite understand why Vivian was looking so intently at this little scene or what she intended to do as she swiftly walked past him. She walked to the bubble maker, took out some change, and bought a bottle to give to the little girl, who looked at her in disbelief at first, then smiled from ear to ear. It was the innocent smile of a child who had been given their most prized possession at a time when they had least expected it. Vivian had knelt down almost to the level of the little girl and they giggled together as she taught her to blow bubbles.

Her eyes danced with laughter as she talked to the girl. Hers was a beauty Andre had never seen before. A heart as soft as hers was not to be fooled around with; he knew that she would get emotionally attached, and right now emotional attachment was not on his list of priorities.

After saying a fond farewell to her little friend, Vivian came back beaming.

He kept his observations from this little scene to himself and they walked towards the pier, where colourful boatmen offered an array of generous deals. The boats were small, like gondolas, with a sofa-like seat at the stern and a small extra bench in the middle. They chose a boat with a seat covered in beautiful red cloth, with mirror-work and embroidery in threads of every colour of the rainbow. Andre gave Vivian his hand to step inside the boat and guided her to the seat without letting go.

They sat on the boat with the lightest breeze touching the water around them. Swans and ducks swam to the sides as the boat moved. As the boatman rowed, the oars left little ripples, which slowly died away behind them, returning the lake to calmness as though they had never been. Andre sat close and held her, pointing to a tree whose branches were partly in the water and partly on the bank. A lift in the breeze would move the branches back and forth in the water, creating a gentle tableau of nature at play.

He was relishing the closeness, enjoying her warm breath close to his. The boat ride lasted an hour, and they huddled close. Andre asked the boatman to go round once more, and Vivian looked at him.

'What?' he said. 'I like holding you and you don't seem to object in the boat, so boat it is.'

She averted her eyes, scanning the lake and the boats, looking as far away from him as possible.

He laughed as he said, 'You look a bit self-conscious!'

'Absolutely not,' she replied, her voice full of mock indignation.

God she looks sweet, he thought. Dappled sunlight played on her face, making her eyes look a shade lighter. He wanted to caress the tiny mole on her chin and run his fingers through the golden streaks of her brown hair. 'Utterly gorgeous,' he murmured to himself, completely absorbed in looking at her. Besides her beauty, there was something else which drew him to her. He did not understand the feeling – he had never felt it before. He wanted to listen to her unpretentious talk, look at her captivating smile and lose himself in this world where only the two of them existed.

'How come I never saw you in the expat bus?' Her words broke the silence.

'I don't live in the expat colony, I stay with friends. It means I'm much nearer to campus; I just go back on weekends to see family.'

As they talked, Vivian looked at him closely. He was not very tall but Andre had an aura about him; his eyes were the focal point of his face, deep and beautiful like the waters of a lake in the night, dark and glistening. She felt she could drown in those eyes and she did not want to be rescued, for there was an impeccable pleasure in drowning.

They sat there, fully at ease, a couple in love, talking and living these precious moments.

He told her stories about his childhood, where he grew up, his favourite food, and so the list went on … He belonged to a small town called Atrani, on the Amalfi coast in southern Italy.

'Interesting,' she said, quietly observing his face, his thin lips, as if carved from stone, and a nose slightly plump for the sharp face. The stubborn chin. The beautifully cut thick black hair. She was surprised at her own thoughts; never had she noticed a guy the way she was noticing Andre.

'We had a glass factory in Murano, near Venice. It was opened by my father and mother …'

There was an abrupt stop. Andre seemed surprised he had taken the story that far.

She gently touched his hand and said, 'It will all be fine.'

Surprised at her words and her ability to understand him, he held her hand, their fingers entwined as he gently kissed her knuckles before rubbing his chin on them.

'I've been blabbering,' he said, 'and you haven't even said a word. I know I'm a good-looking guy but you don't need to be so mesmerised.' He laughed, and she knew he was trying to change the subject – the moment he had spoken of his mother, his voice, normally filled with such conviction, had become low and faltering, as he shifted his gaze to somewhere beyond the horizon. She did not want to press him as she clearly saw it was difficult territory.

She told him about her grandmother who also happened to spend her formative years in Italy.

'Wow, that's a coincidence,' he added.

She smiled as she spoke; 'My grandma specifically asked all her grandchildren to call her *Nonna*. She always said, "It's my Italian link".' Her eyes became a bit lost at that statement, but she quickly changed the subject and started talking about her goal of studying medicine and becoming a doctor. How she wanted to work in the forgotten and poverty-stricken areas of the third world and provide ordinary people there with medical care.

She spoke with passion and tenderness in equal measure, telling him about her trip to Africa.

He nodded and observed the dedication in her eyes when she talked, her head slightly tilted. He sat there, noticing every bit of her, her long eyelashes which so added to the beauty of her brown eyes, her nose, which he could not quite place as being pointy or long – all he knew was that for him, it fitted her face perfectly. How he wished this ride could go on and he could just sit all day looking at her and feeling the essence of her. As much as he was smitten by her beauty, he was equally impressed by her career plans and her determination.

Career plans … Dammit, I need to tell her; she has to make an informed choice. It's just not fair otherwise. These thoughts successfully dampened his spirits and brought him down to earth.

'Vivian, there is something you should know …'

'There is?' she asked, hopefully.

'I need to leave in five weeks. The glass business I told you about? Work on the factory will start soon. I'll have to finish the remainder of my course in Murano. If things go as planned we can give new life to the factory.'

As he spoke, sadness intruded on Vivian's face, and the fingers which were resting in his hand so comfortably suddenly trembled. They were already so attuned to each other that he could see what was running through her mind, and rightly so – their worlds were far apart. But that was not what Andre wanted to dwell on right now. Although he could see apprehension written all over her face, he knew he could convince her, and he would. Meanwhile, they had to seize this time, this time together, which felt like gliding through the air, floating on clouds … free from the baggage of the past, from the hardships of the future; existing simply in the present, just the two of them. On the other hand, was she ready to take that plunge? He looked at her, but she was lost in the horizon once more.

Rubbing her palm with his thumb, he said, 'Where are you?'

'Nowhere,' she replied, but her smile did not have the same twinkle.

His hands slipped to the back of her shoulders and drew her close.

'Vivian, my life right now is not a clear path, and there's a lot at stake. I can tell you that I love spending time with you but what the future holds isn't something I know nor something I can predict. What I don't want to do is lose this valuable time with you.'

Love was not a word he should have said, but it was a bit too late to think now. She was listening to him so intently, looking at him with such puppy-dog eyes that he wanted to hold her close and lose himself in her.

She adjusted herself, leaning against him a bit more, and said,

'I understand.' Nothing more was needed.

By the time the trip was over, night had fallen and the city was lit up, nestling below the light-studded mountainside.

They slowly cycled the hilly road back to the campus in silence, living and breathing every moment, dismayed at the thought of separation as they neared the hostels, and another night of longing, of sleeplessness, of love that was blooming wildly in their hearts.

When they arrived, neither of them wanted to leave the other and they sat on the bench outside the auditorium, talking. Sometime before sunrise, the exhausted couple fell asleep on the bench.

Andre was woken by the voices of students going in and out of the auditorium. In something of a panic, his eyes scanned the place for Vivian, who was peacefully sleeping on the wooden bench beside him, oblivious to her surroundings. He did not want to wake her up. What he wanted was to snuggle up with her, but they were becoming surrounded by people, so he stroked her hair and her cheek, and called her name until she stirred.

Almost sleepwalking towards the girls' hostel, Vivian murmured,

'I'm fine, I can manage, I can walk … Don't worry about me.'

He put his arms around her and whispered, 'Sleep, *cara*, sleep. I'll come and ask somebody to wake you up after a few hours.'

She was resting her head on his shoulder as they walked, her eyes closed, following him. He wanted to lift her in his arms and carry her but at the same time did not want to lose this precious moment when she was trusting him blindly and following wherever he led her. He was sure she would simply drop if he left her at the hostel door, so he snuck into the hostel, walked her to her room and tucked her up in bed. He planted a kiss on her forehead and then looked at her to capture the image of this beauty, sleeping like a princess, her hair spread on the white of the pillow. He could not stop himself – he bent down and gave her another kiss and stroked her hair, and she barely stirred.

'If you want to be with her, then you'd better jump out of the window, or you'll be leaving her *and* the university.'

Andre swung his head and saw Devyani standing in the doorway, smiling.

'I just came in to witness the romantic love scene,' she said. 'But I also saw the warden on her way. Boys are most definitely not allowed.'

He felt himself blush like a fool, and saying a quick thank-you for this valuable piece of information, he jumped out of the window and walked away from the hostel.

Outside, he passed Lenny, and the look he gave her was enough to warn her never to attempt anything like that again. Still, he said,

'If I ever see you near Vivian again, you'll regret it more than anything else on this planet.' His face was so full of anger and disgust that Lenny turned on her heels and walked away as swiftly as she could.

The next day, he was waiting for Vivian with the bike.

'Hop on.'

While slipping on sideways she scrunched her nose and said, 'I'm hungry. How about we eat first?'

The last few days had been about walking, talking, and enjoying each moment together. As a result, they had never made it to the cafeteria at times when meals were being served.

'Lunch is packed, my lady!'

'So where are we going?'

'Surprise, sweetheart.'

She hung on to *'Sweetheart'*.

He stopped the bike near a taxi stand and said, 'The place is about sixteen miles east of Nainital, so a bike would have taken too long.'

She got down and climbed into the cab. Andre put his arm around her shoulders, leaving not an inch of space between them. He seemed absolutely comfortable sitting so close, whereas Vivian was somewhat hesitant but tried her best not to show it.

They reached a dreamy little town and the taxi dropped them next to a boat hire station. Andre quickly scanned the map before taking her over to a waiting pedal boat.

'You have the day planned?' She stepped into the boat, which wobbled as she sat down.

Beginning to pedal next to her, Andre said, 'I checked with the local guys and they suggested this place. It's supposed to be prettier and low on tourists.'

'They were right, it's stunning.'

She threw some pieces of bread for the ducks, and they crowded round the boat, competing for the treats, flapping noisily and turning in little circles. Andre guided the boat away from the town and towards a narrower part of the lake, where trees on both sides almost touched each other in mid-stream. The branches droopily caressed the waters while the faint smell of wet leaves floated in the air around them. In a moment of silence, they stopped there and sat looking at each other, feeling the unspoken bond. It was a spectacular moment of happiness, a fleeting glimpse of times to come, an image of dreams together.

He attached the bow rope to a wooden pole that stood in the shallows on a little spit of land, then took out a blanket borrowed from the hostel, laying it under a willow tree. Vivian's face became anxious and her eyes homed in on the blanket as she stood there under the tree, not knowing what was coming next.

'Relax, don't look so worried.' He came close and tucked a strand of hair behind her ear. 'I have some cake and my favourite poetry book. I thought I might read to you, if you like, and sitting here to read seems like a better idea than trying to do it on a wobbly boat.'

'Oh … yeah. Yeah, definitely, that'll be great,' she said, relief flowing through her.

They sat there talking, eating chocolate cake and drinking coke. When he thought she was sufficiently relaxed, he took a small book from his bag.

'I've read this poem so often, but now I have a face to relate to when I read it.' He looked deep into her eyes, came forward, held her hand, and with the other hand flipped the book open. 'Here goes.'

'She walks in beauty, like the night
Of cloudless climes and starry skies;
And all that's best of dark and bright
Meet in her aspect and her eyes;
Thus mellowed to that tender light
Which heaven to gaudy day denies.'

'It's lovely.'

'I think parts of it were written for you.'

He smiled, still holding her hand, and for a moment it seemed as if he was coming forward to kiss her, but then he stopped. A raindrop fell on his hand but he ignored it and said,

'I guess we need to make the best of dark and bright!' As he read on, she smiled. His touch awakened sensations in her which were unknown; his slight caress on her palm was leagues from anything she had ever known. She remembered that he was to leave in five weeks and maybe he had wanted to keep some distance – but then she saw him again through the trickle of rays, reading poetry to her with so much tenderness, and she wondered if this was forever. Her heart was swelling with emotions as she listened to the lines. The cold air had never smelled so sweet.

She was in a different world, one which belonged only to the two of them, and she knew in her heart that it was a real and tangible world, and not of her imagining. Was she taking all of this too quickly? To say she was becoming emotionally involved would be an understatement, and to be in that position so soon was definitely not a good sign. With a guy who was to leave in a few weeks and who may or may not be as involved as her …

What am I doing? He has no choice, he clearly said that; then why the hell am I getting involved? It's all too complicated. Still, she could not free herself from the strong current that was sweeping her in an unknown direction.

Tiny raindrops started filtering through the trees.

'Looks like it's going to rain,' said Andre.

They packed up and got back in the boat, and Andre pedalled much faster this time.

She looked at him. 'Your t-shirt is soaked.'

Before he could reply she turned her face to the rain and laughed, with her hands outstretched and her palms facing upwards as if to welcome the deluge.

He drank in her excitement, her happiness, and the rain no longer troubled him. In the space of forty-eight hours, she had taken his emotions on a rollercoaster ride, had his heart hammer at her slightest touch and, more than anything else, filled him with extreme happiness and contentment. Laughter echoed off the slope that rose from the shoreline and they lived and breathed every moment of this enduring togetherness.

Completely drenched by the time they returned the boat, their shivering brought them even closer. Despite all the practical thoughts swirling in his head about no emotional attachments, she was pulling him in.

They rode the taxi back, got onto the bike, and Andre took her back to the hostel to change. When the rain stopped, they did some more aimless walking, with Andre's arm tightly clasped around her shoulder and hers around his back, whispering to each other in the darkness of the night, feeling each other's presence and the love that enveloped them, which neither of them were ready to accept.

Chapter Eleven

Sitting on a stone bench outside a small and picturesque temple, he looked at her with dreamy eyes and said,

'You look gorgeous.'

'I know, I always do.'

He kissed her cheek.

'What was that?'

'I thought it was pretty self-explanatory. A kiss. You need another one to understand?' His eyes had a cheeky glint in them.

Before she could say a word he kissed her cheek again, held her hand, rested it against his heart, and walked with her up the temple staircase.

The place was so quiet that they could hear each other breathe, but Andre's heart was hammering in his chest. He wanted to tell how he felt – properly – but he kept reminding himself that their worlds were too far apart.

Andre also saw signs of apprehension and sadness in her eyes. There were so many emotions in those eyes that even though he could normally read her well enough, he felt a bit confused. As they walked out of the temple, she said something which made his heart ache.

'There is so little time, Andre.'

'I know.' He said it very gently, as he could see she was as troubled as he was.

'What you don't know is that I can't help but love you.'

The hand which was rubbing her back stopped, and the grip unconsciously tightened around her waist, drawing her closer. He looked at her with a contentedness that spoke volumes.

Very softly he said, 'I know that as well. But why are you crying, my *cara*, I'm not that bad!'

'It's not you, Andre. We want such different things in life. It can never work. And to top it all off, you need to leave ...'

He cupped her face in his hands and looked at the moist chestnut eyes and the undeniably red nose.

'Hey, don't you think you're jumping the gun here? Let things take their course, we'll take it as it comes. I can always go back and forth.'

What was he talking about? Going back and forth? That was never in his plan, but his mind had already started thinking of options when he heard those magical words.

In those few minutes, he had worked out a skeletal, if not fully functional, plan. All he wanted to feel at this moment was Vivian and the fact that she loved him. The thought was making every nerve in his body sing. He wanted to be with her, to protect her, make her belong to him completely. He looked at this beauty with the red nose, who was crying because she wanted to be with him, and a smile tugged at the side of his mouth. He knew she belonged to him – he just had to convince her. He would have kissed her at this very moment had she not been so upset.

'No. I know it can never work out.' She was almost sobbing, and part of her felt like an absolute idiot. She was, after all, talking about a guy she had only met a few days ago, who had not even expressed his love. She was amazed at the compelling force that had made a girl like her actually take the initiative and express her love outright. In the past, she could barely say hello to a guy without him taking the initiative, and here she was opening her heart to someone she had practically just met. *What a fool I have been.*

He whispered, 'Baby, give it a try. Give it a chance.'

He spoke with such evident sincerity that Vivian did not know what to do. She was torn between her mind and her heart.

The rain had begun to show its presence again, in the form of a slight drizzle, with occasional cloudbursts, but that did not bother either of them as they stood there, in each other's arms.

He gently held her face close to his and said, 'I don't want to be apart from you.'

She could feel his breath on her cheeks. Terribly conscious of their closeness she said, 'Me neither. But—'

'Shhh.' He put his finger on her lips, brushing them gently with his thumb. He had been aching to kiss her all day and now the simple touch of her lips threatened to sweep him away.

Two raindrops were resting on her lower lip, which made them look all the more inviting. He bent his head and kissed her for the very first time, feeling her warmth in the cold rain. His fingers moved slowly through her wet hair, his mouth brushed against hers, lightly coaxing, more a request than a demand, delicately exploring the contours of her lips, feeling the essence of her, taking in her softness. With one hand he gently pushed her wet hair behind her ears, his fingertips touching her neck, gliding around the neckline of her t-shirt, while the other hand slid slowly down to her waistline, drawing her closer. Her soft lips and the warmth of her body were driving him crazy and the thread of control he was trying so hard to hold on to was close to breaking.

She barely knew how to kiss.

'Never been kissed' is impossible. She is too attractive for that. Kissed by idiots would be more likely. But she was responding, her hands drifting away from his shoulders to explore his hair. Cold, trembling fingers brushed against his neck, creating sensations which the most expert hands would be unable to stir. His lips pressed further, asking for more, urging hers to part, and she melted before his insistence. He felt her parted lips and the kiss, which till now had been light and coaxing, started to become passionate and demanding. His tongue felt the warmth and lusciousness of her lips and went further, exploring her mouth, wishing that time would stop and that this would go on forever. He

was taken to new levels of desire; deepening the kiss, he drew her even closer, enclosing her in his arms protectively, signalling that she belonged to him.

She was kissing him back and she was driving him mad with desire; the touch of her skin beneath his fingers and the touch of her lips on his own, the taste of her mouth mingling with his was too enticing. He was lost, lost in the fragrance, in the velvety touch, in the love which she was giving him. Lost in this heavenly moment.

Andre's touch took Vivian to a different world. His urgent lips and the strength of his grasp sent shivers running through her. It was a rapturous delight, an overpowering emotion which she had never felt before. The sensations that he invoked made her lose track of time and space and all she felt was him, his fragrance, his warm fingers and, more than anything – she dared now to hope – his love. His firm hands were resting on her waist and she could still feel the warmth on her skin through her rain-soaked t-shirt.

As they paused, his breathing heavy and uneven from the kiss, desire was running wild in his eyes, and he kept looking at her with a gaze that wanted more. She was still held close in his arms as he whispered,

'I love you, Vivi. I love you so much.'

The words created a fresh stir, filling her with unbounded happiness.

'It'll be fine, my darling, don't worry.' He hugged her close and she felt secure, loved, believing every word.

With eyes gleaming, he whispered, 'You know you taste like heaven. I have never felt this good after just kissing.'

Happy and flustered at the same time, she pinched him and he giggled.

'*Just* kissing?' she said. 'So, you have "tasted heaven" ...' She smiled a smile full of mischief.

But his smile was altogether different – his eyes betrayed the tenderness and passion within, his fingers gently caressed her lips, his voice softened when he spoke.

'Yes. I tasted heaven and I think I am going to taste some more.' He closed his eyes and kissed her once more, a kiss filled with undying passion and ecstatic love.

The night flew by in the sweet words she said; they cuddled together on the stone bench outside. By morning Vivian was exhausted and it was time for the trip back to Delhi. They had to pack and get back to the bus.

'I just need twenty minutes.'

'Alright. I'll see you right here.' He spoke with the tenderness and conviction of a man madly in love. His gaze followed her as she disappeared inside the hostel, constantly looking back and smiling.

The pickup point was filled with students travelling back, excited, tired, thrilled – a whirlpool of emotions. Andre and Vivian stood in a corner holding hands, trying to remain aloof and apart from the rest, in their own world.

They boarded the bus back to Delhi, and an exhausted Vivian slept, leaning on Andre's shoulder as he sat, utterly content. She was all he wanted in a woman and she was next to him, sleeping peacefully on his shoulder, her hair tickling his neck. He was only twenty-two – how strange that he should feel so sure so young. He looked at her and she slept like a child, absolutely calm and peaceful, trusting in him completely. He just had to work out a plan to make their disjointed worlds meet, though he couldn't bring himself to believe that it was possible.

Right now, he just wanted to live in this peace.

Chapter Twelve

In a few days, Vivian was back home. Her parents' faces reflected their delight – and in her father's case, relief.

Vivian couldn't contain her excitement, and news of her trip spilled out immediately. She described at length the beauty of the place, the lake, the temple, the markets, the sunset which made the lake glitter, the lights which had illuminated the entire mountain. She went on and on, and her parents sat on the sofa with mugs of coffee and nodded occasionally.

Every mention of Andre's name invited a frown from Carlos. He turned his face towards the window, looked at the ceiling, every movement clearly telling Vivian that he was absolutely uninterested in Andre or in anything to do with him. Vivian understood – Carlos still treated her like the five-year-old girl who had played basketball with him, who could barely ride a bike, and here she was talking about some man. He could not help but get annoyed. Maria looked much more relaxed, smiling gently whenever there was a mention of Andre.

Vivian could gauge Maria's expressions and had a feeling that she knew what was going on.

Is it true that mothers know everything? Is it the way I say his name? Not letting it bother her, she thought to herself that even if her mother knew, it was fine, she had nothing to hide.

She had not slept properly for days, all the late-night walking had tired her out considerably, and later, dreaming about Andre, she quickly drifted off to sleep.

After managing a good eight hours, she tried to analyse the madness of the past couple of days. Thoughts about practicality, Andre leaving in five weeks, their different career goals, all started playing on her mind. Her thoughts were clouded with worry about the future. She knew for certain she would not be able to handle a five-week relationship – she would be the idiot who would wait for him however long he was gone. But still the longings of the hammering heart were overpowered by the demands of practicality.

There will be continents, not even countries, between us. His goals are clear, so why am I trying to get involved in something which has no future? Why am I even thinking about the future? We've just met.

The more she reasoned with herself, the more it made sense to part ways. They were to inhabit two worlds which could never coincide. How she wished that she could wave a magic wand and this beautiful dream could come true.

Physically shrugging herself back to reality, she decided on pragmatism.

She was determined to tell him as soon as she returned to college.

But when she did see him again, her heart leapt and she felt incapable of saying anything which would cause pain in those entrancing eyes. He gave her a warm and lingering hug and planted a kiss on her forehead, completely oblivious of what was coming next.

'Did you sleep well, sweetheart?'

She nodded and tried hard to smile. His choice of words sent a tingle down her spine – she could melt even at the sound of his voice. As they walked towards the football ground, her hands were already locked together from the pent-up emotions, while one of his comfortably rested on the curve of her waist.

As they reached the pitch, gathering all her courage, she said, 'Andre, there is no point starting something which can never work.'

He leaned against an old tree at the side of the pitch, with his hands tucked into his pockets and one leg crooked backwards, resting on the trunk behind him. Suddenly, her carefully rehearsed plan of action went out the window. His dark eyes went darker, filled with surprise, almost panic, and as a result, words started coming out in a confused mumble.

'I was thinking that … well, I think it is very … of course you're right, it's not very practical.'

With a tremendous effort of will, she said, 'You obviously have your own plans and I have mine, and they don't coincide.' She was twisting her fingers now, but she continued, 'And ... well I think there's no point starting something we can't continue.'

He listened patiently, showing little expression.

'Is that it? Or is there anything else you want to add?'

Her heart raced. *There are a million things I would like to add. To begin with, I love you, I can't help it. I know we have differences but God I want to make it work somehow.*

Getting a hold of herself, she spoke the next words with as much control and poise as she could manage.

'No, that's the gist.'

'And this is what you truly want?'

'Yes.'

The finality of the word seemed to hit her much harder than him, and the tears gathered in the corners of her eyes came rolling down her cheeks in an uncontrollable stream.

His eyes did not leave her face for even a second, as if he was certain she would change her mind; as if he was absolutely sure of his power over her.

'You cannot melt me by looking at me.'

'I'm not saying I can,' he said, in a tone which was more amused than angry. He stepped forward and pulled her towards him, gently stroking her back and her hair, offering an unspoken comfort as she sobbed. 'Baby, you belong with me, and none of your practical thinking is going to change that.' He placed another kiss on her forehead and said with great tenderness, 'Surely you don't believe you'll be able to stay here without me?'

She looked at him and then buried her head in his chest.

'No.' How could she live without him? It was just not possible, and the pleasure of being in his arms was a far greater thing than anything she had ever experienced.

Once her sobs had subsided, he cradled her face in his hands, kissing away her tears. Placing his mouth against her ear he said,

'We started this and we will make it work. Trust me.'

That breached her last remaining defences and she surrendered, lost in his eyes. She saw the future in them, saw the trust which he was asking her to put in him and the love which he wanted her to feel. Instead of fear or sadness she felt only happiness, and a dream of the two of them together started taking shape.

He whispered, 'So, can we start now?'

'What—'

His lips were on hers and he kissed her in a way that was both demanding and nerve-tingling.

She felt the same shiver running all over her body as he came close, taking control, as if she belonged to him completely. Her mind stopped working; all the fears and doubts were converted into passion, a heightened passion which made her draw herself closer to him and slip her hands towards his neck, caressing his hair and feeling his fire with an intensity that threatened to drive her crazy. She knew she was treading a narrow and dangerous path but she loved it and wanted it as much as Andre.

As they stopped, he looked at her and, in a husky voice, whispered,

'I guess that's the start sorted.'

A smile hovered on her lips and she whispered back, 'I guess.'

'We can bridge the gap, my love, just give me time. I'll travel back and forth, get my absences approved by the dean – given my situation that won't be difficult. Don't go asking what situation, I'll tell you soon enough. For now I just want to kiss you.'

Chapter Thirteen

Next day, Andre was waiting outside the college. He sat on the low brick wall that divided the pavement from the trees behind. Holding a few red roses, he patiently waited for Vivian to appear, and waiting had never felt so sweet.

As she appeared in the distance he stood up, and as she drew close he saw the face of a woman beaming with love. The love which he saw in her eyes he knew wasn't imaginary; it was there, solid and strong. He handed her the roses and held her in the circle of his arms, hugging her close.

Resting her head on his chest she asked, 'How did you know I like flowers without the wrapping?'

'Sixth sense. It's finely tuned when it comes to you.'

It became increasingly difficult to attend classes. All they did was walk around holding hands, sit and talk for long hours.

Andre would take her to his apartment, which he shared with a couple of other guys. It was very modern and tastefully done, and as tidy as any bunch of guys would have kept it. Andre's room was large, more than enough space for a double bed, a table and a chair, along with a large mahogany wardrobe. The bed was by a window, outside which a tree with white flowers swayed even in the slightest wind. Three walls were painted plain white and one a deep blue.

On one of their apartment days, as they were lying in each other's arms, Andre said casually,

'Vivi, I have actually never taken you on a proper date in Delhi, have I?'

'You're right, muppet.' She turned to rest on her elbow and gave him a wink.

'Muppet ...' He frowned. 'Seriously, Vivi, muppet – I hate that.'

She giggled. 'Alrighty, I won't call you muppet.'

'Too late. You need to pay for this mistake.' He crawled on top of her, tickling her till she was in fits of laughter, and then kissed her in the very same places, completely losing himself.

'How about Wednesday?' he said. 'That gives you a day to come up with a believable lie.'

'Lie? About what?'

'About being late going home, dumb head. I'm taking you on a date.'

'Oh ... sounds interesting! Muppet!'

More laughter echoed from the room, with Andre tickling her a bit more and Vivian desperately trying to reciprocate.

On Wednesday, she was slightly more dressed up than usual, but nothing extraordinary. She didn't want to drop any hints to her parents – she had told them that there were extra lectures and that she would go straight to her medical class from college.

That little lie had her insured till about 8:00 p.m. Wearing a knee-length, lemon-coloured A-line dress, linen with Croatian lace, she left the house.

When he saw her, Andre stood up to take a good look. The lemon colour added a soft glow to her face and her curls were left loose, just the way he liked them. The pearl dangler was swaying back and forth between her tresses and a dainty necklace made of pearl and yellow topaz sat against her collarbone. Normally she didn't wear makeup, but he could see that she had used a lip gloss today, which made her lips look even more inviting. Looking at this dazzling beauty, his heart swelled with pride; she looked so innocent and so gorgeous that he just wanted to fill her with his love. He had to stop himself from kissing her the moment he saw her and all the passion he felt was transferred to his gaze.

Vivian looked a little self-conscious, and when he said, 'Let's go before I forget that we're going out,' her cheeks flushed with colour.

'So where are we going?'

'Surprise, *cara*. Patience.' He held her hand and led her to a cab. Opening the door for her, he whispered, 'Somebody has dressed up. You look lovely.'

'Thanks.' She smiled and looked away.

The taxi negotiated the crowded streets to their destination, Hauz Khas Village.

As they got out she said, 'Oh, I know this place, Devyani told me about it.'

'Telling and seeing are two different things, darling.'

She scrunched up her nose and nodded as he paid the cab driver.

They walked along a narrow, crowded street with a colourful market on both sides – lines of stalls selling clothes, jewellery, shoes, mainly women's fashion, along with an array of restaurants. Andre saw her looking at everything and, drawing her close, he said,

'Shopping later. I know where we're going.'

Giggling away she said, 'I wasn't thinking of shopping.'

'I'm glad, because we're not wasting any time on that. I just need to pick up something. Do you mind waiting for a few minutes?'

'No worries, but what do you need to pick up?'

'Surprise!' He smiled as he disappeared into one of the shops. He came out with a packet which Vivian tried to steal a peek into.

'Why can't you tell me?' She tried to tilt her head in the direction of the packet and Andre pulled it further away, laughing.

'It is absolutely nothing, but I'm loving seeing you so uncomfortable, not knowing what's coming; a part of me just wants to take you in circles.' He laughed and pulled her close as they entered a park, and what Vivian saw there made her forgot all about the packet. There were dozens of deer running around, tiny rabbits frolicking in the grass.

'Oh my God, are we really still in the middle of a busy, bustling city?'

'Yes, my dear, we are.'

They walked past the deer, onto a narrow path which snaked around the long trees that covered the path in a green canopy.

A monument of some kind stood in the middle of the park. Barbed wire blocked the way to the narrow staircase on one corner of the square structure, and Andre carefully moved it aside before quietly sneaking her in.

'What are you doing? This isn't allowed, surely?' She spoke in a hushed tone.

'Hurry up.'

She squeezed through and he quickly put the barbed wire back. They walked up the stone steps.

'Where are we going?'

'Shhh … keep climbing.'

She did as she was told. As they reached the top, he gave her a hand and they emerged onto a huge terrace. They walked close to the edge and neither said anything for several minutes.

The view was spectacular. Beneath a blue sky with a few wisps of white cloud lay a small lake surrounded by lush green trees. Further ahead stood the fabulous Hauz Khas fort on one side and the skyscrapers covering the skyline on the other. It was a beautiful mix of a lost world, nature and a modern high rise city.

'This is gorgeous. I never knew this view existed.'

He opened his bag and took out a green and black check blanket, spreading it on the stone floor. He had to make a conscious effort to hold himself back – he had promised her a date and they would have a date. He gave himself a mental shake.

God, why does she have to look so beautiful? I'm a lost cause.

She looked at the cans of Coke and the burgers and her favorite chocolate cake which he was taking out from the same bag she had tried to peek in earlier and smiled.

'You have planned.'

He said nothing. His eyes always became dreamy when he thought about her – dreamy, with traces of passion. It was something which only she could read in his eyes.

'What's going on in that head of yours?'

He gave her a peck on the cheek and said, 'You. I would have brought champagne, but knowing you it would have been difficult to walk you down the stairs.'

Vivian never really drank; for one she was too young according to her father, but also, she had not quite acquired a taste for alcohol yet. Andre sat close and they talked about Nainital, about their magical times together, about cycle rides, about the future and, inevitably, the glass factory. Vivian noticed the sudden change in Andre's tone at the mere mention of the factory. She knew he was silently upset about it and she wanted him to share that feeling with her, so that she could ease his pain. So instead of changing the subject she decided to confront it head-on.

'Andre, why is it you always get upset when we talk about the glass factory?'

Andre knew she deserved an answer. He had never talked about it with anybody – not even the friends he had been living with for two years – but there was something about the way Vivian asked that made him want to get it out of his system. He softly laid a kiss on her forehead and stood up, to stand at the edge of the terrace. His gaze turned to the horizon.

"When I was fifteen my mother was diagnosed with cancer. It was the hardest moment of my life.'

The statement jolted Vivian. Never in her wildest dreams had she thought that the reality of Andre's pain was so dreadful.

He continued, 'I clung on to the thin ray of hope which the doctors had shown us. Papà thought private doctors were better so he went that route, which eventually led to selling off everything we had to pay for the treatment. By the time I was sixteen, I was actively engaged with all the dealings of the factory and running them single handed. Papà and I used to alternate our shifts in the hospital and in the factory. Over the years, we did all we could. The treatments gave Mama a few more years but not the life which I so wanted for her.

'When she died, we were broken, emotionally and financially. The only thing which we were left with was the family home near Murano and a small room in the factory. The business was moving towards closure. Then Papà got this offer in India and he took it – it paid well and would help keep us afloat.

'That glass factory was built by my parents together. Mama used to design the pieces, and my earliest childhood memories are of her little office, papers and designs scattered everywhere and Mama sitting in the midst of it all in a swivel chair. I used to go there with my grandma after school and do all my homework while she finished her work.'

Andre felt an unfamiliar constriction in his throat. Telling someone was not only a new experience but somehow an enormous relief. It was as if all the pent-up anger and frustration was finally being drained from his system. A smile tugged at his lips as he said,

'As a reward for doing my homework, she used to put me in her swivel chair and twirl me around.' The faint smile vanished as he said, 'We did everything, Vivi, we did everything we could but it didn't work. You know what my mama's biggest fear was when she was leaving us?' He turned his head slightly to look at Vivian, who was gazing at him intently, her face almost drained of colour. His hands thrust deep in his pockets, he looked up to hide the tears which were burning at the back of his eyes.

'It was me she was worried about. She was in great pain but all she bothered about was me. Before dying she made a diary for me, and against every year she wrote what I should be doing. She said, when she was not there, I could read it and it would be just as she if she was guiding me through that coming year. She asked me to read only that year and not the years ahead.

'You know what she wrote for when I turned twenty-two?'

Vivian could hear his voice becoming knotted and she got up and put her arms around him from behind.

'What did she write?'

'She wrote, "Fall in love with the aspects of the girl you can't see, because they are the most important." She put a little x.' He turned, rested his head on her shoulder and whispered, 'I have the best girl.'

She lifted her eyes to see the haunted gaze of the man with whom she was madly in love.

He said, 'I want to revive the glass factory, it is what my papà did, it's what my mama did, and it is what I should be doing. It belongs to my parents, both of them. I want that glass to go places, I want to see it gleaming in the finest stores, I want to revive the business for Mama and Papà.'

She softly placed her hand on his jaw, so full of tension, and whispered,

'I'm positive you will. I love you, Andre, I love you so much.' It broke her heart to think of Andre as a young boy, willing his mother to live; she wanted to take away all the sadness from his heart and fill it with love – her love. She said, gently, 'You are a very special person, Andre. You can do absolutely anything.'

A new intimacy developed that day, an emotional bond which was too strong, too overpowering for two young people. Vivian understood for the first time the depth of his motivation, but at this moment she didn't want to dwell on it. Her only concern was to make Andre feel better.

As they stood glued to the spot on the terrace, she pressed a soft kiss on his lips. Never in the past had she initiated a kiss, but today she felt differently; she wanted to kiss him with all her heart, take away all the pain. Andre raised his head, his eyes full of surprise, and after a couple of seconds of separation their lips joined again.

They sat there quietly, Vivian gently rubbed his back, and time and again gave him affectionate pecks on the side of his neck where her head was resting. And then she laid her lips on his, kissing him with a tenderness that was even more enticing than passion. Her hands were softly caressing the skin of his neck and shoulders. As if that was not enough, she nipped his earlobe and started exploring the details with her tongue exactly as he used to kiss her. What had he taught her, he thought; it was sweet torture! She gently pressed the sides of his neck with her lips before passionately kissing his neck until he felt he was ready to explode. He opened his eyes and looked at her face, the face that made every bit of his heart ache, the face that he would never be able to forget. The moment took over and he kissed her lips again.

Somewhere in a mingling of lips and breaths she found herself horizontal on the blanket and felt Andre's weight on her. He nuzzled her neck, kissed the back of her ear, feeling and tasting every bit of her mouth and brushing her parted lips with his own.

Gently pulling her hair back, he kissed the sides of her neck, the little shallow of her collar bone, while his fingers gently tugged on her ear and then slipped down to hold her waist. He slowly removed her necklace and Vivian almost shuddered as he slipped it away.

'Relax, my love, I'm just removing the necklace,' he whispered hoarsely, a craving burning in his eyes as he locked his mouth with hers once more. He kissed her neck again and this time she heard herself moan for him. Andre made desire flow through her body, passion run wild in her, passion which she had not even known existed. His tongue touched every possible place in her mouth, exploring every tiny detail. She felt he wanted to go further but somehow he stopped himself.

He so wanted to go further, but his boundaries were firm. He knew that no matter how much she loved him, she was not ready, and he would be the last to make her feel guilty or sad or regretful. If she was able to drive him insane just by kissing him, he thought, they would surely lose control if they went any further. The thought made him ache, for he so wanted her to belong to him completely, to make love till both of them were utterly drained, but this was not the time and this terrace was definitely not the place.

Their bodies were entwined until the chill in the breeze gave them some hint of the passing time.

'I want to show you something,' he whispered in her ear. He sat up, taking her hand and leading her by the waist, making her sit between his legs and lean back against him. She had her head turned sideways, still looking at him and breathing heavily, her hair ruffled. He pulled her closer, and digging his nose into the nape of her neck whispered, 'Look ahead.'

She turned her gaze as Andre had asked, though deep inside she just wanted to be in his arms, take in his fragrance and enjoy the familiar melting feeling which she always had when he held and kissed her. But what she saw was indeed breathtaking. The sun was slowly setting, leaving a soft golden glow filling the trees behind it. Shades of red and orange from the sunset seemed somehow mixed with the colour and depth of the water. The entire place was bathed in a golden light which caught the tips of the leaves, transforming the tableau in front of them into a thing of magic and wonder. It was perfectly peaceful and quiet, and they sat there listening to the sporadic chirping of birds and to their own breathing – almost, it seemed, to the beating of each other's hearts.

'This is so serene,' she said, quietly. 'I can't think of a better place for a date. Thank you for bringing me here.'

'You are welcome. Anyway, you can always pay me back.'

He took the necklace and carefully clipped it on again. Lazily dragging himself up, he started to pack their stuff back into the bag. Meanwhile, Vivian stayed where she was, happy to sit a while longer.

'Not after sunset, *cara*. I don't know how safe that would be.'

She got up obediently and they made their way down the stairs. Once again, Andre removed the barbed wire and put it back behind them.

'I had the most wonderful day, Vivian,' he said.

'Me too.'

When he dropped her home she was beaming.

'I am sure,' he said, 'Maria will be able to tell which class you were off to.' They both laughed as he bid her goodbye.

Vivian went straight to her room, saying that she was tired, in a desperate attempt to hide her beaming face and her slightly dishevelled state. The taste of his kiss was still alive in her mouth and the warmth of his hands on her skin. Looking at herself in the mirror, she noticed a love bite on her neck which made her smile even more.

Changing to sweatpants and a high-necked jumper to hide her hickey, she came to the dining table for her meal. A story was quickly established about the extra class, a story that didn't warrant any kind of questioning or doubt from either Maria or Carlos.

Post-dinner and after a short chat with her parents, she retired to her room. The calendar hanging on the wall again offered a reminder that he would leave in a few weeks, and her whole body tensed. She knew it was a short-term thing. Andre had told her to live in the present, but she was going beyond that now. With every passing day new layers of emotions were developing. Tears started to spring from her eyes at the mere thought of separation, but then Andre's words, that he would travel back and forth, returned to her, giving her the reassurance she needed.

She decided to give him a call – his voice always did wonders for her. She wouldn't discuss what was going on in her mind. Instead, she told him about the love bite. His tone suggested he was very pleased with his work, and there was an excitement in his voice when he said,

'I can't wait to see it tomorrow. Does it hurt?'

'No, of course not.'

That fetched a little laugh from Andre, along with a promise that she would be getting a few more of those.

They talked about the day, about the sunset, about kissing on the terrace under the sky, about mundane things. She sat huddled on her bed, clinging to every word he said, words which worked as a balm to soothe her heart and mind.

The next day, as Vivian unwrapped her scarf, Andre said,

'Oh my God, it's really blue. I think it needs treatment.'

She was still trying to interpret that statement when he started kissing her in the very same place.

'Doctor Andre at work. Do not disturb.' He looked up and smiled, his mischievous eyes sparkling.

Chapter Fourteen

Time flew by, and the day came when Andre had to leave for Murano. It had been the fastest five weeks of his life. He didn't want to leave her.

What if she gets tired of waiting for me? No; hell, I'll come back in four weeks. I'll stay with her, make her feel loved. God, I need more time. He cupped his head in his hands as he sat waiting for Vivian on the concrete wall outside the college. When she came he could see the lines of worry on her face. Fear of losing her gripped his mind but when she spoke, it took him by surprise.

'Andre, I'll wait for you. Even if it takes months, years … I don't care. I'll wait for you. I don't think I've loved anybody the way I love you; I don't think I ever could. So don't worry about me, go set up your factory. I'm there with you, always.'

He was unable to say even one word, for what she had made him feel was beyond words. It was beyond time and boundaries. He took her to his apartment and, on this last day together, they once again enjoyed the same feeling – of dissolving, of becoming one, breaths mingled, souls entwined.

He left for Murano full of her love, to carry his family's buried legacy forward, to pick up the remains of the past and shape them into the future.

Without Andre, her life felt empty, her heart felt hollow. She waited for him. And when he called, listening to his voice felt as though he was applying a soothing balm to her soul.

'How are you?' he asked.

'Dreadful without you. I'm missing you.'

'Oh Vivi, don't even go there, I cannot begin to tell you how much I'm missing you. I love you, sweetheart. Every day not seeing you is a complete pain in the ass.'

She giggled at the comparison. 'It's so nice just to talk to you, Andre. Your voice … it almost feels like music to my ears.'

'What do you mean, "almost"? It better feel like music, not just almost.'

Both of them giggled. They talked about mundane things. And when they hung up she felt a wild delight, as if infused with a new exuberance, a new life.

She tried to concentrate on her medical entrance exam studies, thinking that this was the time and she would try to complete as much as possible while he was not around. He had to come back after four weeks for some work, just a few days, but she was literally counting the minutes. Time passed at great speed when he called, and after every call the clock returned to an unbearable crawl.

Sometimes thoughts about how their relationship could ever work would come into her mind, but over time she learnt to set them aside. She put a heavy lid on reality, and occasionally it would bubble and steam but she always managed to keep it in place.

Carlos was looking remarkably happy, and with a certain eagerness in his tone he told the family,

'My old friend Alberto is coming with his family in four days. I have a fabulous plan for you. We will all leave on the twenty-fifth of this month for a safari to the Jim Corbett. I've heard it's great!'

Vivian's spirits immediately plummeted. Andre was coming back on the twenty-fifth and she had to be there. It was a disastrous plan for her – nothing about it was "fabulous".

'I can't go, I have something at college I can't miss.'

'Vivian, it's just four days, it's no big deal.'

'It is a big deal, Dad …' Her mind was working overtime to come up with reasons why she couldn't go, to somehow excuse herself from the plan. 'I … I … have my interim examinations.'

'Interim examinations? What exactly are those?'

'They … they are between terms, not the regular exams but a preparation for the main ones. I … I can join you for the weekend, that way I won't miss the exams.' Weekends, it occurred to her, she and Andre could never meet anyway as she had to be at home. Her hands felt moist and her feet went cold. She hated lying to her parents but it was not just any other day, it was the end of four long weeks of torture, of not seeing Andre, and there was no way under the sun that she could not be with him.

Maria was staring at her.

Carlos was annoyed. 'I have never heard of interim exams.'

'Maybe it is just an Indian thing …'

'I have already spoken to Alberto and both Matias and Sebastian are coming as well. You love them, don't you? And Sebastian doesn't even set fire to things anymore.' Carlos was looking for a nod from her.

'Yes I do, but I cannot miss my exams.'

As much as Vivian respected 'uncle' Alberto, she hated his two sons. They were intolerable; the elder one, Matias, was only interested in hitting on her and most of the time his conversations were directed to her breasts. If Andre ever saw him, sure as hell he'd hit him. And the younger one was a complete freak. His hobby was burning things; he burnt everything from leaves to toy trucks, and the reason Vivian hated him so much was that as a child he had burnt her favourite doll. He was forever in her bad books after that, and now he and his brother would have to be tolerated for four full days – or two if she could skip the first two days.

Carlos gave up and Maria said, 'I'll call Kristoff, he'll come and stay with you here for a day.'

'There is no need for that, I can stay with Devyani. I'd prefer that.'

By now her sweaty palms were clinging to the hem of her skirt under the table. Maria looked at her and Vivian suspected that her mother knew what nonsense was being cooked up, but without further argument she said,

'That's fine, but only for a day. You are coming to Jim Corbett the next day, with Kristoff.'

'Very well.' Vivian took a deep breath and looked at her plate, silently applauding herself for the entire performance.

I guess the play rehearsals helped in real life too. She smiled inwardly as the pesto chicken melted in her mouth.

Chapter Fifteen

Finally, the day of Andre's arrival in Delhi came, and Vivian was there to pick him up at the airport. He said nothing, but hugged her fiercely and then stood back to look at the face whose absence had driven him insane for four weeks. Four weeks when he could not get her out of his mind. She would pop up sometimes, in the middle of meetings, or when he was finalising designs, sometimes even when he was on a call, and leave him bewildered and full of longing. And now she was in his arms, beaming and very sentimental.

Her voice hoarse with emotion, she said, 'I missed you, Andre, I missed you so much.'

'Me too.' He pulled her close, his fingers interlaced in her hair, his other hand gently rubbing her lower back.

The journey back to the apartment did not feel long with two people sitting in a cab, lost in each other. When they got to his apartment and after he had freshened up, she handed him an envelope.

'What is this?'

'It's a memo.' She grinned. 'What do you think it is?'

'It could be a million things. How am I supposed to know?'

'What happened to the hyperactive sixth sense? Four weeks and you lost it.' She laughed, and Andre stared at her, half in admiration and half in annoyance.

'Don't try and act cute.'

'I don't need to. Born that way.'

He said, finally, 'Can you please tell me what it is now? Now that you've had your share of teasing for the day?' He held her neck in the crook of his arm.

Her tone changed from naughty girl to woman in love. 'It's a few lines I wrote for you, something which I felt – in fact have been feeling – for a while now. I actually wrote it before you left, wanted to give it to you then. But I felt so … you know, disoriented, that I forgot to get it for you.'

Opening it carefully, he pulled out a purple sheet of cartridge paper with his name painted in shades of yellow, overlaid on which were a few lines in a beautiful hand.

The sun departs and the moon takes its place,
I drift from reality to dream, losing control of my
conscious mind, to slip into the depths of my
soul.
And all I find there is you. The longing in my
heart wakes me up wishing for this night to end.
I want to stay in the heaven where I can find you,
where I can feel you not only for today, not only
for tomorrow,
But for a lifetime and beyond!

And at the bottom of the sheet was written, in italics, *'Andre, I love you – a lot, lot more than you can ever imagine.'*

He looked up at this woman, whose eyes had all the love in the world for him, whose soft hands were gently resting in his palm and who was comfortably sitting, snuggled in his arms. Andre read the lines again, his heart filling with the depth of meaning, with the beautiful gesture she had made for him, only for him. It was unknown territory, and for the first time the emotions welling within him for a woman were proving to be beyond his control. The passion that had enveloped him made him believe that true love, which he had always mocked as the stuff of fairytales and fiction, something manufactured by Hollywood, did exist. It was not something which happened every day – it was once in a lifetime and it was happening to him now.

'Vivi, you make me feel so special that sometimes I doubt my own existence, my whole self, and whether I'm worthy of your love.'

'It's mutual, darling.'

'God, I can't believe I'm behaving like one of those clingy Hollywood stars in some love story who cries and gets emotional about everything. Vivian, what the hell are you doing to me?'

'My *Die Hard* guy is becoming a wax candle; what has Murano done to *you*?' Her eyes laughed again. All he did was look at her, in the way that only a man truly in love could look.

Then from nowhere he said, 'Marry me, Vivi. Whenever you want, but marry me.' He was shocked at himself. He was twenty-two years old and marriage was not in his plans, but suddenly everything seemed to be pinned on what Vivian would say or how she would react.

Her eyes widened in shock and for a moment he thought he had said it too early, but then the shock was replaced with softness and a suppressed smile.

'I did not know a few lines could get me a marriage proposal.'

'They can. And what do you have to say about it?'

She looked down and for a moment he wondered if she was going to evade the question. A few seconds felt like a decade, with every muscle in his stomach knotting, but finally she spoke and it was like music to his ears.

'I have this to say. I would love to. Anytime you say.'

Relief and happiness swept through his system, freeing up the knots and soothing every tensed nerve. The words of the poem were playing in his head, and combined with the softness with which she was holding on to him, they ignited emotions deeper than he could handle. He began kissing her, but it was not enough today, he needed more. His hands moved down her soft cotton shirt, feeling her curves, and when he looked at her again he murmured,

'I can't stop today.'

She lowered her eyes in silent consent. The shyness in those brown eyes brought a tender smile to his face, and his hands for the first time slipped under her shirt, feeling her soft warm skin. The touch of her bare skin felt like a shot of cocaine, drugging his mind completely, rendering him insensible of anything but the experience of this magical moment between them.

He felt a slight tremor as his hands moved across her belly, caressing it softly beneath the shirt. He held her with his palms resting firmly on her waist and his thumbs making little circles around her ribs, as his lips explored the smooth dewy skin around her neck. Dragging his lips away to meet hers, he kissed her luscious lips as his fingers, free for the first time, swept restlessly across her navel to her back, drawing her closer. His head lowered as he kissed her collarbones and her neck, and then slowly he unbuttoned the shirt.

She became so tense that he knew he had to relax her, and he gently stroked her back and kissed her again until she was kissing him back with the same passion. He returned to the buttons, kissing every inch of skin the moment it was exposed. She shivered as the shirt fell open and the cool air hit her skin, but then his sweltering body was against her, his lips pressing on hers in an urgent need.

For Andre, all thinking stopped, his mind registering only what he was feeling with every passing second, and he wanted more. He kissed every inch of her body, which felt like hot satin under his firm hands. Her hand, which had been resting on his chest, unconsciously slipped around his waist and her fingers pressed on his skin as he was kissing her, with desire mounting every second. He was amazed at the powers of this wonderful, inexperienced brunette, who by a simple touch could set him ablaze with passion. His hands tugged at her hair and glided along the nape of her neck and her shoulders, then further down her bare back, while his lips explored hers.

With his every touch she shivered like a little rabbit. He skilfully moved across her body, his lips caressing every bit of her skin. He knew how much he wanted her and he had to let her feel it too – the same fire that was driving him mad. As he went lower, Vivian moaned and curved. Heaving with desire, she clasped him tighter as they made love for the very first time. She wasn't aware of anything but the mind-numbing sensations which Andre had stirred in her. Losing herself in him completely, she felt every moment, every touch, shared every breath.

Afterwards, they lay there wrapped in the sheets, playing with each other's fingers while Andre rubbed his nose on her shoulder and held her again, tenderly. She wanted to live in this moment, in his arms, smelling him, feeling him, hearing his heartbeat. If there was heaven it was right here, right now in his arms, and there was nothing more she needed, just this, now and forever.

One hand wrapped around her waist, and with the other he tipped her chin, which broke her train of thought as he said,

'Vivi, do you know your cheeks were so flushed with colour when we were making love that for a moment I wanted to stop and just look at you and admire this new beauty, seeing it for the very first time …' He brushed away another strand of her hair and continued, 'There were little droplets of sweat on your neck, which was curving with every kiss, and my God you look breathtaking when you're aroused.'

'What are you trying to say? I don't look breathtaking all the time?' She gently bit his cheek and laughed.

'I'm saying you drive me mad, Vivi.' The look in his eyes changed and he kissed her again, made love to her again with increased passion and urgency.

After another round which left both of them exhausted, he looked at the woman who was tickling every nerve in him, playing with every beat of his heart and filling every inch of his soul with unconditional love. He had never made love to a woman the way he did to Vivian. Nothing in his past even came close to what they had shared today. In the past, sex had always been exciting, but with Vivian, Andre felt profoundly content. Making love to her felt magical, an act of spellbinding madness.

'I want more of this. More of the strawberry taste of your lip gloss, more of the salty sweat on your skin.' But he knew Vivian had to leave for home. Surprisingly, she had not seemed at all worried about the time and he hated to point it out. 'Darling, we need to go, otherwise you'll be late.'

Vivian wrapped her arms around him and whispered, 'How about I don't go today?'

His eyes widened for a moment, then he said, 'Now that's an idea … Baby, don't tease me.'

She whispered back, 'I'm not.'

'You're serious?'

Rubbing her nose on the side of his neck she said, 'Absolutely. We need to make up for lost time.'

Andre caressed her cheek and smiled into her soft eyes before covering her mouth in a melting kiss. 'Thank you,' he said.

She whispered a faint, 'Welcome', and they both smiled and looked at each other.

As much as he did not want to waste any time on eating, he was sure the beauty he was holding on to must be hungry.

'Let me take you out for something to eat because, my sweetheart, you have a very long night ahead of you.' Saying that, he tried to get up but Vivian held on to him and said, 'How about we just order something and don't go anywhere?'

'I like that even more.'

The night dissolved into her sweet fragrance, the beauty of love, her exotic taste. He kept her up almost until dawn, making love to her again, and when she fell asleep he still lay awake, adoring her.

She slept in the circle of his arms, forgetting the world, forgetting everything but the exquisite feeling of being with the man she loved.

The weather turned, the cold increasing in intensity. Andre had to leave again. Two weeks flew by in seconds and she found herself waiting for him to come back once more. She felt a bleak and persistent emptiness and she shuddered to think what would happen in the future. For now, there was a six-week wait for Andre.

Chapter Sixteen

With her mind lost in Andre, Vivian had almost forgotten that Gloria, her best friend, was due to come as well and was staying with them over Christmas. As a result she was at the airport twice within a week, extremely happy both times – the first to pick up Andre and the second, Gloria.

She almost jumped with joy as Gloria came out of Terminal 3 at New Delhi International Airport, waving frantically at her.

Vivian shouted, 'Hi sweetheart, it is so good to see you, I missed you SO much!'

'Same here. It has been so dreadful since you guys left.'

Gloria hugged her with such ferocity that the girls almost fell over, giggling.

'You look great,' said Vivian.

Gloria had a tanned complexion – very Italian, Vivian always thought – with thick red hair. The girls had more or less grown up together, same neighbourhood, same school, the best of pals although complete opposites. If Vivian was petite and conservative, Gloria was curvaceous, a risk-taker, flamboyant and full of life. Vivian had clear goals in her life in terms of her career; Gloria had some sort of hazy picture which changed on a quarterly basis. She loved dark colours and Vivian loved light.

Vivian also loved everything about Gloria. She knew that beneath all the flamboyance was a deeply caring person, and she admired her attitude to life and the ease with which she could talk to anyone, especially boys, sailing her way through life in a way that Vivian had never been able to.

The short car journey from the airport was filled with the non-stop chatter of two dear friends meeting after a time apart.

Back home, Gloria was welcomed equally warmly by Vivian's parents. The dinner table brought back memories of old times, their school, Barcelona, forgotten friends ... The list went on.

Vivian waited till her parents were asleep before she started talking about Andre.

'I have to tell you something, something amazing, out of this world,' she said, when they were alone in the bedroom.

Curiosity bubbled in Gloria's eyes. 'What? What is it?' She paused, and then the penny dropped. 'Hang on, are you dating? Ooh, you are! Since when? How come you never told me? Who is he? Spill!'

'Oh Gloria, he is the most wonderful guy ever ... you have to meet him, he is out of this world ... absolutely amazing.' She clasped her hands across her chest and fell back on the bed, lying with her eyes closed as if in a dream. Her voice softened as she continued, 'The way he does everything ... it's completely out of this world. Have I said that already? Maybe ... Never mind ... It's as if' – she took a deep breath and a smile spread across her face like morning sunshine – 'I ... can't explain in words, I have never been this happy. He's the one for me, Gloria, I know it, I can feel it.'

For a moment, Gloria just looked at her friend basking in the dream of her new life.

Vivian's voice became softer still as she said, 'I know you must be thinking I'm mad, talking about being so madly in love with a guy pretty much immediately after meeting him ...' Her gaze drifted to the bedspread as she spoke. 'But Gloria, I think sometimes you just know that it's forever the moment you meet that extra special person.'

Gloria was not sure of this, but nodded in agreement.

'He's so different, Gloria, and so astute, and at the same time so tender and so loving. Even the way he says my name is special; it's so full of love and tenderness.'

Vivian talked on and Gloria listened. She heard the words 'great' and 'out of this world' a dozen times. And, finally, Gloria spoke.

'Listening to you, there are two things I can make out ... Number one: great. Number two: out of this world. So it sounds like Mr Andre is greatly out of this world ... That makes him an alien ... Vivian, are you in love with an alien?' She burst into fits of laughter, but Vivian frowned.

'Shut up, that's mean. I'm not telling you any more.'

'Oh Vivian, it's as much fun as ever to tease you. I'm so happy for you, you seem truly blessed.'

'I am, I really am. You want to see a picture?' Before Gloria could answer, Vivian took a photo from her wallet of the two of them sitting on a bench in Nainital, and thrust it in her friend's face.

'Not bad looking, I must say. For an alien.' She rolled on the bed, laughing again.

'Can you drop this alien nonsense? He's really cute and sweet and … Oh Gloria, I don't think anyone can make me as happy as he can.'

The girls talked into the small hours and Vivian told her every detail of their love story and how Andre was working on rebuilding the glass factory. For the first time, there was apprehension on Gloria's face, but Vivian was so lost in her world that she didn't catch it.

She went on, 'Do you know, Gloria, he even has a name for his factory. "Vetrofond". Nice name, don't you think?' She hesitated and looked hopefully towards Gloria, who nodded. Content that Gloria liked the name, she went on talking about Andre.

At three in the morning, the girls left that conversation for some sleep, as Vivian had college the next day.

When she left in the morning Gloria began thinking about the two of them and their differences. Gloria knew Vivian, and how she would only ever act from the heart, and only see the positives. She was unable to see the differences between herself and Andre – vast differences, it seemed to Gloria. She decided to talk to Vivian, for she genuinely cared for her and did not want to see her hurt.

In the evening, as the sun hid in the western sky and Vivian came back from college, the two girls got to talking and Gloria mustered up the courage to speak up.

'Where do you see this going, Vivian?'

'What do you mean?' Vivian knew exactly what she meant but nevertheless continued, 'Andre has told me that he'll travel back and forth, I'm sure I mentioned it to you too.'

'You did but you guys want such different things in life, have you thought about that? You seem to be running into it head-on, without even looking. He leaves again in two weeks. He has to work in Murano and you, eventually, in the third world. Have you, I don't know, measured the gap between the two of you?'

Even though she did not want them to, Gloria's questions took Vivian back to the last day in Nainital, when she had asked herself exactly the same things. The lid which she had carefully kept on reality was suddenly being removed, and the ugly apparition of truth had started to emerge. A wretched feeling grew inside her. She dreaded every new word which Gloria spoke, for they were true and she knew it; she had known it from the beginning. Vivian had no answers, just a silent sadness.

Chapter Seventeen

Next day, when Vivian met Andre, she told him about the conversation with Gloria. Silence followed, a very uncomfortable silence. Unable to bear it, Vivian, with her head bent low, finally said,

'Andre, can I ask you something? If it came to it, would you leave your glass factory to be with me?' She knew it was the wrong thing to ask, but she asked nevertheless, for she needed assurance that it would all work out.

Andre went quiet for a long moment, and when he did speak she heard the reticence in his voice.

'Vivi, don't you think we are taking this too fast?' He was trying to defuse the situation but feared it was beyond his control now.

Her voice full of pain and anxiousness, she said, 'Well, you wanted to marry me. Tell me, how did you think it would work?'

He had no answers. As he looked into her eyes, which were swimming with tears, all he could manage was that he had not thought about it in such detail, or looked so far ahead. He knew Vivian wanted security for the future, a definitive yes, but for some reason he was unable to supply that. He knew she was thinking about a future together and so was he – somewhere – but he felt it was way too early to sort the details. The more immediate issue, though, was how to keep Vivian from all this talk of the future, and how to rescue her from the pit of mindless complications into which Gloria had thrown her.

But the pit was much deeper than he had anticipated, as he came to realise over the next few days. She came up with random questions like, 'Where will we settle down, which country will we choose?', all of which annoyed him considerably. It was not that he did not love her, but he was missing the smiling Vivi, and all this future talk was wearing him down.

From the moment she raised the issue, Vivian felt as if she was starting to lose Andre, and that played havoc with her heart. Every time she asked him something related to the future, he gave flippant answers or ignored the subject completely by saying, 'I haven't thought it through in such detail.' She just could not work out a way to proceed. What Gloria had asked her made perfect sense, but reconciling that with the reality of the future was something of a struggle. She had never cried so much – out of despair, out of fear, out of the unknown.

It was the last day – Andre was due to leave in the morning. Vivian could not sleep, worries for the future dancing in her mind, occupying every iota of space in her consciousness.

When she arrived at college in the morning, her eyes were red and swollen. Andre looked at her pain-stricken face. He felt guilty to have turned a laughing, happy girl into a wreck. She didn't even try to say hi.

All she said was, 'Andre, I can't go on without knowing what will happen to us. I know we've had hardly any time together, but I have difficulty imagining a life without you, and this uncertainty is killing me.' She turned her face to hide the tears.

Andre wanted to reassure her but could only say, 'Don't talk like this, Vivi. Let me think about it and I'll have the answer when I come back.'

He knew from the look on her face that he might have no choice but to try to look into the future, and to make a decision right now on whether it made sense for the two of them to continue. Holding her close for a very long time, he tried to ignore the reality and listen to his heart, to make his mind stop, to just feel the soft touch of Vivi's skin.

Come evening, Vivian had to get back home. He hated not only that she was leaving and he would not see her for almost six weeks, but that he had to take a decision, a decision which would decide their fate.

Chapter Eighteen

Andre left for Italy. He worked his heart out in the factory, but Vivian's words continued to haunt him. Occasional calls mainly focused on whether he had decided anything; he would take the conversation down a new path and Vivian would follow, but he knew the question lingered in the back of both their minds.

The decision he had to take was beyond him – deep down he knew the answer, and he knew the outcome. Somehow, he had known it from day one, and he felt guilty for he knew Vivian had hoped that things would work out, as he had too. He had always ignored that tiny voice, but soon there would be no option but to listen.

Although his physical self was in Murano, his heart was with Vivian. He had promised her.

The day before they were to leave, as he walked towards his father's study, Andre decided to speak to him.

Andre felt the chill as he entered the room; it was colder than other parts of the house because the window was always partially open, allowing the smoke from his father's cigar to escape. The study was fitted out in oak, with every bookshelf, every panel finished to a high shine, reflecting Sergio Paolo's considerable taste. He loved reading – his library held a fine collection of all genres, collected over many years. It was among the few things that were left when they had sold most of their belongings. Each book was preserved in pristine condition because he and his wife had bought most of them together, and for him they stood as reminders of the beautiful times they had shared. A large part of his day at home was spent in this room, which he had designed. Against one wall was a big, glass-topped oak desk, behind which Andre's father sat in his favourite leather chair.

He moved the book he was reading to the side in order to see his son's face and saw at once that Andre was distraught. He waited for him to speak, as everything about Andre suggested that he was here to discuss something important. Andre sat down on the other side of the desk, and there was silence for a while as he scanned the room, played with the paperweight on the table, then finally looked up at his patiently waiting father and said,

'I'm in love.'

'That's wonderful, Andre. Who is she? Italian or …? Anyway, it does not matter.'

'I want to marry her.'

'You want to what?' Sergio's tone reflected his utter astonishment. But he collected himself, relaxed his frown and said, 'You realise, son, that you are twenty-two?'

'I'm very much aware of that, but I also know that she is the one.' The statement was delivered with considerable clarity and authority for a twenty-two-year-old, and Sergio was not just surprised, he was shocked.

'That's how you feel when you are young. It's normal. Take it slow. You have just started your life.' Sergio strained to speak casually, lighting another cigar and filling the room with tobacco smoke.

Andre tried to explain how Vivian wanted to be a doctor and go to Africa and work for the poor, and how they wanted different things in life. Unable to accommodate the idea of marriage, Sergio tried hard to listen to his son, who seemed to be in a state of extreme wretchedness.

'Why don't the two of you take it as it comes? You are both so young. Why not—'

'Can you leave the age angle for a moment?' Andre was up and pacing round the room. 'I have dated before and I know what it is to date and I also know that we are young and I'm twenty-two and she eighteen.'

His tone reflected his frustration; his papà did not seem able to understand the emotional turmoil in his heart. He told him how much he loved her, but that he did not want to carry on if they were unable to work things out for the future because that would be much more painful for her in the long run.

He came back to the desk, and resting his hands on the glass top, he spoke quietly and firmly. 'She trusts me, Papà, to make the right decision for both of us. I cannot break her trust. It has to be the right decision for both of us and that's what I need your help with.'

Sergio, still smoking his cigar, observed him though narrowed eyes. He felt the anguish and urgency in Andre's voice, and he saw the sadness which had fallen over his son's face like a shadow.

He thought for a while, giving Andre time to recover before he spoke.

'How attached is she to this dream of hers?'

'As much as I am to mine.'

'Hmmm. Andre, if you ask her to give up on her dream, I'm sure she will, if she is as madly in love with you as you claim. But there will come a day when she will regret it because she wanted that dream so much, just as you will regret it if you don't set up your factory, as is your dream. And that day will be much more painful than leaving her today. You cannot see it clearly now, but if you love her you will leave her, for she needs to pursue her goals and so do you.

'She will find somebody who wants similar things in life and forget you eventually. As you will forget her. It's up to you what you do, I can only suggest, but you children are too young to talk about marriage.' He could not help but bring in the age factor again. 'You will fall in love many times, son! It is a natural process in life. Falling in love is not difficult. Trust me, I have gone through all of this and your mother was not the first woman I loved, she was the last.' This last statement softened his tone considerably. 'It will happen when it is meant to happen.'

Andre wanted to cry out that it had already happened. There was no part of him that did not think of Vivi as his own life, a reflection of all his love, his true self, but all he did was stare into space for a moment and then walk out, thanking his father for the advice.

'*If you love her, you will leave her.*' The words were ringing in his ears, and then his thoughts, *We have started this and we'll make it work*, brought only foreboding, and a creeping sense of guilt.

Chapter Nineteen

As Andre boarded the flight from Marco Polo airport to New Delhi, he felt as though he was coming home. The plane landed and so did the negative thoughts, the thoughts of separation, of losing the most precious thing he had. But Papà's words came to his mind: *'If you love her, then leave her.'* With this in his head, he pulled his rucksack from the overhead locker and walked, numb with anticipation, towards the queue for immigration.

Outside, he stopped at the exact spot where once Vivian had given him such a heart-warming smile and hugged him so close. Today, all that were here were thoughts of her, wrapped in a blanket of fear. He had not told her the exact time he would land – he needed time to gather his thoughts before breaking the news to her.

Once back home, his fingers ached to dial her number and, when he did, instead of the familiar tinkle in her voice, what he heard was a voice overflowing with misery. After a brief exchange about his flight, the trip, the factory, the dreadful question came up.

'What did you decide?' Her tone was both gloomy and hopeful.

'I'm coming tomorrow. We'll talk then. How's everything else?'

'I don't really care how everything else is.'

She was right to snap – he had comfortably evaded the question one more time.

He felt already the silent tears which would come with his answer; he could picture her sitting with warm teardrops falling from her cheeks, but saying anything on the phone could only make it worse.

She was waiting for him at the same spot in college where they had sat together so often over the months. She looked so pale and thin that Andre felt incredibly guilty. They looked at each other and he gave her a long warm hug without saying a word. Sitting down, he held her hand and gathered all his courage.

'Baby, it's not going to work. We want such different things in life that our paths will always be separate and I think the practical way out is to part ways.' *God, she looks so dreadful and her eyes... Damn, what am I doing?* He shook himself. *Andre, you have to get through this ... it's the right thing to do.* 'I thought about it a lot. It may not seem right now but maybe it is for the best.'

'Maybe.'

He held her hand and his eyes went dewy as he desperately tried to hold back the tears. She fiddled with the ring on her finger, taking it off and putting it back again and again. He saw her trembling hands and with a break in his voice softly said,

'I'm sorry.'

'It's fine, Andre, you don't have to be. We were in this together.' She spoke as clearly as she could, tears flowing freely down her flushed cheeks. 'The decision you've come to must be for a reason, and I believe you because I love you and will love you to my grave.'

The sun was getting lower in the sky and the rays which had fallen on her face slowly faded, leaving her looking more desolate than ever.

Andre looked at her in pain, for he was the reason for the tears. He could also be the cure, yet he was unable to do anything at this moment for the tears of the woman he loved so dearly. All he could do was to look at her as she curled silently into a shell of despair. Andre knew he had to be the stronger one, because his Vivi was weak when it came to him. He believed that one day it would be alright, as Papà had said – she would meet somebody and forget him and he would do the same.

They sat by the cold, dusty footpath looking at each other. He took her hand and softly held it against his palm, and they walked together to the college canteen, knowing very well that this would be the last time they would walk hand in hand in those ancient college grounds.

They sat at the same table they had sat at so often, but this time opposite each other instead of together, and he tried to tell her how it would be better for them.

Vivian saw the reality of separation taking its shape. His words had hit her like a hurricane hitting a tree standing alone in a barren land, but she had continued to listen without saying a word. The canteen was full of noise, the clatter of plates and cutlery and the hum of conversation between students oblivious to the tragedy unfolding in their midst. The two could barely speak. They just sat there looking at each other, their eyes full of pain and sorrow.

Breaking the silence which had spread its wings between them, Andre said,

'We should go to class.' He would never have said that in the past, and a fresh surge of tears started welling in her eyes.

She said, 'I want to go home.'

'I'll drop you.'

They walked back to Vivian's place and he left her at the door after hugging her close for several minutes and placing his lips on her forehead for one long and final kiss.

She stood at the door and watched him walk away; away from her life and far beyond her reach.

Long after he disappeared, she stood on the doorstep weeping, and then she slowly turned and walked into the house, closing the door on all the dreams she had dared to dream, on all the moments they had shared, all the hope she had nurtured. It was the end, the end of a beginning in which she had had the utmost faith.

She dragged her feet up the stairs to her room and curled up on her bed. She was aware of nothing – not the giggles of the kids outside, nor the pillow under her cheeks, which was wet from all her tears. She stared at the clock, feeling the deadness of the passing time.

She collected herself before her parents were due to come home and plastered a smile on her face. It had to be done – she needed a mask to hide the emotional tornado raging within her.

Days passed, then months. The distance between Andre and Vivian grew. They hardly saw each other, a few telephone conversations here or there, nothing like the way it used to be. But Vivian could not move on from the point of their parting. To everybody else, she was the same Vivian, smiling, full of life, a bright and positive person, but deep inside she had changed, and the change could not be undone. There was a pain which she could not show but which constantly held her in its grip – a mask which she had perfected.

At first, Andre was completely distraught. His friends tried to cheer him up, they took him places and cracked jokes, but they couldn't reach him. He would sit alone in his room and smell the sheets on which Vivi had lain. He would cry alone too, and be as strong as he could be in front of her when they occasionally crossed paths on the campus. Because of the factory, he was hardly ever there. He was mostly in Murano, coming for only a set number of days. As time went on, he continued to miss Vivian, but he also started to enjoy the newfound freedom of a twenty-two-year-old guy, doing the usual things a guy of his age would do.

On one of his spells in Delhi, he saw Vivian from across the road but avoided going to her. He wanted to give her more space, and the time to recover, but also to protect himself from guilt; every time he saw her he would be filled with guilt, for he knew her well enough to see her distress. She was much thinner, and somehow he blamed himself. The words he had spoken about trusting him, about carrying on, would come alive in his head. He missed her, but he kept reminding himself that the decision was for the best and that, over time, things would surely get better.

Chapter Twenty

Vivian buried herself in her studies for the medical entrance exam, for the pain of seeing Andre around college and not being with him was greater than anything she had ever experienced. She wanted to escape to somewhere without the dreams of the past, and her naïve heart told her that by changing the backdrop she would be free from the clutches of those haunting memories.

Her hard work paid off and she was admitted to medical college, a welcome boost in her urgent efforts to erase Andre from her memory.

Medical school certainly kept her occupied. She submerged herself in subjects which she had always wanted to study, and she became well accustomed to the mechanical daily cycle of studying, going home and more studying to achieve a goal which would finally and decisively separate her from Andre.

Any attentions from the opposite sex were religiously fended off. Soon labelled the 'Ice Queen', she concentrated solely on graduating from the university and then studying for her Master's. Dating was something too painful even to think of, and love ... well, she was still in love with the shadow of a man who had left her. It was a while back now but, for her, their love was still alive and breathing every moment; his fragrance was still within her, his touch still awoke sensations in her spine. She was devoid of any capability to even think about a man the way she had thought about Andre; feeling anything was yet more impossible.

Time could not heal the deep cuts of the past, but it did pass, slowly and painfully. It was September 2004, year two of medical school and on one of their regular meetings, Devyani could not help but bring up the topic again.

'Viv, what's happening with you? You plan on fading away? Every time I see you, you're thinner.'

Vivian peeled another banana and dropped it into the mixer with the berries.

'Dieting. I'm trying to get to size zero.' Vivian half-laughed, handing over a peeled orange and trying to change the subject. 'How's college? What's happening with your internship?'

'You're aiming for size zero minus ten. You need to get a hold of yourself, Viv, it's almost been two years. Look at you, you look like a matchstick. More to the point, look at Andre – he's seeing other girls.'

The immediate widening of Vivian's eyes was enough to tell Devyani that she hadn't been aware of Andre's dating. Although she instantly recovered and said,

'I have been on a few dates.'

'Not a few dates, a few *first* dates, which I forced you to. And after each of them, you told me exactly the same thing, that you 'don't feel the same way' as you did for him. Vivian, you have built walls all around yourself. You seem to have no wish to escape, and you're not letting anybody into that space. You need to come out from this emotional trauma, now. Andre has moved on, Vivian, and so should you. You are wasting your time and your life. People's hearts and minds change, and so should yours. It's normal. I'm sorry, but grow up. It was only a couple of months' affair, dammit.'

Devyani was frustrated – she could not understand this bond but at the same time she could see how painful it was for Vivian to hear what she was telling her. And she was equally sure that nothing of her speech was registering when it came to Andre. Vivian was an emotional fool. But at least she had told her the truth, and she hoped that somehow it might lodge in her head.

Vivian was looking so distraught that Devyani did not have the heart to carry on. She tried changing the subject.

'Hey, there's a concert in the college and you have to come. I'll pick up the passes. Don't say no, it's for old times' sake.'

Vivian nodded and replied, 'Yes. Of course I'll come.'

The girls had lunch together, talking about those old times and, before Devyani left, she stressed the fact that she needed to come to the concert. Hugs and goodbyes followed, and left in their wake a somewhat disoriented Vivian. She could not come to terms with the fact that Andre was dating.

Andre would definitely tell me something like this. He would never hide it from me. Maybe they're just first dates and Devyani is exaggerating.

She sighed deeply, as the haunting question threatened to consume her thoughts.

Does he ever think of getting back together? I'm sure he must. All the more reason he wouldn't be seeing anyone else.

With that reassurance, she tried putting the whole conversation to rest, but doubts lurked at the back of her mind. Even now she waited endlessly for his random calls which hardly came, dreamt about a time when he would just come and meet her, hold her, tell her how much he had missed her, how much he loved her. But none of that happened; he rarely called and even when he did, it was very casual, very … detached. Was she just waiting in vain for someone who would never come back, possibly never want to come back? That thought made her stomach knot, made her soul twist. The lump in her throat returned and the twinge of pain gnawed at her heart again. They were so perfect together, it had to have been more than just a casual relationship …

Oh God, I need to stop this, I'm going mad. I'm overreacting. I need to get out, take a run.

She ran till she could run no more. Her heart was pounding, her lungs heaving, but the thoughts were still there, lodged in her stomach like a cancer.

On the day of the concert, Vivian went back to her old college. She had put some effort into dressing for the occasion, pale blue ankle-length dress and matching stone earrings. The desire to cross paths with Andre was carefully wrapped up in her heart, well concealed from the world. She was secretly betting on the chance that Andre might be there for the concert, as Devyani had mentioned that he was visiting for a couple of days.

And there he stood with a group of people, talking and laughing, near the patchy football grounds where once he had kissed her so completely. He had gained just the right amount of weight, his cheeks were slightly fuller than they used to be. But something else was different too, and she couldn't put a finger on it. She stood for a moment, glued to the concrete path, trying to work it out; a subtle change, but a change nevertheless.

Andre saw her, and at first he thought he might be hallucinating. She looked so much thinner ... but she was there alright, standing motionless in a beautiful dress, alone. For a brief moment his heart stirred with longing and he had the urge to forget everything and hug her close the way he used to, but then his senses intervened and he just walked over to her and said,

'How are you? Nice to see you. It's been a while.' Covering his emotions under layers of disguise, he gently hugged her for a brief couple of seconds. When he looked into her brown eyes, he felt he saw pain.

Andre had genuinely tried to move on, but Vivian still looked as if she was stuck in the past. He had dismissed all thoughts of her as they flashed into his mind like scenes from a motion picture, and immersed himself in work. He had dated girls, gone out and done everything he possibly could to move as far away as possible from the lakes and terraces of his memory. To some extent, he had been successful. But he had the distinct feeling that although he had travelled some distance, if not the whole journey, Vivian had somehow stayed behind, sitting on that concrete pavement where he had left her, waiting for him.

He quickly dismissed the thought, telling himself that it was madness to expect a girl like Vivian to wait for him almost two years after breaking up. He was sure that her charms would have attracted many admirers in the medical school, though the mere thought of other men touching her or spending time with her was as a knife twisting in his gut.

Shrugging off the scenes which his treacherous mind was playing, he said again,

'How are you?'

She raised her eyes to meet his gaze and looked into his deep black eyes, and somehow she knew that Devyani was telling the truth. The mere thought choked her, making her feel sick and empty on the one hand, furious with herself on the other for being so vulnerable to a man who she could clearly see had moved on.

'How come you're here today?' he asked.

Devyani's words were ringing in her ears. *'Andre has moved on, Vivian, and so should you. You are wasting your time and your life. People's hearts and minds change, and so should yours.'*

With a physical effort she collected herself and replied, 'The concert. Devyani got the tickets.' Trying to hide the maelstrom of emotions which were raging within, she asked, 'And you?'

'Here for the concert too. I have friends in the college besides you, madam.' He laughed, and Vivian tried to smile. Even as she stood there, the battle between her heart and her mind turned fiercer, but for the first time, with a painful realisation, she acknowledged the victory of her mind over her heart.

Looking at the jumbled expressions in her chestnut eyes, he said,

'Are you lost?'

'No. No, I know exactly where I'm going … I'll see you later.'

'Hey, you just arrived, how about a coffee?' He wanted desperately to pull her into his arms and comfort her for whatever was troubling her.

But she gave him no such chance and, turning round she said, 'I really need to go. Bye.'

Andre was not only puzzled by her behaviour, but very disturbed. Briefly he thought to call after her but she was almost running, and for the first time away from him instead of towards him, as she always used to do, her face bright and eager and her eyes full of love. Today she had been neither bright nor eager, but her chestnut eyes had told of an effort to hide something, something painful, and her face had been drained of colour.

When she disappeared at the turn, he walked slowly along the cobbled path, inwardly cursing himself, his mind leaping to the conclusion that she must be seeing some idiot boy in medical college who would not have wanted her to meet with her ex. God, he thought, what he would give to go and floor the bastard. Even after all these years, he did not like to see her run away from him. Somehow he still wanted to retain some kind of relationship, under the umbrella of "friendship". But obviously, her new boyfriend was averse to the idea of him meeting her.

He closed his eyes tight in sheer disgust at the new addition to Vivian's life. For some reason, he had thought he saw pain on her face, which made him feel like she was not as emotionally involved with the bastard as she was with him, and that thought made his heart twist as well as rejoice. Only Vivi was capable of ruining his mental peace like that.

His friend came to tell him that the concert was about to start and he quietly followed along, glancing again at the spot where, a few moments before, Vivian had stood. Now it was as empty as his life without her.

Chapter Twenty-one

Vivian arrived home disoriented. She had put on a strong face in front of Andre, but deep inside she was a wreck. The belief she had harboured for so long, the belief that he still loved her and that someday they would get back together, felt ludicrous now, and she felt like a fool who had ignored reality at every step. She held back her futile tears and, with stern steps, walked towards the chest of drawers.

I have been the idiot of the century and this madness needs to end. It was two bloody months together, and most of the time we were not even together. She opened the top drawer and took out the package which read 'Andre'. One look at that package and all the sternness evaporated. Her eyes reverted to pools of sadness and despair, and the tears which had momentarily stopped began flowing uncontrollably once again.

She opened the package and looked at each card and read each word carefully as if reading for the very last time. She picked up her favourite and read the lines which Andre had written.

Vivi, life with you is what I dream of. I see our love blooming over years together.
I see the future with you and then I see the two of us getting old together. I see our children in your eyes.
I see you as my life, my soul and this is all that I want – every moment with you in my arms.
Love you forever.
A xx
PS – Think of the willow tree, under which I can read poetry, and when you are bored of me reading, put my lips to better use ... Love you, baby! ;)

And another:

If love should have a name, it will be thine, Vivi.
(I am trying to be Shakespeare here and failing miserably! But I mean every word even though it isn't exactly poetry ;))
You are my life, and even beyond it, if there is something which exists, I want to be there with you.
The way you have made me feel, no one else ever has and no one ever will,
The way you have touched my emotions no one would,
The sensations you invoked after kissing me, no one ever will.
You are my soul, Vivi, my heart and my life.
Love you so much...
Yours and forever yours and only yours for this life and many more to come,
Andre x

Her heart ached at the mere sight of those words and she dived into the past one more time, thinking of those moments when they had kissed and he had taken out these cards from under the pillow. That thought made her want to pull her heart out for the pain that filled it was too much for her to handle.

You have to do this, Vivian, you need to forget him. He has long forgotten what we dreamt of together. With a weak determination, filled with silent sobs, she tore each of the cards into little pieces, one by one. Soon the pieces of paper were scattered on the floor, the names 'Andre' and 'Vivi' torn apart, separated beyond recovery.

Also in the package was a diary with a black leather cover in which Vivian used to write poetry for Andre. The yellowed pages had rose petals preserved between them; a petal from every rose Andre had ever given her. She picked up a petal, felt the crustiness, and moved her fingers over the surface with closed eyes. They reminded her of their times together, of love, of contentment. With those thoughts still in her heart, she opened her eyes to reality to see the dried petals for what they were – dead, just like their relationship, and being preserved for no practical reason.

Emptying the diary of all the rose petals, she placed them on her palm and crushed them, hard enough to feel the pain of preserving something which should have been long forgotten. Each and every page of poetry which carried any mention of Andre or his thoughts was torn up and discarded.

A feeling bore into her heart, a feeling as if breaking up all over again, and this time forever.

The hope, harboured for years, of getting back together with Andre was broken into fragments of reality. In the final battle, the mind had won over the heart. She felt like an idiot.

She had been living in the realm of the past and her contact with the real world had been fading – now she had to move on. The concert incident had changed her, forcing her to rejoin the world.

How could I be so blind? He never even tried to stop me ...

She laughed aloud, thinking of the gap between the way Andre was in real life and the way she'd thought he was. The more she thought, the more she realised it had all been in her imagination. He'd never asked her out again, not once in all these years, he'd never said he had any issues getting over their break-up, he'd certainly never said that he still loved her. The reality was that he had completely forgotten her, he was happy getting on with his life, building his factory, sleeping with other women without any complications. Life was simpler for him without her and she, like a love-struck fool, had waited for him in vain while he found new ways to entertain himself.

She hated herself. This was it, this was the end. She wiped her tears away. She had cried enough – she would never do it again, for him or anyone. No one would be allowed to make her feel this miserable and this helpless again. She did not deserve this much pain and she had no one to blame but herself; that would change. She would change it.

After a few weeks, when Andre hadn't heard from her, he decided to call her to see how she was.

'Hi, how have you been? I haven't heard from you in ages.'

'Nor will you, anymore,' she said, sounding very impassive; unlike her.

'What do you mean?' He was more puzzled than shocked.

'Andre, I can't be in touch with you. This pretend friendship is not possible from my end. I need to get over you and clearly talking to you on and off is not helping. I don't want to be in touch.'

'That's crazy, it doesn't make sense.' He was beginning to get what she was saying, and it was irritating him. He wanted to go to her and convince her that they should be in touch. If he suggested it, he knew she would never refuse him. But before he could even try convincing her, she said:

'Maybe not to you, but it does to me. Goodbye.' And she hung up. It was sudden and it was abrupt and it was unlike the Vivian he knew.

He was still holding the receiver and unable to believe what had happened. A million things raced through his mind. *The bastard she's dating must have told her to stop talking to me.* But then he thought of what she'd said: *'I need to get over you and clearly talking to you on and off is not helping. I don't want to be in touch.'*

Is she still not over me? I doubt that, but then why did she say that? Is she alright? Does she know that I'm dating? I hope it'll all be alright someday, someday when we can truly forget each other and move on.

157

Pictures of a smiling Vivi flashed through his mind. He went and sat on the balcony of his apartment, staring at the white flower tree, and Vivian's voice echoed in his ears. Her laughter, which always used to put a smile on his face, her touch, which made his heart leap – the notion that they might not be a part of his life, or that he might not even know where she was, hurt him profoundly.

But he adhered to what she had asked, and never called her again.

Andre had dated random women, but it was nowhere near what he had had with Vivian. With her there was a deep satisfaction, a contentment, a feeling of love which had filled every part of him, and now there was just a hollowness. When he had made love to her, every part of him was alive – he was in heaven – and now, no matter how hard he tried, that passion never came again.

As he sat beside his current girlfriend, she turned over and said, 'I don't know what you're looking for, but it's not me, I can tell you that.' She lit a cigarette and looked at him as though expecting some sort of statement contradicting her, as anybody would.

He neither corrected nor interrupted her; he just looked the other way. She got up to leave and he did not stop her, he did not feel like stopping her. It was the end of another vain relationship and he sat there, unmoved and unaffected. The only face which came to his mind was Vivian's. He closed his eyes in pain, while the woman dressed and left without another word. He slipped back under the sheets and looked at the ceiling, wondering when he would be capable of a meaningful relationship.

At low moments he wondered if breaking up had been the right thing to do, and whether he should go back to her and ask her to be with him; but then thoughts of her dream would intervene and he would silently put all his hopes and wishes to the side, wrapped in a cloak of disguise.

Chapter Twenty-two

2009

Years passed, and Vivian did not allow herself to cry again for Andre. The defences which she put around her heart turned into walls of solid ice, impassable. Though the cracks ran deep, they were carefully concealed, not to be seen, not to be felt, and definitely not to be acknowledged to the outside world.

After her graduate programme, she completed her Master's from the same institution. Finally, after seven long years of studying hard, she was ready to embark on the journey of her dreams. She accepted an offer from Providence, a charitable organisation that gave opportunities to doctors to go to remote areas of Ghana and work there with the local people. The offer had produced an ear-to-ear smile on Vivian's face and some apprehension on those of Carlos and Maria. Vivian understood why, but they both knew how much she had wanted this, so neither of them objected.

Her emotional father had hugged her close when she left, whispering, 'God bless you.'

Her mother had stroked her hair and was on the verge of tears as she said, 'I'm very proud of you for achieving your dream.'

Not long afterwards, she was on a flight to Ghana – a little chaotic and a little dirty. The air hostess came over with a frown to offer a small glass of water, after she had pressed the buzzer half a dozen times. But to Vivian, the flight was not about being polite or rude, or about cleanliness, it was about the wings which had finally been given to her to accomplish what she had laid out for herself years before.

Landing on the same airstrip with the same bumpy landing, she felt neither nervous nor intimidated, as she had felt with Nonna years before. Now, as a twenty-five-year-old, what she felt was a sense of achievement and pride.

The afternoon sun did not tire her out; nor did the ride in the dilapidated jeep to the remote medical station. After a brief rest, Vivian decided to go to the place where they examined the patients. Instead of a clinic, which she had half-expected considering it had been years since her last visit, it was still the same dusty ground but now with scattered tents, looking more like a military base than a hospital. One concrete structure served as an examination room, with lurid green curtains separating parts of it off.

The room bustled with activity as she stood there near the line of iron chairs. She ran her fingers over the back of a chair and could feel the rust peeling off. There were doctors and nurses coming in and out through the closed curtains, children crying, women trying to pacify them. Far too many people for the size of the room and worlds apart from anything she had experienced at medical school or in the hospitals of Barcelona. Over the years, little had changed. The scale of the place, she thought, had expanded since she had come with Nonna, but there was the same mismanagement and doctors were still scarce.

The closest hospital, she soon discovered, was still some distance away, in the district of Tumu. The hospital brought memories of Nonna flashing into her mind. It was still the only hospital in the region, slightly bigger than it used to be but leagues away from what might be expected in the Western world.

Even now the adults and children in this rural setting lacked the basic medical care which was so readily available in the more developed parts of Ghana. And that is what Vivian wanted to change, to work for.

Work started immediately. Before she knew it she was sucked into this malfunctioning system, trying to make it work and treating patients with what was available. She had never seen so much poverty, so much sadness, close-up; her only encounter so far had been with Eneka when she had come with her grandmother, but now, starting work here, there were so many more Enekas who not only needed treatment but also the mental support to fight the cruel battle of life.

Every day, coming home, she felt blessed for having parents who loved her and who had been there for her, unlike those of the children in the orphanage who were either abandoned or had lost families in various disturbances. She started working at the orphanage after hours, teaching children not only regular subjects but about humanity, about hope and about a happy future, trying to soothe the damage by not letting their present be affected by what had been robbed from them in the past.

The medical team went to a small village as part of a vaccination programme. It was providing basic immunisations for tuberculosis, diphtheria and other diseases, something readily available in the developed world and in developed parts of Ghana but unheard of in this tiny village, where vaccination was a foreign concept.

As their vans stopped on an uneven track near the village's cluster of mud houses with thatched roofs, Vivian emerged to a scene which filled her heart with pity and guilt, but most of all annoyance at the disparities of the world. The women were clad in single pieces of torn cloth; the children were left without any clothing at all. Some of them were crying for food and some were too weak to cry. Standing at a distance, she saw a mother weeping, sitting on the ground as the little boy next to her continuously asked for food. Vivian did not understand the local language but she did understand the pain she saw in the woman's eyes, looking at her child with a haunted expression because she had no food, and the helplessness of the child who asked for it.

She walked towards them, took out the sandwich which she had brought for herself, and gave it to the child. His dried lips opened and the tired eyes became wider as he took the sandwich and ate it very quickly, as if he feared she would change her mind and take the sandwich back. The woman just looked at her, gratitude filling every speck of those sad eyes. Then she touched her hand in a silent gesture of thanks.

Vivian had to control the tears stinging her eyes, for what she had just witnessed was the harsh reality of everyday life, which would be part of her own life from now on. The happiness that a sandwich had given to the mother was far greater than that the biggest diamond could have given. It was at that moment that she realised people here needed food even more than they needed vaccines.

After a full day in the tiny surrounding villages, she went back home exhausted, not physically but mentally. She had to do something more; being a doctor was only treating one part of the problem. At this juncture, she needed to be more than that, she had to be a human, treating the basic issues of humanity she encountered. She sat in her room with her head hung low, and the tears which she had stopped in front of the African woman came flowing now.

Curled up on her wooden bed, she started working through possibilities in her mind, ideas springing from the hope of making a difference in this world. She was restless that night, her sleep broken by interwoven thoughts about the incidents of the day and ideas of how to help.

Next morning, her head was still awhirl with thoughts from the previous day. She got up earlier than usual and immediately launched into writing a list of ideas to make a difference to the place. She worked on it for a few more weeks, perfecting it before sending it to Providence management. The much-awaited acknowledgement, along with the go-ahead to start a campaign which she would call 'Food4All', came back in a brown envelope delivered to her office desk. She was profoundly pleased with what she read and her faith in the organisation grew.

Unconventional, and with the minimum of red tape, Providence was run by people who really cared about what they did and truly believed in it. One of their major criteria for new employees was that they fit with the group's style of working and that they accepted their value system – primarily a passion to make a difference where it was needed the most. As a result, new ideas were always welcome and people like Vivian were supported. If confirmation of that were needed, she was holding it in her hand today.

Vivian started work on her campaign almost immediately. There were two main areas she wished to promote. One was child adoption, not in the conventional sense but in terms of being financially responsible for the upbringing, food, health and education of the child – that meant raising money to start development in these remote areas. The other was using food that was wasted in restaurants in the big cities. She got in touch with several big companies and came up with multiple proposals showing the ways in which they could help provide the very basic necessities of life to these people. She involved colleagues, friends and anyone she could find who was interested in volunteering.

She worked hard for a good two years on that campaign and as a result it was a success. The charity raised considerable funds, bringing help to numerous families. Vivian herself was responsible for six children in various rural locations. Her aim was to be able to provide basic meals for the people of that tiny village and many more villages like it.

She spoke to restaurants and hotels all over the region, asking them to donate food that would otherwise be thrown away. In such a hot climate this was a logistical challenge, but ways were found for the food to be carefully packaged and transported to the poorest nearby areas.

'It sounds awful,' some people told her, 'eating leftovers,' and she would say,

'It doesn't sound so awful when you haven't had food for days. It is, unfortunately, our society which has created this terrible disparity where some people eat and throw away while others eat what they have thrown.'

She believed passionately that wasted food could be turned into saved lives.

It had been barely three years since she had joined, but she was now a key volunteer at Providence, travelling extensively and working long hours. She believed in what she did and she loved it.

Chapter Twenty-three

2012

Vivian's workload was increasing and so were disturbances in the area. Her parents had started worrying about her, but she was adamant that she would continue to work there. All the people in the village adored her, especially the children from the orphanage. During one of her classes at the orphanage, a little boy made a sketch. Vivian looked at it and could not quite understand it at first, but later, when the boy explained it to her, her heart was filled with admiration. The picture showed various people, young and old, lying down as if in pain, while an angel floated in the air.

The boy told her, 'You are the guardian angel, taking care of all the people here.' She was deeply touched by the ten-year-old's simple sketch.

The attentions of her male colleagues never bothered her – her focus was work and that's what she concentrated her energies on. To Vivian, life was about working with these people and providing the basics every human deserves. Emotional involvement wasn't something she ran away from; she just did not feel anything for anybody in that way. No matter how many men stared at her, no one could make her feel self-conscious the way one look from Andre could, and she hated every bit of that fact. Ignoring it was the only option she had, and she fought thoughts of him whenever they entered her mind.

During lunch break, one of her colleagues told Vivian, 'You must meet Samuel – Sam. He's the manager for operations in the African region.'

'Why should I meet him?' Vivian asked, chewing bread and speaking at the same time.

'Because, Vivian, he's by far the most handsome man you'll ever meet.'

Vivian raised her eyebrows, looking at the woman in front of her as she dreamily went on describing Sam.

'He's got a body to die for and charm that could make the terrorists campaign for world peace, if they were women. If I wasn't married to Alex, I would have made the first move!'

Vivian laughed aloud. 'Go ahead, you get charmed while I go back to my ward.'

'Come off it, Vivian, don't dismiss him. Check him out – apart from anything else I'll need your support in case I faint after seeing his entrancing, sparkling blue eyes …' The girls laughed aloud and she continued, 'He actually joined Providence as soon as he completed his degree in medicine, and ten years later he's part of the top management in the charity. He's the youngest member of the board, his work is always dynamic and his ideas innovative. That part might just interest you.'

'Wow, you've done some extensive research on this character. As much as I'm intrigued and would like you to continue your description of this superhero, I need to go and attend to my earthly duties.'

'You're awful at lying, Vivian. You are not at all intrigued. I think what you really want is for me to stop describing him.'

Samuel was fiercely passionate about what he did. To get a better understanding of the challenges they faced, he had started staying at the camps. He visited the station and decided to work there for a while to get an idea of what he was managing. He had always been very hands-on, and to understand the environment which he was managing was very important for him.

In his regular round of introductions to the team members, his eyes rested on a lovely brunette, who was bent down beside a little girl, talking to her about some upcoming race. As he walked up to her, she raised her head and looked at him with the most innocently beautiful eyes he had ever seen. She stood up and he realised he was standing too close; she swiftly took a step back and smiled. He extended his hand and said,

'Hi, I'm Sam, and you are …?'

'Vivian. Nice to meet you.'

He felt she'd had to swallow a giggle. 'Anything wrong?' he asked.

'No, it's just that I was talking about superheroes with the little girl and that was still on my mind.' She struggled to keep a straight face and turned to walk away. 'Nice to meet you,' she said over her shoulder.

Sam watched her for a moment. He was thoroughly intrigued. He had heard about the work she had done for a campaign, one she had not only instigated but fiercely promoted. But when he looked at her he was floored – for some reason he had expected a much older person and a much stronger one, but what he saw was serene beauty. The laughter dancing in her beautiful eyes still made him smile, as there was a jaunty, slightly impish look in them which lit up her entire face.

Vivian had worked hard to control her laughter, the image of a comic book superhero with cape and mask uppermost in her mind. Instead of listening to anything he had said, or inspecting his fabled good looks, she had put everything into keeping a straight face.

God, Vivian, you are hopeless, she told herself.

Sam organised a dinner for all the doctors one day as an after-work social. It was nothing flamboyant, just a meal at a nearby café, with some locally produced alcohol. Sam saw Vivian but instead of the suppressed giggle which he had seen the other day there was a cool smile on her face; nevertheless, he went over and started a very casual chat.

'Somebody told me you were from Barcelona. Me too.'

'Really? How interesting!' was all she said, before excusing herself to get some food.

'She is a tough nut,' Sam murmured to himself, watching her hips sway as she walked away. It was difficult for him to accept that he wasn't getting much back, as normally his charms seemed to work on the opposite sex.

A few minutes later he tried again. 'So, Vivian, what inspired you to come and work here?'

'Nothing so very different from what inspired all these people here,' she said; nothing more, not even a slight inkling to carry on a conversation.

He didn't try further as he could see it was a lost cause. As they talked around the table he gave her a few more glances, but without any response. Despite this, his interest and curiosity increased. Whether it was the fact that for the first time he was not getting any attention back, or whether he was genuinely intrigued by her, was something he couldn't yet put a finger on. But she definitely caught his attention.

Work gave him more opportunities to interact with her. As he was working at the station one morning he heard obscenities coming from outside the cloth window and saw two of the young lads who worked part-time at the camp having some kind of argument. The argument went from heated to fierce, then physical, and then to his amazement he saw Vivian just jump in. This petite doctor just dived in between two full-grown lads and shouted at the top of her voice,

'Stop it! Now! Is this what we need? Don't we have enough of this already? Why the hell are you two fighting again?'

Sam wanted to jump out, but surprisingly enough she seemed to have things under control even though she was half their size. The smaller, darker-skinned one said,

'He started it. I was working, and he started sweeping all the dust to where I was standing.'

The other one said, 'I was just sweeping the floor, doing my job. Why does 'e 'ave to be such a ger'l …? Dust e'ritating 'is nose?'

'Stop it,' Vivian said again. 'Show some respect to the people around you, Berko. Last time I'm warning you.'

It was funny to see her commanding such a big guy – and he was listening, too.

'Now both of you, I don't want any ruckus. There are sick people around and you guys are not helping, shouting at the top of your lungs.'

Both of them muttered a sorry and went in different directions as Vivian disappeared into one of the tents. There was a soft smile on Sam's face from the whole incident. He was still smiling to himself when the patient he was examining said,

'You like her, don't ya? But she doesn't pay any attention.'

'No I don't, she's a work colleague. Just admiring her bravery.' His voice sounded defensive even to his own ears.

'Good, becaoze I have known 'er fo' three years. She does not pay attention to anyone who makes a move on 'er … Different, she is, and I tell ya—'

'I know,' he said, smiling to himself.

He had just finished with this patient when Vivian came in, flushed from what he assumed must be the heat of the conversation and being outside in the hot sun. The anger which he'd seen on her face had been replaced by immense softness as she said hello to the woman he was examining. She asked about her children and her health, before bidding a warm cheerio.

Sam was still standing there when Vivian turned to him, and he almost faltered since he was blatantly staring at her.

'I ... I wanted to speak to you about the new MRI machine,' he said. 'I know we really need it to be brought in.'

'Go ahead,' she said, folding her arms and leaning on the wall as if she knew he was bullshitting.

'Maybe over a cup of coffee this evening?'

She levelled her gaze on him before replying, 'I prefer to discuss these things during working hours,' and walked away.

He watched her go and wondered if she was generally this difficult or if he was a particular target. Recalling what his patient had told him, his conclusion was she *was* difficult. Beautifully difficult, though, he thought. Surprisingly, instead of getting annoyed over her cool behaviour, he was smiling to himself when he called the next patient in.

He started engaging more with her for work matters, trying to keep the conversation, as much as possible, professional. The moment the conversation slipped to something personal, Vivian would withdraw into herself, and he did not want to lose the opportunity to interact with this gorgeous woman, who he found utterly mesmerising, as well as fiercely passionate about the work they were doing.

One fine morning they all noticed more military activity in the area than usual. In the three years Vivian had been here, military presence was quite normal, but today there was way too much.

Around noon, a mind-numbing, deep, rumbling sound reached the base, and during the complete silence that followed, everyone seemed rooted to the spot, and a palpable sense of fear enveloped the base. A violent gust of wind swept across the open ground between the huts and tents, and as their ears readjusted after the deafening noise, cries of help were heard through the smog which filled the place.

People started madly racing about in a state of panic, engulfed in horror. The pillar of fiery smoke and dust, mixing in the air above, created a heavy cloud, looming over all of them. Thousands of particles floated in the air around like deadly rainfall. From the commotion and the polluted air, coupled with the sound, Sam guessed a blast had happened close to their base, or even inside their base; he hoped not. Even though he was inside his tiny tent, the scene outside was fully visible from the small tent window.

Armed military personnel emerged out of nowhere and began herding everyone into a small room. The whole scene had changed in minutes. Soldiers were everywhere, and people were screaming, and running blindly through the clouds of dust looking for loved ones. Sam stood for a minute, frozen, holding on to the flapping entrance of the tent, trying to come to terms with what had happened. As his senses returned from numbness, his first instinct was to look for Vivian, who he could see at a distance, trying to get children together in one place.

A loud voice came from a door on the opposite side of the open ground:

'Hurry up, over here!'

People were blindly responding, not that there were any other options. Sam ran to Vivian, who was holding on to the group of children and trying to make them walk to the open door. He picked up a couple of them and they all walked together, yelling for the children to stay close.

'Keep walking, quick over there.' A man in uniform was talking to one of the young doctors, who seemed to be in a state of hysteria, which was not helping.

Once everyone was inside, the same soldier gave orders to secure the place. The doors and windows were jammed shut, and after that all Sam heard was voices shouting commands.

'Recon Squadron, stay put and guard this place; Foxhound Squadron follow me, we head south. Shelldrake Squadron, you cover northern side.' The echo of footsteps started to diminish but still the anguished cries of people not far away could be heard from inside the room.

They were all huddled in a tiny space, in which the only light came from a small light bulb in the middle of the ceiling. Sam's mind was working feverishly as he tried desperately to look out through a crack in one of the window shutters, but not much was visible. He glanced down at Vivian, who was trying to do the same, all the children huddled close to her. He could hear her slow breathing as her eyes tried to find the right spot to get a view between the window and the frame.

Strangely, at that point, the fear that had engulfed him minutes ago took a back seat, the noises outside became more distant and the soft smell of her flowery perfume started to fill his senses. He had never been so close to her; her thick eyelashes were moving steadily, as if in anticipation that things would get back to normal. Even with just a dash of lipstick on those terribly inviting lips, and no makeup, she looked incredibly attractive. Her hair, like dark honey, was tied loosely with a few strands falling on her face, complementing the colour of her eyes. And as if in a trance, he unconsciously bent towards her, smelling her.

He saw her hug a small child very tight and gently rub her back, telling her that all would be okay. There was a tenderness in that gesture, a sense of genuine care, not that it was uncommon in the field he worked in. Most of the people who worked there were sincerely motivated to make a difference to society. But somehow she was different and in that moment, a strange feeling stretched through his body.

Oblivious to how long he had been looking at her, his thoughts were interrupted by one of the military personnel saying,

'It's still not completely safe. You can go out now but please return to your quarters and stay indoors.'

'God, I hope no one is hurt,' said Vivian.

'Yeah,' was all Sam could manage. His mind was still racing with what he had seen; the beauty who he had so closely observed; the same beauty who was slowly filling his consciousness.

She approached a man in uniform and her voice was thick with concern as she spoke.

'Are the children in the orphanage safe? Can I go there?'

The officer looked a little surprised and said, 'I'll escort you.'

'Thanks, but who would escort these children to their homes?' There was a quiver in her voice when she said, 'How about you escort them and I'll go on my own.'

Sam was about to offer but the officer interrupted. There was a strange look on his face which Sam could not quite decipher.

'I'll ask my colleague to escort you,' he said to Vivian. 'It's best to stick with military personnel right now.'

Vivian gave clear, crisp instructions to all the children to do as the military men asked, before giving a warm group hug. Even though she was pretending to be calm her movements were fidgety. But her need to take care of those children was so great that somewhere she had hidden her fears. He saw her eyes getting watery when she told the kids, 'Everything will be fine.' If they were tears, they were carefully concealed.

As she walked away with the soldier, asking numerous questions, Sam stared after her and wondered if his observation was correct. Her fingers were entwined behind her back and were being constantly twisted and turned as she moved briskly with the officer, nervously looking all around. The more he observed her the more he realised how scared she was.

When he got to his house, he felt as if Vivian had bewitched him. He could not get her image out of his head, her face hopeful and scared at the same time as she tried to look through a crack in the shutters, her hair messily tied back and her smile, when she spoke to the kids – so much more genuine than when she spoke to him. The last bit irked him. He had to win her over, she was too unique to let go.

'Beautifully unique,' he said aloud, and smiled.

Chapter Twenty-four

The next day was hectic, full of work due to the devastation of the previous day. People with various injuries, some minor and some horrific, walked in or were carried, one or two at a time, until every bed was full. Vivian was working flat out and Sam kept coming to her workspace.

'What's with you today?' she said, on his third or fourth visit. 'Can you please let me concentrate on this ward? You're interrupting me every ten minutes.'

'Well, I need help. How about you let Alex take over your ward and you come and help me. We have too many people in my ward.' He spoke in a very professional and impassive tone, trying not to react to the telling-off he had just been given. Alex, who was bent down examining a patient in the same room, looked at Sam, confused, but did as he was told – and so did Vivian.

They worked together until midnight, by which time Vivian was exhausted.

'Why don't you take a break?' Sam said, gently, as he saw Vivian tilt her neck back and roll her shoulders.

In a tone that had considerably softened, she replied, 'There are too many people, Sam. You can't possibly handle this on your own.'

'How about a quick coffee?' he asked, impulsively.

'Not now, maybe when the second team comes in.'

The second team came and they handed over the shift and took a short walk outside, away from the odour of medicine and disinfectant. There was still a faint whiff of explosives in the air, but it was nice to breathe in the open as opposed to the enclosed tent. Even in these adverse circumstances, he was itching to ask her out. The logical part of his brain said a firm no, but the idiotic part, seemingly of its own accord, went right ahead.

'How about dinner when things settle down a bit?'

'Maybe. I can't think about anything right now.'

Before he could coax her any further, they were interrupted by a shout for help. They both rushed in and got back to work.

And so it went on throughout the night. It filled her with anguish to see so many people hurt and wounded, some crying in pain and some crying for the pain they felt at losing loved ones. Either way, the faces reflected agony and grief. She wondered whether she would ever recover from the wretchedness she saw all around.

A demanding work schedule and a heavy heart tired her out completely, and around dawn she went to her tiny house and slept soundlessly till a frantic knocking woke her up. It was more work, as another blast had taken place in a nearby village and more injured people needed treatment. She ran without even taking her morning coffee, and was caught up in the day immediately.

Next morning, she called her parents, who were now back in Barcelona for good. She talked to them for a long time and felt much better, as did they, as they had been very worried about Vivian after seeing the disturbances on the news. Even after nine years she had an impulse to call Andre but that urge was kept tightly on a leash.

Days went by like this, and the line between day and night was increasingly blurred. She worked round the clock to help as much as she could. After a few weeks, the place settled down somewhat and work started, very slowly, to get back to normal. Vivian was getting more sleep and the mornings, instead of starting with a frantic scream or an urgent knock on her door, started with her usual coffee.

The whole experience gave Vivian a feeling of contentment with her life, which had been lacking ever since her separation from Andre.

On a warm windy day when the harsh dry air was baking the already barren land, Sam came up to her and asked,

'Hey, do you remember the dinner?'

'Which dinner?' she asked, sensing the direction in which the conversation was going and continuing her work.

'The one I want to buy you.'

'Why is that?

'To eat food?'

'I do that every day anyway.'

181

'Come on, don't be such a nut. It's just dinner and I'm a nice guy, honestly.' A smile swept across his face, and then he added the clincher: 'Plus, I need to understand a few details about the orphanage for the next project.'

Finally she looked up. He was wearing a crisp white shirt, with the cuffs folded back, and beige trousers; his blue eyes returned her gaze and were filled with an amused smile. His muscular shoulders were almost blocking the entrance, and his head was slightly bent to accommodate the lintel.

'Fine,' she said. 'I won't be going to the orphanage tomorrow. Possibly then.'

His smile broadened at this acknowledgement, and with a gleam in his ocean-blue eyes he said,

'I'll pick you up and then we can go together.'

She just nodded and went back to what she was working on.

Sam left as Alex emerged. He had obviously overheard the whole conversation, as he was smiling.

'This one is persistent; not like me – I gave up on you a long while back.'

'You were smart, Alex.' She laughed. 'No point being persistent.'

'The bugger will learn the hard way,' he said. 'I don't like the guy.'

'Alex, I'm not going out with him. One dinner and he'll realise what a bore I am and not try anymore.'

'Oh, yeah. Standard pattern – I forgot.'

They shared a laugh before the conversation turned to the more serious topic of vaccines. Alex was one of the few guys with whom Vivian was very good friends. Initially, when they had met, Alex had hit on her like any other guy, but once she said no he had found someone else fairly quickly. That had removed physical attraction from the equation and laid a solid foundation for a strong friendship.

Even before she could finish her work the next day, Sam was there.

'So can we go now?'

'Hmmm.'

Clad in plain jeans and a t-shirt, her hair in a clasp at the nape, she looked to him more like a college girl than a woman who was running an entire division of Providence.

He apologised for having to take her to the small coffee joint which was the only option for dinner, and she smiled a brief acknowledgement. Sam tried some small talk about the orphanage, about work, but he was impatient to ask her out properly. Too soon, he kept telling himself. After some random topics including sports and horses he said,

'You are different, Vivian. I have never met a woman like you.'

She took a sip of her drink and nodded without expression, as if she had heard that statement many times before.

'I really like spending time with you …'

'Hmmm.'

He was acutely aware of the coolness which was evident in her tone when he started talking about personal matters, but he still wanted to ask her out.

'Would you like to go out with m—'

'I'm sorry, but I'm not looking to go out with anyone. We work together. Let's just keep it that way.' As she spoke, she looked sideways at a tree a few feet from their table.

Sam got the message and changed the subject to make her feel comfortable. It was the shortest, most awkward proposition he had ever made. And the first time he had been so heartlessly turned down. His good looks and muscled physique had never been so brutally ignored.

They finished their dinner and Sam dropped her off before going back to his house, thoroughly disoriented. He knew he was falling for Vivian but all he could see in her eyes was indifference.

She's tough, he thought to himself before trying to divert his mind to think about the hospital.

Vivian was exhausted and went to sleep immediately, dismissing thoughts about Andre which somehow always entered her mind whenever anyone asked her out.

Next day, she got a call from Devyani, asking her how she was after the recent blasts. The call filled Vivian with genuine delight; it had been a while since she had spoken to any of her friends from college. The telephone, kept in a common area on a small wooden desk, saw continuous babble and giggles from the ladies.

Andre's name was mentioned, along with information on the latest girl he was dating, which produced a pointed silence from Vivian's end. In an effort to lighten the atmosphere, Devyani said,

'So, are you dating some hot doctor?'

'No, no time. There is so much work, so much to do.'

'Oh come off it, Vivian, you need to start seeing other men, it's been years. It's time for a relationship.'

'I will, when I'm ready and when I get time.'

'Alrighty, let me reframe the question. So, is there any hot doctor chasing you? There has to be, Vivian, don't you dare lie.'

Vivian had a good laugh and told Devyani about Sam.

'What the fuck, Vivian? Date him. Give it a try … duh. You really should.' Devyani was one of the few people who could order her about like that.

'It doesn't work like that, Devyani.' Her sigh almost covered the words and a certain sadness loomed over that sentence, very audible to Devyani's ears.

'Viv, it will work when you let it work. It's time. It has been nine years.'

Vivian took a deep breath and inwardly acknowledged what Devyani was saying before telling her to change the subject. They talked some more about Devyani's research, her super-rolling love life and their original travel plans, sharing giggles and trading friendly insults.

The conversation left Vivian thinking that Devyani had a point. She was stuck in time, unable to move on. She had gone on a few first dates but nothing more – that was all she could handle as the past always came alive during such times. She knew it was time that she moved forward. Thoughts of

Andre, of their love affair, their time together, had covered – almost smothered – her, and she wondered where the nine years had gone. How had they passed so quickly? It almost felt as if they had broken up only yesterday, and today Devyani had reminded her it had been nine long years.

Her mind started going over the same old ground – had it been something special with her, or just another affair like the ones he was having now? Possibly just the latter. He might be loving every woman the way he had loved her, and she was a fool to think anything else. How many times in the past had she thought that he would come for her, ask her why she'd left, and make her feel loved again in the way that used to fill every inch of her soul. Times when she had thought about how he would kiss her, make love to her, just be with her.

Small dreams, however precious. And the passage of time had finally made her realise that they were just empty dreams, far removed from reality. She hated that part of her, that part which still carried the wreckage of the past.

I have to stop this. I can't think about him. For God's sake it has been nine years – how can I still be having this conversation in my head?

'Everything ok?' Sam was standing in the doorway.

'Yup, just a call from back home.' She put on a smile, as wide as possible. 'How's the kid in bed sixteen? I did give him a morphine injection … hopefully it helped.'

'Doing much better, but we need to operate. We'll be taking him to Tumu soon.'

186

Vivian had to go back to Spain for training and so did Sam. They were to fly to Madrid for the training programme, after which Vivian would go on to Barcelona.

They took the flight together. Sam tried some small talk, but after a while Vivian yawned and said,

'I think I need to sleep, flights tire me out.' She closed her eyes, allowing her head to fall to the opposite side from Sam, which he took to be a pretty clear signal.

For the rest of the flight, and in the airport, he did not try any further conversation.

For Vivian, it felt good to be back in Spain, and she was excited that she would be able to spend time after the training with her family in Barcelona. It had been a while since she had seen her parents – work had somehow taken over her life and she missed them.

The training programme was for a full week. Doctors from around the globe flew in to attend. Sam was very popular in the group, with women hitting on him quite openly.

One of the doctors came over to Vivian while they were waiting for a seminar.

'Why don't you go out with him – he likes you a lot and he is a wonderful man. If he asks me, I won't even think twice.'

'Go ahead, help yourself,' Vivian said.

After a long day, Sam insisted on dinner again.

'I promise I won't hit on you,' he said, and laughed.

She was about to say no when she thought suddenly about what Devyani had said. She had to make a start somewhere. She had lived within her shell, denying herself any possibility of change.

'With that condition established,' she said, 'let's go.'

Sam took her to a lovely Spanish restaurant, a cosy place lit up with fairy lights and candles. A jazz band played live music and the waiters served bubbly on the house as a welcome drink.

Getting out of work mode, enjoying this taverna with a few glasses of good wine and delicious food, Vivian felt good. Sam did not pass up any chance of impressing her.

'I thought we talked about not hitting on me.'

'I can't help it, your beauty makes me a compulsive hitter.'

They both laughed, and it occurred to Vivian that it had been years since she had shared a laugh over a good meal. They talked about work, families, the colleges they went to.

'Your travel record is impressive for someone so young. My life has been pretty much all in Barcelona, from birth to education and then work, for a long time. It's only in the last couple of years that I've done any work-related travelling.'

She told him all about India, but tried not to venture too much into the early days of college. Instead, she concentrated on Sam, hearing him talk, looking at how his long fingers moved as he spoke. She could see he was really good-looking, and there was an honesty about him that gave him considerable charm. His thick blond hair was beautifully cut and styled – he was what her mother would have called 'well presented'.

The dinner ended on a pleasant note. They walked back together to the hotel, talking and laughing, and it was a nice change for Vivian as she had succeeded in enjoying herself rather than perpetually thinking of Andre. As they walked, she noticed for the first time how tall and muscular he was. There was a grace in his movements, whether it was walking or while asking her for dinner.

At the hotel, she said goodnight and went straight to her room before Sam could ask her for a coffee.

The next day, he asked her for dinner again. 'Same place?'

'Again?'

'Yes, again. I can't help it, you've bewitched me.'

She laughed, and genuinely tried to start enjoying the time spent with him instead of remembering ghosts from the past. She had to break the first date barrier.

And it worked. They went several times for dinner or coffee, always followed by long walks and chat.

The training over, she went to Barcelona to see her family. Her parents' faces reflected their delight after such a long absence, and her father became visibly emotional when he saw her. They hugged each other tight and he kept talking about how relieved he was to see that she wasn't hurt.

They sat down for their usual coffee and conversation, something all of them had dearly missed, and for the next several days Vivian felt as if time was turned back and she was a teenager again, completely oblivious to any sort of suffering and sadness in this world. She was pampered every minute she was there, with her mum making her favourite dishes and her dad 'taking care of everything' for her. They went out on long walks and she played basketball with her dad for old times' sake – little things that made the days beautiful. It felt like a much simpler world and she loved every moment of it.

The few precious days of her holiday passed too quickly and it was time to go again. She had noticed for the first time that her parents were ageing a little, so she said goodbye with a heavy heart at the airport. They met up with Sam and there was just time for her parents to say a quick hello before they boarded the flight to Ghana.

Conversation on the flight was much more two-way, in contrast to the monologue of the flight over. Vivian was much less hostile, more open, than before. Sam had enjoyed the whole trip thoroughly – for him it was a step closer to knowing the girl he wanted to be with.

Back at work it was life as usual, except for the fact that the after dinner walks continued and so did the conversations.

'You know, Vivian,' said Sam one evening, 'you are the only woman who has ignored me so brutally. God, my ego is in pieces.'

Vivian stifled a laugh. 'Am I?'

'No. I get ignored on a daily basis … what do you mean, "am I"?' They shared a laugh as they walked towards Vivian's house.

'Do I get anything to soothe my ego?' There was a gleam in his eye.

'Hmm … For the pain I have caused you? I think so, yes. Tomorrow, I can work an extra shift for you while you have a leisurely lunch.'

Sam stood there, pretending to frown, but he did love the sound of her laughter.

After a couple of months of dinner, chats and working together, Sam tried again over a cup of coffee.

'Can you think about being with me now?'

Silence followed his question. A million thoughts about Andre crossed her mind, and then she thought of Devyani's words and she heard herself say,

'I can give it a try.'

Sam's face lit up, and a hug dissolved, for the first time, into a soft and tender kiss.

Vivian lay there after Sam left, thinking about her situation, and her eternal love for Andre. She knew very well that it still existed, but she also knew that he was in the past and that it was completely insane to think anything would ever work out between them. And here was a guy who was head over heels in love with her. The options were clear and she had to make a choice – it was long, long overdue.

Devyani was right, she told herself. She had to start dating properly – there had been nobody since

Andre. She looked forward to her new life because she was tired of carrying along the corpse of a dead relationship. She started enjoying the fact that she was not chasing a ghost anymore, and that there was somebody right beside her to whom she could talk – not somebody who would only ever be her companion in her dreams.

From then on, she became ever more welcoming to Sam; she encouraged him many times and enjoyed him for who he was. Sam was loving this new outlook of hers – she was so much more gentle and inviting. It was like a new Vivian, and the more he found out about her the more he loved her.

Months passed by, and then they had been dating for two years, during which time their relationship continued to strengthen. Not much changed at work save for Sam's proximity, which greatly increased. She looked forward to spending time with him instead of avoiding it. She was getting there slowly and steadily, and Sam could see it.

One evening, as they went on their customary dinner date, Vivian noticed something was different. Their table was set up in a different corner, and there was a white tablecloth on it – she was used to the bare wood. There was a little vase of flowers in the middle, and a small candle, which was flickering in the breeze. She looked at Sam and wondered what was going on. The people who ran the café smiled and spoke quietly amongst themselves, as if they knew something she didn't know. Then Sam bent down on one knee and said,

'Vivian, you fill my life with love. Your face is one of unparalleled beauty; your laughter makes me smile and when you are sad it breaks my heart. I'm not perfect, but you can make me perfect just by being with me – I'm incomplete without you, without your love, without your presence, without your smile. Be mine, now and forever.

'I'm not a poet, Vivian, but that's how I feel deep within. Marry me.'

Vivian was enchanted by his lovely words and by the earnest look on his face. Her brown eyes lit up when she saw the ring he held out towards her. She looked at him and she knew he loved her and always would. She smiled and extended her hand. He put the ring on her finger and kissed her, forgetting they had an audience in the coffee shop until everyone applauded.

Looking at the ring glinting on her finger, Vivian said simply, 'It's beautiful.'

Chapter Twenty-five

It was holiday season and time to go back home. Vivian flew to Barcelona; Sam was to follow in a few days. Unlike previous fleeting visits, the plan was for Sam to meet Vivian's family formally and talk about the wedding. When Vivian had spoken to her mother about Sam, the reaction had been immediate – and positive. She did not mind saying how pleased she was that Vivian was finally talking about men and not work.

The day Sam was to arrive, mother and daughter went on a cleaning and cooking spree. By evening, the house looked immaculate. Carlos was asked to make sure that, when he sat down, the cushion arrangement was not spoiled – in disgust, he spent most of the day in the garden pruning the hedge.

Sam was on time. Vivian opened the door to find him standing with a bouquet of fresh flowers in one hand and a bottle of champagne in the other – and nervousness spread all over his face.

'Relax, you're not walking into the enemy's base camp,' she whispered, closing the door behind him.

He managed a forced smile – and met the entire family with the same smile plastered on his face.

For Vivian it was hilarious – she had never seen him so nervous – but her father was already scrutinising him. They all settled themselves around the family dining table and Maria set out a selection of tapas for starters, alongside a jug of sangria. Vivian looked at Sam, and from his expression it was clear he could have done with the whole jug …

Sam felt he was under constant surveillance. He answered questions about his background, family, education … the list went on. Just when he thought the question and answer session from the old man was over, and he raised his glass for a much-needed sip of sangria, another one was fired:

'So, how were your grades in med school?'

This was absolutely the limit. *How the hell, in a marriage proposal, do grades come into the picture?* He was sure he saw a grin on Vivian's face. Once, their conversation had been limited to work and life in Africa. But now it was all personal, down to – bloody hell! – grades. But he didn't lose his cool. Instead, he smiled and replied,

'I was in the top five percent.'

'So was Vivian.' The old man smirked. 'She was a top performer throughout and not only in academics – in sports as well. She used to play excellent basketball. Do you play a sport?' Sam was nodding, but before he could reply the old man continued, 'I went to see all the matches and the way she used to shoot was stunning – a pure pleasure to watch. It is rare to see someone play so well.' His smile was wide and proud, but Sam was neither genuinely smiling nor feeling especially proud. He felt annoyed.

He admired Vivian, but this was a bit over the top; the way her father was describing her was as if she was some miracle born to them. Sam was a very successful guy – a very *good-looking* and successful guy – but he was being made to feel as if Vivian would be obliging him by marrying him.

'Dad, it wasn't that big a deal, I just played in the school team, nothing extraordinary.' Vivian was trying to help.

'Of course it was extraordinary, I went to all your matches and no one even came close to the way you played.'

Vivian obviously gave up as she changed the subject. 'Sam plays excellent tennis.'

'Not excellent, just okay,' said Sam, managing another sip of sangria.

Vivian tried to be the lubricant, intervening at strategic moments to prevent friction and steering the conversation in the right direction.

But the old man was not giving up. 'How will you handle settling down, with all that travel?'

Suddenly, the conversation was taking a more serious tone. Vivian had been clearing the table for the main course but she stopped at that question and said,

'It's the same for me as well, Dad. We'll manage.'

'This is what I'm asking, Viv – how *will* you manage if both of you are travelling all the time? Sam, what do you think?'

It was a good question and Sam knew it.

'I guess I'll try and pair up with Viv every time she's travelling, and vice versa, and we'll try to cut down travel to an extent.' Then he added the winning point: 'Vivian is much more important, so if career needs to take a back seat, then that's how it will be. No two ways about that.'

That put a smile on Carlos's face.

Sam tried his luck with flattery, praising Maria's culinary skills at length. As the cod and paella was finished, the initial hesitation and tension eased too. Everyone became more relaxed, more accustomed to each other's presence, but Vivian could see that Maria's emerald eyes betrayed a less than positive reaction to Sam. They were filled with concern, as though something was troubling her, something on which Vivian could not quite put her finger.

From the question and answer round the conversation moved freely to Africa, then economics and the stock market. By the time they got to the American economy, Sam and Carlos were laughing together. The jug of sangria was refilled.

'Ready for dessert, Sam?' asked Vivian, tilting her head a little.

'I'm so full, I don't think there's any space left; the cod was delicious.'

'It's rice pudding,' said Maria. 'The only thing Vivian knows how to make!'

There was a general chuckle. 'We'll be a rice pudding couple for breakfast, lunch and dinner,' Sam said, and they all laughed.

Neither Carlos nor Maria could fault Sam. He was a great guy from every perspective. His eyes had an honest love for Vivian, and that was the one truly important thing her parents were looking for.

Vivian knew how difficult it must be for them to trust somebody with their daughter. She was the single most precious thing in their lives.

The evening progressed well and the rice pudding added the right amount of sweetness to the conversation. Sam invited them all to his house to meet his side of the family. He was doing well – he laughed and talked with her parents naturally, something that Vivian enjoyed watching. The only thing that bothered her was the look her mother was giving him.

Vivian and Sam took their leave after coffee; she walked alongside him when they went outside. There was a long sigh from Sam.

'What?'

'I was nervous as hell.'

'You did famously well, why were you nervous?'

'There was so much at stake.' He smiled softly, cupping her face and looking deep into her chestnut eyes. Then, aware that Vivian's parents were looking on, he gave her a gentle kiss before waving goodbye.

As they were clearing the tables, Vivian said to her mother, 'Did you not like Sam?'

'He's a great guy, but there was something that bothered me. I can't quite put a finger on it – something didn't feel right.'

'Go on, Ma. What is it?'

'I think it's the fact, sweetie … that you are going to marry him, that's all!' she said, and laughed. The tension disappeared in the tinkle of her laughter and the clatter of coffee cups once again filled the house.

One meeting led to another and it was not long before the two families became busy with detailed arrangements for the wedding. Vivian was a bit overwhelmed, albeit excited. It was a new feeling, a feeling of being loved, of being cared about, rather than just hoping ...

Chapter Twenty-six

All dressed up for the Venice Biennale, Andre stepped into the grand entrance of the historic Gritti Palace. It was one of those rare occasions when he was without a date, as his girlfriend had had to fly out for work and he was not keen on asking anyone else to accompany him. He loved the palace – a nice mixture of history and culture restored in the Venetian style.

But before he could admire the splendour of the place, he spotted Lenny. He'd known she was in Venice as she had developed a habit of calling him, trying to catch up, something which Andre had successfully evaded every time. But now he had no option as she was standing right in front of him in an atrocious gold gown, smiling that annoying, devious smile. Andre always found it sickening to talk to her for some reason, even now – years after what had happened.

'What are you doing here all by yourself?' Lenny asked.

'I actually just came in,' Andre replied, planting a kiss on each cheek.

They entered the main hall together, something which he absolutely did not want, but there wasn't much choice. To his relief she excused herself, saying she wanted to get someone over to meet him. Andre relaxed and continued to mingle; he knew most of those present – more or less the same people who came every year, with a few exceptions.

As he was talking to an elderly couple, Lenny patted him on the shoulder and, without bothering about the conversation he was engaged in, launched into an introduction to her current boyfriend. Andre knew him well – the son of an airline tycoon, he was as spoilt as Lenny and the two of them were, he thought, perfect for each other.

Out of nowhere, Lenny asked a bizarre question, all the while playing with her hideous diamond necklace.

'So, are you flying to Barcelona next month?'

'Why would I be?' Andre replied, as politely as he could, catching the waiter's attention for a drink.

'Are you not invited? Vivian is getting married.' Lenny smiled the kind of knowing smile that made him want to break her teeth.

All sound around him seemed to stop; only the revelation that Vivian was getting married echoed in his head. Anger and hurt started to boil within him, though he knew he had no right to feel either. She was not his, not after twelve years, not anymore…

He felt as if the place was suffocating him now. He stared blankly at the waiter who was offering him his drink, turned, and walked out of the grand salon and out of the hotel, without any parting courtesies and heedless of Lenny's call from behind.

Sitting in his car, he thought, *She never even told me* … Then a wry smile covered his face. *Why would she? I never even tried calling her or finding out how she was. God knows I wanted to, though …*

He closed his eyes and his head flopped back onto the leather headrest. A familiar feeling bored into his heart – the feeling of losing her again. It did not make any sense, but that was how he felt. A wild thought ran across his mind, that he might somehow run to her and put a ring on her finger and hear the words 'man and wife'. As reality sank in, he wondered what had stopped him all these years. He questioned once more the finality of that fateful decision.

And as he sat, surrounded by memories of Vivi, the decision felt stupid and meaningless. If only there was some way to reverse it … While they were breaking up, it had never occurred to him that even after twelve years he would be still longing for the same woman. He always knew it would be difficult but this kind of difficult was not something he had expected. And now it was too late. He had no wish to cause turbulence in her obviously settled life. He knew she had had difficulty coping with the break-up but now she was engaged to another man – she must have moved on, and saying anything could only cause her pain.

When he got home he went straight to his room, cursing himself for his situation and bewildered as to why he was still being affected by it all.

Slouching on the couch, he removed his bow tie and stared at the ceiling.

'God,' he said aloud, 'it's been twelve years. I need to get her out of my system.' Closing his eyes, he wished for her happiness and wellbeing. But it was hopeless. Even after all these years, he felt like a lovesick schoolboy when it came to Vivian.

He opened the cupboard by his bed and took out the box Vivian had given him. Gently taking out a frayed and flimsy sheet of paper, he read the poem she had written for him. The beautiful, forward-flowing hand, the few heart-warming lines, made him feel loved again. A strange, warm feeling filled his heart, a feeling of her presence, of the warmth of her body and, most importantly, of the oneness of their souls; something he had never found in any other woman. Unshed tears burnt his eyes as he touched the paper, tinged yellow at the edges after all these years.

He kissed it and folded it again, returning it to the same flat, wooden box on which Vivi had carved her name. He had thrown away most of the things from his time in Delhi but there were still a few memories carefully preserved. In the same box were their photographs from Nainital. As he closed it, his fingers traced the name, unevenly carved on the side, and memories from the past engulfed his aching heart.

It had been a cold evening in Nainital and the two of them had gone for a walk around the town. Browsing the market towards the end of the day,

Vivian had seen a rustic-looking wooden box and asked the shopkeeper how much it was.

'You like that?' Andre asked.

'It strikes me as a box for storing memories. I had one like this when I was a child and I used to keep my most precious things in it. I still have it with me, and the most beautiful memories return every time I open it. Can I buy it for you?'

Her face was so full of earnest innocence that it was impossible to say no.

'Of course, but you need to inscribe it in some way, because I don't really get this system of keeping memories – you keep them in your heart, not in a box.'

'But there are always some for which you need a box,' she said as she paid the shopkeeper. 'How do I inscribe it?'

'Think, baby, think …' He gave his familiar naughty, boyish smile.

She asked the shopkeeper if she might use a small knife which was sitting on the counter, and scratched the word 'Vivi' on the side of the box there and then. Then she kissed it and handed it to Andre with a smile.

'There you go,' she said.

'I love it. It's special now, I'll keep it always.'

He had kept his promise; the box was his most treasured possession. Vivi was right, he thought. Sometimes you do need a box to store your memories. This little fragment from the past left his heart brimming with love. The idea of Vivian marrying was relegated to the back of his mind and his love for her had taken over. He had had his fair share of women, but it was a constant struggle to find the passion, the magic which had once come from just a single kiss.

Now, he was annoyed with himself for ever expecting to find heaven when he had already found it and given it up. He had lost that desire, the desire to be with someone for the rest of his life, finally reconciling himself to the notion that history could not be repeated.

Nowadays, it was more a question of having a companion than of finding true love.

Chapter Twenty-seven

On a Saturday afternoon two months before the wedding, Vivian was busy selecting the floral decorations for the big day when she got a call from Sam. What he said put her into a state of shock and frenzy, and she left the flower shop and ran to her car. Before driving off, she made two calls, to her parents and to Gloria, and all of them had the same reaction.

She stopped the car in front of the Hospital Universitari de Bellvitge. She had a few hasty words with the receptionist and went straight to the emergency wing of the hospital. After showing her badge, she was led to the waiting area outside the theatre. Her heart went out to Sam when she saw him sitting there with his head in his hands. The slight touch of her fingers made him look up, his face so full of grief that she instantly hugged him close.

She gently brushed his hair for a while before asking, 'How did this happen?'

'He was going to meet a few of his friends to give out invites for our wedding. On the motorway a lorry hit his car – at least that's what the police have told us. I haven't told Mother yet, she'll be hysterical. The doctors had to do an emergency operation.'

Every time a nurse went in or out he pressed her hand unconsciously.

She said, 'It will all be alright, have faith. Your father is a strong man – you both are – and I know he'll pull through.' She pressed a kiss on his forehead.

As the team of doctors and nurses finally emerged, Vivian felt the sweat on Sam's palms. One of the older doctors came forward and said,

'The good news is he's out of danger; the bad news is it will take a minimum of six to eight months to recover. We have put a plate in his left arm as it was quite badly broken, shattered in places, but it is his back which is the biggest problem. A few bone fragments have become lodged close to the spinal cord. We have done what can be done at this stage, but back injuries take time and patience. He might have to undergo further surgery. As of now, plenty of rest and careful monitoring are the order of the day.'

The doctor sat with Sam for some time, explaining the details. When he left, Sam walked briskly towards the recovery ward, where he found his father lying unconscious, surrounded by drips and tubes. As he stood beside his father's bed, Vivian stood behind him, her hand on his shoulder. She felt his muscles, which were flexing spasmodically.

They went back home and when Sam broke the news to her mother, which was another herculean task, she was hysterical, as he had rightly said. After a whole day of madness, Vivian decided to stay with Sam, as he was exhausted, both mentally and physically.

The next few days were a never-ending cycle of hospital visits and managing Sam's mother at home.

One evening, as they were sitting on the porch of Sam's house after a particularly long day, Vivian said,

'Sam, don't you think we should postpone the wedding?'

He stopped rubbing the back of his neck and looked at her, and gratitude filled those ocean-blue eyes.

'You're okay with that?'

'Yes, totally!'

'Actually, Vivian, I would be quite relieved. Dad's condition has been eating me up but I just didn't have the heart to talk to you about postponing. Thank you for understanding.' He squeezed her hand and settled back into his rocking chair.

Vivian didn't mind. She understood the situation. If, God forbid, her father had been in a similar condition, weddings would have been the last thing on her mind.

When Sam's father improved, they decided to have an engagement party – a small get-together with a handful of close friends and family. The party was in Sam's back garden, with beautifully set up, dainty arches covered with white flowers and lit with fairy lights.

Sam watched as she stood below one of the arches, dressed in a flowing light blue gown, talking to a mutual friend. Sunlight glinted on her face and her silver earrings added sparkle to the soft glow spread across her striking features.

As soon as he saw she was on her own, Sam walked over and said quietly,

'Did I tell you how stunning you look?'

'As a matter of fact you did not.'

He squeezed her shoulders and leant in to whisper in her ear. 'You look ravishing.'

They were the perfect couple, laughing and talking to their guests. Sam greeted everyone as they arrived with a well-practised smile, but he faltered when Gloria came in, wearing a deep-neck black and gold gown. Sam curtly acknowledged her and she continued in full force, hugging and kissing Vivian.

'Oh my God, Viv. You look so beautiful!'

The girls chatted and when Gloria went to get a drink, Sam said,

'She couldn't find anything more suitable to wear?'

Vivian waved at Gloria and then gave Sam a nudge. 'She's looking lovely. Just a bit of a bold dress from the top but that's Gloria.' She laughed. 'Besides, she can carry it off.'

'Fine, if you say so …'

In the weeks immediately following their engagement, Vivian spent much of her time with Sam. Slowly, she learned to love him – he was a wonderful guy and he took care of her in every possible way. She did everything she could to make him feel loved, but there was a part of her which she knew nobody could manage to touch, not even Sam, so rigidly sealed off was that area of her vulnerability.

The problem was that for Vivian, something in her had become dormant the day she had run out on Andre in college. It even had an effect on their lovemaking; Vivian knew it, and she suspected Sam knew it too, but was kind enough never to say it.

Slowly, Sam's father's condition improved, but this improvement coincided with an increase in Vivian's workload. She was about to depart on her third trip in a month to Africa.

Sam was annoyed. 'What's going on? You've been pretty much out the whole time, and you seem to be travelling every month.'

'I'm so sorry, Sam, but there's just so much work, you know how it is.' She was trying to force the zip on her bag.

'I know exactly how it is and I also know you take on way too much. Viv, we need to start thinking of ourselves as well. With this schedule you don't have time to think for yourself; how will you ever find time for me – or us?'

Vivian gave up the struggle with her bag and held Sam's hands. 'Please, Sam, try and understand. You know work means a lot to me – those people need me. Not many people can do what we do, and if we don't do it, who will? You have seen the way things are. Someone has to take care of them.'

Sam just nodded and said, 'I would like someone to take care of me as well.' Then he walked away.

The sad truth was that when it came to a choice between Sam and her work … well, work meant a lot to her, and she felt, today, that Sam realised it too. This was not the first confrontation they had had on the topic and she was sure it wouldn't be the last.

It's all a part of staying together … I guess.

Chapter Twenty-eight

No sooner did Vivian return from Africa than she had to travel to London. She was planning to attend a conference on extending medical facilities to the poorest areas of the world, a topic about which she cared deeply. Thankfully, Sam was setting off on his own travels so there were no pre-trip arguments. Providence was one of the key participants and she was to give a presentation about its work in Africa.

She was travelling from Ghana to Frankfurt and then to London. Her flight from Ghana was delayed. As the flight landed, she hurried down the escalators, dressed in a plain black skirt with black tights and a white shirt.

She walked briskly towards the check-in counter, where a stern-looking lady, dressed in an indigo suit with blonde hair tied up in a bun, was sitting behind the counter. She handed over her ticket and passport. The lady sounded as cold as the weather there as she spoke with a clipped English accent.

'Madam, you are late.'

Am I in Frankfurt or London? Vivian explained that her connecting flight had been delayed. The lady barely took any notice and continued her speech after the brief check-in procedure.

'Please hurry and make your way towards the gate. We will not hold up the flight if you cannot make it to the gate.'

'I'm sure that won't be necessary.' Vivian spoke with a calculated tone and was gone in a flurry.

As she was running through the security gates, tannoy announcements were becoming more frequent, but the smell of fresh coffee and gourmet food made her want to dally in one of the lounges. After the long trip from Ghana, a coffee was just what she needed to set her up for the rest of the journey. The departure lounge glittered with the wine and cosmetics of the duty free shops, people milling around, shopping or looking. But she had no time for either and kept on running towards Gate 3, her boarding gate.

Gasping for breath, she ran on the moving sidewalk, hearing the last call for boarding. The airport was big and felt even bigger as she ran. Finally, a glimpse of Gate 3 brought a sigh of relief.

'Are you Vivian?' A man dressed in a deep blue suit was addressing her from behind a counter.

'Yes,' she replied, still running.

'The last passenger to board is here,' he said into a microphone, a frown accompanying the statement as he made a final check of the passenger list to confirm numbers.

'Madam, we held up the flight for you.'

The suited guy looked at her as if he had given her a life-saving drug and she owed him for the rest of her life.

Trying hard to sound polite and catch her breath at the same time, she said,

'I cannot thank you guys enough. Really appreciate it ...'

There was another leg of running on the skywalk, with the ground staff accompanying her, and the hum of the aircraft became more strident as they stepped out onto the apron.

As she stepped inside the plane, the air hostess seemed to slam the door closed behind her, shooting directions to her at the same time. Moving down the aisle, she looked for seat number 19C and tried to catch her breath. It seemed to her that the passengers' eyes were upon her, accusing her of causing a delay in take-off. The airplane smelled of disinfectant and looked much cleaner than the one on her flight from Ghana.

The man sitting in 3B was reading, his face half-covered by a newspaper. He had glanced up when she entered, and his wine glass had remained still between his lips as his eyes had followed her. He could not help getting up from his seat and following her blindly down the aisle. Finally, she reached her seat.

'Would you like help putting your hand luggage in the overhead locker?' asked a friendly steward.

'I'll manage, thanks,' she said.

As she took her bag in both hands a voice came from behind.

'Can *I* help with that?'

She recognised the voice immediately, and when she looked back, a swarm of emotions competed with the dazed expression that filled her chestnut eyes. Her cold hand brushed his warm palm as she handed over the bag without a word – a touch vividly remembered from so long ago.

'Sir, we need to take off, can you please return to your seat?'

Andre asked the man sitting crammed in the middle seat, 'Would you like to exchange your seat with me please? I am at three-B, in business class.' He did not bother looking at the man's surprised face as he swiftly got up and moved away.

Even after all these years she looked as innocent to him as when she had been an eighteen-year-old undergraduate, only now a subtle layer of charm and sophistication had been added. Her eyes, when she had glanced up to meet his gaze, still caused every muscle in his heart to ache. With the brown curls tumbling down her shoulders, her cheeks flushed from exertion, she was the woman Andre had loved like no other, and here she was, sitting next to him on a one-and-a-half-hour flight to London. Sweet taste of fate!

'How are you, Vivi?'

Andre had asked the question, but all he wanted was to hold her close, smell her hair, kiss her and adore her. He was surprised by his reaction because now she was married, he was dating, and it had been years since their break-up – but at that moment it was like the clock had been turned back and he was just Andre the boy, madly in love with Vivi, the girl of his dreams.

Her face had softened so much when she heard him say her name … He knew she loved that name.

For her part, trying to control her drumming heartbeat, Vivian stood transfixed by the face which had been embedded in her soul since time immemorial. Her heart had galloped the moment she had heard that rich baritone voice. Unable to comprehend what was going on or how, she tried to calm herself, in vain. She dropped into her seat without speaking, her head tilted towards him, trying to come to terms with this unlikely turn of events. Her emotions were brimming over, but the situation around her kept them hidden.

She thought she saw the same emotions in his eyes that had been there when he was twenty-two but she had seen them so many times before and, every time, circumstances had convinced her otherwise. Over the years she had programmed herself to trust what was concrete and not what she felt, and today, even as she saw those feelings in his eyes, accepting their existence was not an option for her.

Yet the constant hum of the aircraft, the clamour generated by the passengers, the security announcements from the cabin crew – all of it took a back seat, none of it was audible. Her heart could hear only the voice from the past echoing in her ears. Belatedly realising that he had asked a question and she had not even replied, she said,

'I'm fine. How are you?' Drawing a deep breath, she almost felt like telling him how miserable she had been all these years without him, then Sam came into her mind and she felt a creeping sense of guilt.

'I'm good,' he said, looking at her so tenderly that Vivian could have fallen in love with him all over again.

She could not believe they had met again, not after so many years, not on an airplane, sitting next to each other. But God, was she loving every moment! She saw his deep black eyes and realised how much she had missed looking into them, how those eyes meant the world to her, how she could see her future in them. She noticed that his complexion was more tanned than it had been in college days, and the innocence on his face had been replaced by rugged sexuality. His charm was as intact as ever – the way he talked, his flirty swing, they were all just the same. He was dressed in navy blue trousers and a cream and blue checked shirt with the buttons open at his neck. The side of his neck was very visible, where Vivian used to love to burrow her nose and take in the scent.

Shrugging herself back to the present, she glanced down at their arms, touching on the armrest, a touch which was still special, which stirred buried emotions from years past. She was appalled at herself for thinking along these lines; even after all these years, Andre was still instilled in her somewhere – she knew it deep inside, but to accept it was different. Trying hard not to fall prey to that irresistible force of attraction which Andre was emitting, she said,

'You didn't have to change your seat, it can't be very comfortable sitting in the middle.'

'It's not at all comfortable,' he chuckled, 'but I would give away anything to sit next to you.'

Why did he have to be so charming?

She tried continuing the conversation very neutrally, even though she was thoroughly elated after his last statement.

'So ... em ... are you going to London?' She was having a hard time coordinating her mind and her voice, feeling as if his mystical eyes had cast a spell on her, as always.

'I would be surprised if I wasn't, considering the flight goes to London.'

Vivian giggled, not just at the stupidity of the question but the fact that his sense of humour was clearly unchanged by the passage of time.

He watched her laugh. She could laugh and make him forget the world.

'It's good to see you, Vivi, after all these years. You still have the college girl charm.' Those brown locks, he thought, through which he loved to run his fingers ... Those luscious lips which he could have kissed this very moment; the long, slender neck ... how he wanted to run his fingers–

Blocking his chain of thought, he cursed himself for acting like an immature, idiotic boy, losing all control after one look at a girl.

'Thanks.'

They got to talking and the years past were put aside, the walls of time were taken down and the words were picked up from where they left off.

'I managed to open the glass factory in Murano just the way I planned. You should come and visit, I would love to show you around.'

'Well done you. I've been working in and out of Africa. It's a different world, requiring such different things to the shallow material things we so depend on in the West. You should come sometime – *I'll* show *you* around!'

They talked on, making up for all the years, bridging the chasm.

'Congratulations on your marriage.'

'Thanks.' *He doesn't know*, she thought. She had the urge to tell him that the wedding had been postponed, but why make a fool of herself? He had obviously moved on – he had moved on years ago. It was of no consequence to him.

'So what about you? Are you married?'

'Nope, just dating, marriage isn't for me.' He sipped from his wine glass and stared blankly at the seat in front.

His words confirmed to Vivian that he would never be interested in settling down. He liked to date. They had dated. It was as simple as that.

There was an uncomfortable silence, broken by the cabin crew's announcement to fasten seat belts for landing. It felt as if they had just taken off.

The plane touched down and taxied to the parking stand, and people began getting up and making their way to the door.

'Can we be in touch now? Or would that still be a problem?' He looked at her with such hopeful eyes that it was impossible to turn him away – but for the sake of self-respect she said,

'What would you prefer?'

'I want to stay in touch with you. Please, Vivi, don't say no.'

Her heart had already agreed – those beseeching black eyes could make her do anything, even now.

And she was not just surprised, she was bewildered. In one-and-a-half hours Andre had stirred an array of emotions in her which no one had done in years.

I'm engaged to a wonderful man, a man who loves me, who genuinely cares about me. What the hell am I doing?

They exchanged numbers and email addresses.

'I'm in London for a conference for two days,' she told him.

'I'm here for some work. I'll give you a call.'

They went in different directions but had one thing in common – neither of them could think of anything but those days in college.

This wasn't normal, thought Vivian – it had been twelve long years and though time, so they say, makes us forget, they were still stuck there, stuck in that magical year.

Andre watched her go, and he realised how empty his life had been without her. He stared out the window of his taxi, reflecting on all the time he had spent without her, setting up the dream factory, building a business. Such mundane things to have kept him apart from her. Now, suddenly, none of it made any sense. As the taxi slid through the city, the time lost in chasing a dream took on a life of its own and began to torment him. What was success? Certainly not those last days in Delhi, leaving Vivian for the nth time, being unsuccessful for the nth time...

Chapter Twenty-nine

2006 – New Delhi

It was December 2006. Andre's dad had finally been posted to Rome and the family was moving back to Murano.

On a cold winter's night, Andre was packing his belongings when he stumbled upon a carton on which he had written Vivian's name. He opened it gently for he knew exactly what was in it. Small things he associated with her – cards, letters, poems, a small wooden box …

He read through them, kissed each in turn, and placed them carefully in the open fire. The paper turned from white to brown, slowly curling at the edges, becoming smaller, disappearing … Everything she had written for him with such feeling was being turned to ash. One after the other, his eyes moist with tears, he put them in the fireplace.

His eyes fell on the card that Vivian had given him on his birthday, and he opened it to read the lines which he had read a million times before.

You are the sound in my ears,
You are the hope in my eyes,

You are the love which fills my heart;
You, and only you, can ever make me feel this
way,
Because it is you with whom my heart is tied and
my soul is one..
Love you forever.

His hands trembled as he dropped the card into the flames, but he had no choice – these were the remnants of a relationship which had ended, and he had to go on with his new life.

All that was left was the little box and a purple-edged sheet of paper with another poem in Vivian's hand. He read it again, remembering those hours when he and Vivian had been together – the time when she had belonged to him. He took the poem in his hand, pressed it to his heart, and sobbed the silent tears of loss. She had given him the poem the day they made love for the very first time, when they had first spoken about marriage. How could he throw away that poem? It was more than just words written on a piece of paper; the story of love was behind those words.

He folded the poem and placed it inside the box, resolved to keep it but never to look at it. Then he selected three photographs of their time in Nainital, and solemnly added them to this love-filled repository. He sat there, desolate, watching the flames consume almost every dream they'd ever shared. His heart filled with anger, with regret at not stopping Vivian the day she ran, the day she said she never wanted to speak again. He wondered if the decision actually made any sense at all. He knew it must have hurt her and maybe practically it was the right decision, but now, after all these years, it did not feel right, and he wondered why. There was something more that troubled him, something which he knew deep inside but had never confessed to himself.

There had been more than just his father's influence behind his leaving Vivian. He had been tired of second-guessing what might happen in the future and it had seemed like an easy way out for someone who wanted to explore the world, who was just twenty-two, who wanted to have fun. He was truly in love with her but there was some part of him that was not ready to talk about marriage or settling down with as much conviction as Vivian wanted. He knew he wanted to marry her – he had even asked her – but talking about it all the time and being emotional about it had somehow worn him down. By the same token, however devastated he had been by the break-up, he had felt a certain sense of relief – relief that he could spend his time the way any normal young man would, not worrying about marriage or the future.

Now, though, with the poem fresh in his mind, he felt awful.

What did I do? I lost the most precious thing I've ever had and didn't even tell her the whole truth. Maybe she wouldn't be able to take it anyway. She trusted me so much ...

He buried his head in his hands. After she'd left, he'd realised that passion and love, which Papà had said happened all the time, almost never happens at all. Once, with Vivian, then never again. He was twenty-six now. He wondered if she ever thought about him; or perhaps she had forgotten him completely and moved on.

I hope she has forgotten me, for a happier life. I hope she does not have to go through any more pain.

So, they'd moved to Rome and Andre had gone back to Murano to continue the work of the factory. His father continued in his job; Sergio thought it wrong to leave when he had made a commitment. Besides, in the factory he would be haunted by memories; Andre knew that that was the real reason his father felt unable to help him in what he had set out to achieve.

The work towards his dream had started immediately. He'd tried to apply all his entrepreneurial talent to the glass factory, but it needed a lot more than that. He combined his father's experience and his own hard work. Andre literally slept in the factory, working harder with each passing day. Orders started coming in and one led to another. After just a couple of years, they'd needed a bigger place to expand their manufacturing capacity.

He bought a parcel of land just outside Murano and found himself standing there one afternoon, his hands in his pockets, looking out across the empty space, feeling the breeze and smelling the grass – and, somewhat incongruously, the fumes from the other factories that surrounded him.

A sense of pride filled him. He owned this place. He gazed up into the sky and whispered,

'Ma, I have our dream back where it belongs.'

But as the breeze moved his shirt, and the sun's rays touched the tips of the grass, lending them a golden tint, his thoughts shifted unaccountably to the time in Nainital when he had looked, fascinated, at Vivian, with sunlight slanting across her face and glinting off her hair. Now, closing his eyes, he felt the warmth of the afternoon sun on his face. The breeze, the fragrance, filled his nostrils and heightened his senses. All of it reminded him of Vivian, the way she had filled him up, and now all that was left was the thought of her and a heart-wrenching emptiness.

Dismissing these thoughts, he'd turned and walked to his car, his head already full of plans and layouts, production processes and worldwide sales.

Months became years but Andre's enthusiasm for the factory did not diminish. He wanted everything bigger and better. He put in his days, he gave away his nights to see the glittering glass from his factory go off to all corners of the globe. He was immersed in his work, oblivious to everything else. Sometimes he would see Vivian's face in the stem of a glass or the rim of a plate, and each time his heart would melt and his mind would shut out the image.

He dated women – he was ever the charmer – but his heart could find no solace. There was always an emptiness in some distant recess, a desire for more, like an unfulfilled wish. He wondered what she had done to him. What chord did she touch in his heart that the sweetest music played and all other relationships paled into insignificance? *I have dated so many women; there should be someone who can strike that tune again* … He tried hard, but his heart won over his mind every time when it came to women, and in due course he gave up even looking for that perfect love. He knew he had to forget Vivian and that's what he did. With the passing years, thoughts of her had become fewer, the feel of her touch started to slowly fade, her fragrance became less strong.

Chapter Thirty

2013

The car stopped outside his hotel, breaking his train of thought. The hotel concierge opened the door and he checked into a luxury suite. As he changed, Vivian was on his mind. He wanted to sit for a while and just be lost in thoughts of her, but work was calling – his phone had already beeped several times and he had ignored it. It finally rang for the third time in a row and he picked up, spoke for a few minutes and then went downstairs for his meeting.

When Vivian reached her hotel there was already a group of people waiting for her. She quickly got on with her schedule, looking at her mobile phone once in a while. The day was extremely busy but time, for her, was passing slowly, thoughts of Andre flashing into her mind. She couldn't wait till evening, when she would hear his voice again.

This is stupid, I'm not eighteen, I cannot behave like this. He's in the past – I'm much more mature now.

When the phone rang she was the college girl again in a second, panicking to pick up.

'Do you want to catch up for a drink?'

'Sure.' She struggled to sound as calm as she possibly could.

'I'll pick you up from your hotel at six. Will you be free by then?'

'I should be, otherwise you can wait.'

'Okay,' he said, a hint of amusement in his voice.

She wound up her work as fast as she could, keeping a constant eye on her watch and phone. After her last meeting she dashed upstairs to her room and took a quick shower. Her hair was still dripping wet when Andre called to say he was waiting for her in the lobby.

She quickly slipped on a plain black dress with thin lace straps, which sat gently on her delicate shoulders. A dash of lipstick and she was ready to go.

Nothing too revealing, nothing too sexy, she thought to herself, remembering how his eyes used to make her self-conscious. Hopefully that was a thing of the past.

In the lift, which had mirrors on three sides, she constantly checked her appearance, feeling a little foolish and wishing she had time to dry her hair.

Breathing in deeply and exhaling very slowly, she endeavoured to look as calm and relaxed as possible, though her heart was beating at an astonishing speed.

'You are not a teenager going on a date. Calm down,' she murmured. 'You are engaged to be married, for God's sake.'

Andre had barely been able to wait for the clock to reach six. He had been all ready by five, walking up and down the road outside the hotel. A small flower shop caught his attention and he wandered over. In the window was a heavy aluminium vase containing red roses. He knew how much Vivian liked single stems, without any packaging or decoration – just the way nature intended. In another life he had gotten her roses and she had given him the sweetest smile. He brushed his hand across the petals, lifted out a single stem, hesitated, and quickly put it back.

'Get a grip, Andre,' he murmured. 'She's a married woman.'

He entered the hotel reception at five-thirty, hardly able to wait for the clock to strike six before giving her a call.

When he saw her coming, he could not quite believe his eyes. She was the same serene, untouchable goddess, with the most heart-warming smile and dove-like eyes. Wet brown tresses left tiny droplets of water on her skin. He shuddered at the sight of her bare shoulders. If time, he thought, could have been turned back …

Controlling the urge to caress her shoulders, he hugged her briefly, and for that moment both of them closed their eyes. The sound of Mozart was drowned for those seconds by the silent exchange between them. Her smell, the familiar touch and warmth, returned from the past and held him spellbound, like an exquisite haunting. Brushing his nose past the wet locks and inhaling a breath of her intoxicating fragrance, he said,

'You look as lovely as ever.'

'Thanks.'

In a voice coloured by his inner thoughts he asked, with a boyish smile,

'What do you want to do?'

She read that look and was completely flustered. Trying to ignore the double meaning, she said,

'I thought you were taking me out. You should have planned.'

'I normally plan the second date!'

He didn't have to mention Nainital. After a brief exchange of smiles, Vivian went over to the concierge's desk, took a few pamphlets and spoke to the manager for a while. Andre waited patiently, unable to take his eyes off her.

She came back with the pamphlets in her hand.

'Most places are closed. We can start with Covent Garden, and then—''

'Let's just start – see how it goes.'

They rode to Covent Garden in a black cab. There were street performers, along with an array of exclusive shops and restaurants that lined the surrounding path. They aimlessly walked through the covered part of the beautifully decorated market, which had stalls selling jewellery, clothes and lovely artefacts. Lost in the ever charming cobbled streets of London, they reached the Royal Opera House, opposite which was the statue of Plazzotta's Young Dancer. Vivian stood and admired the statue, while Andre concentrated on looking at her.

She caught him staring, folded her arms and said, 'What are you looking at?'

Folding his arms in exactly the same manner, he replied, 'You. I have seen Bernini in Italy; today I need to look at what I *don't* get to see.'

The words caused a visible stir in her. She was not expecting such a direct answer, and he had not intended to supply one, but with Vivian his impulses were always unpredictable ... She quickly turned her face to hide her smile.

He could see she was trying to distract herself, touching the bronze, sliding her hand over the curves of the statue, talking about the patience the artist must have possessed to come up with such a piece, but it did not work. She had her side towards Andre and her hair partially covered her face, but he could feel that she was smiling – he would have bet a million euros on it, and just that thought gave him happiness. Even after so many years, he could still make her smile despite herself.

They walked around the square and Vivian suggested dinner on the Thames. He nodded like an obedient child. Then something came into his mind and he smiled and touched her arm.

'It's a good plan. Are you dropping a hint?'

'A hint?'

'A boat. On the water. Remind you of anything?'

'I didn't think of that.' She lowered her eyes and her voice dropped.

'I know. Let's go,' he said, holding her arm and taking her towards the Strand.

Vaguely conscious of the web which Andre had begun to spin around her, and increasingly uncomfortable under the scrutiny of those dark eyes, she said,

'I don't know, though, if we can just go without a reservation. Do you still want to go?'

'Let's see ...' Still holding her hand, he turned and stood in front of her. 'Vivi, sometimes we need to just let things flow – see how it goes instead of pre-deciding each and every step.'

She felt a chill run down her spine. For an instant she felt like an idiot, forcing him to take a decision when they had just started dating. Instead of evading the web, she had jumped right into it. Her deepest feelings had been awakened, and her mind issued a warning signal.

The boat for their trip on the Thames was very different from the cosy craft at Nainital – much bigger and much more formal. Dining was at circular tables with white linen, each decorated with orchids and a small candle. There was a live band playing soft music. The two sat on a table in the corner and talked, about work, about their lives. Both carefully avoided the past.

'Tell me more about Africa, Vivi, I've never been there.'

'What is it you want to know? If you're looking for your regular tourist guide then I'm not the person,' she giggled.

He raised an eyebrow and stared at her. She continued,

'But if you want to know about the work which we do there to support the local population, I'm your best bet!'

She smiled again as he said,

'Let's go with the second option for the time being.'

Her voice underwent a change as she said, 'What is needed there, Andre, goes beyond the realms of the medical profession. The people are in need of the basics in life. Malnutrition is so widespread that it breaks my heart; to see people in the western world throw food away so easily. Do you know that in children under five, almost seventy percent of deaths are caused by an infection compounded by malnutrition? Diseases like typhoid and malaria, which are so easily treated in our world, are life threatening there. To survive a day is a constant struggle for most of them, and that's what Providence is trying to change. It's a slow process but I'm sure we'll get there.'

He was looking at her so intently that she felt connected to him, as before, by some invisible force. She reminded herself that for him it was all a memory, nothing else, and he was just a very attentive listener.

'You tell me about your business; how has the journey been so far? Although the Rolex clearly tells me that you are doing well,' she laughed.

'I'm glad you still notice me.' He grinned and Vivian faltered. He gave her just enough time to recover before adding, 'Tough, very tough, but at the same time it has been very fulfilling to see it coming together piece by piece. We bought the whole factory back, which was sold due to Mama's treatment. It cost me twice the money but it was worth every penny. Since then I have bought three more places to set up production work.'

He spoke passionately about designs and production of fine pieces of glass as she listened, observing the dedication in his eyes. The conversation, as always, moved with ease throughout their dinner.

The captain on the boat was reciting a story about the Savoy hotel. When he said, 'Dreams come true at Savoy,' both of them looked at each other. With the sentence still hanging in the air, they deliberately shifted their gazes to the city of London, which looked much prettier at night, the lights reflecting off the water adding an element of mystery. The graceful bridges, the history-soaked buildings on the bank, the majestic Big Ben and the colourful London Eye – it was like something from a picture postcard.

After dinner, they disembarked at the pier and started walking slowly to the hotel. Wandering in silence by the riverside, flashbacks to Nainital, unspoken but somehow acknowledged, gripped them both. Vivian wanted to hold him and cry her heart out, but all she did was smile quietly, keeping a tight lid on her emotions.

As he left her at the hotel, Andre said, 'Can I see you tomorrow, same time? I promise I'll plan the evening.'

She smiled and said, 'Yes,' when every instinct said "No!"

It was Andre. The man she could never refuse – how could she possibly say no?

She walked through the doors, and when she looked back, Andre was still standing there.

She went up to her room desolate and broken, half in sorrow and half in bewilderment as to why she was still so emotionally bound to this man from another life. It did not make any sense. She was a smart, practical woman who had travelled the world.

What I had with him was a trivial affair, for a brief time, that's what people do in their teens; then they forget it. The world is so full of sorrow and remorse, this is nothing in comparison. He chose to part ways – it should have been finished.

'Then why the hell am I still thinking about it?' she said aloud. The tears were flowing down her cheeks. Getting emotional about a man she broke up with years back was utterly crazy – it was lunacy. But the painful fact was that no matter how hard she had tried to forget, that love was still there; the peace and solace which she'd found in him could never be found in another. She was terribly scared, the ice walls which she had built around herself were melting at an alarming rate, exposing her weak and vulnerable heart, and that thought was terrifying. She did not want to get burned again; it had taken her years to get a hold of her life and the prospect of meeting Andre tomorrow was playing havoc with her feelings.

She dug her face into the pillow and lay there until her phone beeped. A message from Sam.

Hope you're doing well in London, missing you here   ...
Love Sam

Her guilt increased and so did the tears. The phone beeped again; it was Andre this time.

I had the most wonderful time I've had in years, can't wait to see you tomorrow. A

She was being torn between her heart and her morals. *It's madness to even tell him that I'm not married ... Vivian, wake up! He even said on the flight that he doesn't want to settle down. And how could I possibly think of hurting Sam, especially when his dad is still recovering? No, I can never hurt him. Whatever it was between us, it was a long, long time ago. No point digging it up.*

The battle raged within her, and somewhere in a lull between fights, her eyelids closed.

The next day was busy, with the conference in full swing. But thoughts of Andre and the walk by the Thames kept crowding her mind. She was looking forward to the evening, and dreading it too, because she knew it would take her a step closer to Andre.

It's the last day, and then I won't see him again. It's fine. But every practical bone in her body told her it had been a mistake to agree to meet him that night.

She finished work well before 7:00 p.m., and when Andre came she was all dressed up and ready to go, in a deep scarlet evening gown with a Carmen neckline – she had actually gone out and bought it at lunchtime as Andre had specified black tie. A thin necklace with American diamonds clung to her neck, adding a slight sparkle against her smooth, tanned skin. She had tied her hair up neatly at the back, making the little hanging earrings with diamond studs very visible.

He had never seen her so formally dressed. Vivian was always the college girl in casual attire

236

and here she was, a girl who had gorgeously blossomed into a woman. She looked … regal.

God, he thought, *she can still make me lose my head and she doesn't even need to do anything.* There was just one thing not right for him – the chignon was too tight, too severe. He loved her hair hanging loose on her shoulders, covering parts of her face, and he fought to control the urge to pull the hair pin which was holding it in place.

'You look stunning.'

'Thanks.' She tried hard not to blush. 'Why did you ask me to dress formal? Where are we going?'

'You'll see.'

Andre was dressed in a double-breasted deep navy blue pinstripe suit with a crisp white shirt and blue tie. He extended his hand and her fingers curled tentatively around it. A fuzzy feeling went through Vivian, and she stared at their joined hands for slightly longer than she should have.

Their taxi stopped in front of the Royal Opera House. As she got down she looked at the magnificent facade of this historic building, standing here in the centre of this bustling city. The surrounding architecture and diffused lighting made the building look even more spectacular. Walking inside, she paused to take it in – the interior boasted an equal degree of opulence.

'Wow, this is lovely.'

'Wait till you see the opera, *cara*.'

Vivian looked at him and smiled from the depths of her heart. She had not heard the nickname for a very long time.

She walked on, slightly scrunching up her evening gown. 'So which opera are we going to?'

'Your favourite.'

That was when she stopped abruptly, unable to believe that he had remembered. She thought back to their time together and recalled the conversation in the warmth of the afternoon sun in Delhi.

'Andre,' she had said. 'Some day, when we travel together, I want to go with you to see *La Bohème*.'

'Why?'

'It's one of the most beautiful operas ever composed. You should know – it's Italian.'

'Why haven't you seen it till now?'

'I have, but we must see it together. It's a beautiful love story and when I think about it, I always think you are my Rodolfo.'

'Okay, baby, if you tell me who the hell Rodolfo is, I'll take you to *La Bohème*.'

They had laughed, and Vivian had told him the story of Rodolfo and Mimi …

Andre only had to touch her shoulder gently to bring her back to the real world.

'Where were you, *cara*?'

'Nowhere. Let's go.'

She lowered her eyes so that he could not read the love that felt like a veil drawn across her eyes; he had remembered such tiny details.

The opera started and Andre leant in towards her and whispered, 'I wanted only to see it with you …'

'So I'm not the only idiot who remembers that conversation,' she said, trying hard to speak evenly, her voice becoming clouded with unshed tears.

'No, you're not. I'm your partner in crime.'

'Are you?'

'I am. Always have been, always will be.' He moved even closer and whispered, 'Gift from Rodolfo to Mimi.' He took her hand and gently kissed it. 'You are my Mimi, no matter what.'

He was stunned at his own directness, the sheer audacity, for she was a married woman. He knew it was the wrong thing to say but for once he could not hold himself back. The love he had for her had been kept carefully hidden all these years – he had always thought that was the best thing to do – but today, having recognised in her the same state of anguish, he wanted to tell her how he really felt, to drop the disguise. He owed it to both of them.

Buffeted by an unexpected current of emotions, Vivian could not concentrate on the first act at all. All she heard ringing in her head were his words: *'You are my Mimi, no matter what.'*

Her heart was hammering and the speed at which her emotions were flowing was overwhelming. All these years of yearning, the moments when she felt she was alone – none of it was true; he was right there with her, just on a different continent. As the realisation sunk in, her eyes began to moisten and a smile of pure bliss covered her face. Only Andre was capable of affecting her like this and there was an impeccable pleasure in this sweet torment.

They watched the rest of the opera in total silence. Their fingers were intertwined in the darkness, as though in closure of some eternal pact. A peace swept over her, knowing that she was as special to him as he was to her. Several times, he moved his head close to hers, just to feel her hair and take in her fragrance. She knew exactly what he was doing, and that brought another smile to her face.

The opera was followed by dinner at a fancy restaurant which Andre had booked. After dinner there was music and, taking her hand, Andre led her onto the dance floor. He held her waist and drew her close with the same authority he always had, as if she belonged to him. He brought his face close enough to her bare shoulder that a slight shudder ran through her body, and she closed her eyes and pictured a grassy clearing by a distant lake ...

The band played on and they talked in whispers into each other's ears, until they heard the opening bars of 'Love is all Around' and Andre began to hum, just as he used to when they dated.

I can't believe they're playing this song, of all the songs in the world, she thought to herself.

Andre read her mind and said, 'Quite a coincidence, huh? Things have always been magical with you, and I guess they'll continue to be ...' He stared into her deep brown eyes.

Her vision became blurred and somehow she managed to wipe away a tear without Andre noticing. When the music stopped, they stood there looking at each other, silently confessing that the love they had felt so long ago was still alive. His tender gaze broke the last remaining defences, and tears which had been locked in till now started to seep through. Andre gently dabbed them with his fingers. He did not say a word but she could feel the million emotions embedded in his heart. The silence was golden, it was pure – and it was brimming with happiness and pain.

He escorted her back to the dinner table, and Vivian knew she had to ask the question which had haunted her all these years. If not now, she would never be able to. Events since yesterday had given her an idea of the answer but her mind was not ready to believe it. She had been so wrong in the past that even now, when Andre was clearly reaching out to her, she was scared to accept the facts. Mustering all her courage, she said,

'You never thought about me in all those years?'

His eyes opened wide.

'Can you honestly believe that's possible, Vivi?' He paused for a moment, gathering his thoughts. 'I have never loved anyone the way I loved you, and I guess it's the same for you ... Except for your husband, I'm sure.'

She nodded; her face reflected that she was beyond guilt now.

'Did you never think of us getting back together?' she asked.

'I was stupid. I thought you loved your dreams more than me, that if you didn't achieve what you wanted, you would regret it.'

Vivian wanted to get up and hit him. How the hell could he be such an idiotic fool? *Love my dreams more than him ... Seriously?*

She resisted the urge as Andre continued, 'I thought about you for years and tried forgetting you for years. God knows what you did to me, Vivian … Anyway, then I heard the news of your marriage and it broke my heart all over again. I wanted to come and tell you how much I loved you, to ask you to marry me and not him.'

'You had plenty of time. Andre, seriously – you had twelve years. I thought you never wanted to get back together.' She stifled a sob. 'We could have worked it out, it wasn't that big a deal.'

He looked at the pain in her eyes and the feeling of wretchedness grew. He felt like a self-indulgent idiot – he had not done anything for the girl he loved and had lost her for no reason at all. He wanted to pull her into his arms, stroke her hair and comfort her, tell her that he was there for her, but instead he looked away – it was killing him to see her so distraught.

Then she raised her tear-filled eyes, which made him break all the rules. He got up, took her by the hand and led her onto the terrace of the restaurant, where he encircled her in his arms and held her tight. She held him too, wrapping her arms around his shoulders, and the stream of tears became a torrent.

A part of her was disgusted at herself. Here she was, a successful, strong, career woman, and in his arms she was eighteen again. All the pent-up emotion, the grief, came out as they held each other, and then she felt tears on his cheeks that were not hers. He too seemed to be stricken by the pain of their separation, and it dawned on her that, more than anything, he had been weighed down by guilt. She softly placed her hand against his jaw and said,

'Don't blame yourself. It's okay.' She said it so gently that he forgot the real world. She was distraught – but still she was trying to make him feel better.

Removing the hairpin that was holding the chignon, he let her hair tumble down her back and dug his fingers into her thick curls. Living and breathing the moment, he brushed a kiss against her lips. In his head, he knew it was wrong, but his lips started coaxing hers and when she responded the familiar taste and smell took him to another place, a place without limits or guilt. Desire began to build and his hands slid down to her waist and drew her even closer.

Vivian felt the familiar shivers – her body was responding and she was so lost in the moment that she neither stopped him nor questioned him. She kissed him back with all the passion, all the love she felt for him. All the years of yearning were transformed into a rousing kiss, her tongue exploring his, their passions charged with pent-up emotion.

Andre was unable to hold himself back. It was as though he was reclaiming her, marking her as his domain. His skillful fingers were running all over her bare back, while his mouth moved from her lips to her ears and then to her shoulders. He lifted her hair and kissed the sides of her neck, and she clung to him as he kissed her neck and then went back to explore her warm, inviting mouth.

When they stopped, she still clung to him, resting her head on his chest and listening to his heartbeat. They both stood a while, in this precious moment.

After a few minutes, a waiter appeared and asked if he should lay their table outside. Andre smiled briefly, and nodded – it was almost a welcome intrusion, a chance to think and not just to feel, as what he really wanted was to make love. He felt her longing too. If, after all these years of separation, they still felt so strongly about each other, they should surely be together – he ached to tell her so, but her situation was … complicated. She was married. Part of him felt like a selfish bastard. How could he think of creating this storm in her life, asking her to leave her husband – whoever the idiot was – and come with him? His heart was debating with his head when Vivian interrupted.

'Andre, no matter what we feel for each other, this is not right. I'm eng– married to someone else, and he is a very … nice guy.'

Nice guy? Pangs of jealousy shot through his body. He stared at the horizon, trying to hide the pain in his eyes.

She continued, 'There are people who trust us and love us. You have a girlfriend and we are not teenagers anymore. It isn't right to hurt people. Can I repeat what you told me years ago?'

'What?'

'Let's live in this moment, please don't try and shape anything or think about the future. Let's cherish this time, given to us by fate.'

He nodded. Every word she said was right, but he hated right. He would accept right one more time, but it wasn't going to be easy.

They ate sitting next to each other, outside on the terrace, the breeze gently brushing Vivian's hair and Andre tucking strands of it behind her ears. He wrapped his jacket around her as she ate and that one familiar gesture brought a smile to her face. Acutely aware of this intimacy, Vivian knew that she was making things much more difficult for herself, but the sweet pleasure of being in Andre's arms was greater than anything she'd ever wanted.

Walking back to the hotel, Andre could not let go of her hand.

'When will I see you next?'

'I don't know.' She wanted to say, *anytime you want.*

He brushed her hair from her shoulders and gave her a peck on the cheek.

'It was a magical evening.'

'For me too.'

'I'll miss this like the other million things I miss about you.'

She looked at him, love mixed with surprise. He had always hidden his emotions for all these years, and now he was giving way so easily. Trying to put off the return to reality, she told him that he could come to Barcelona – or Africa – to see her. To her amazement, he said he would prefer Africa.

'Why? Barcelona is so much closer to Italy.'

'I cannot see you with another man.'

He hugged her, hailed a cab and disappeared into the darkness, while she stood there digesting his answer. Finally, realising she was still standing in the same spot even though the cab was long gone, she turned around and, with slow and heavy steps, went into her hotel.

The walk to her room took forever, and when she got there she sat motionless on her bed, trying to move but unable to do so, her body failing to respond to her commands, as if it wanted to stay in the moments after the opera and had been unwillingly dragged to this cold room. The open suitcase reminded her of the need to pack for the early morning flight home. The fragrance of Andre had to be packed away as well, back in the casket of her heart, where it had been entombed for years. Tears followed one another down her cheeks, only adding to the cloying pain that filled her heart.

And then images of Sam set pangs of guilt running in her mind. She felt like a spineless woman who had given in the moment Andre had expressed the slightest inclination towards her. Two days, and he could not only sweep her off her feet but twirl her in the air. Her heart tried to come to her rescue, telling her that her actions were those of any woman who had been deeply in love.

Love ... Still! No, get some sense, Vivian.

She closed her eyes and a picture of Andre came alive, of the two of them walking together, holding hands – his closeness, his eyes, his smell. If she squeezed her eyes tight, it was as if she could bring him closer. Vivian behaved like a little girl, giving herself the time left before morning to relive these magical moments. She lay, eyes closed, immersed in Andre, refusing to allow her mind to corrupt any of the serene memories she was inhabiting.

Andre could not come to terms with the brief reality he had seen and felt. His mind and heart raced to Vivian and the fact that he could not physically do the same was tearing him apart.

Now back in his hotel room, he did not know what to do. Silent tears shimmered in his eyes and he sat there while thoughts of Vivian engulfed him, wondering if they could have really made it work as she had said. All these years he had convinced himself that she was part of a life beyond reach, that their love was strong but over. But meeting her had shown him the reality – that love was not something he could cut away or remove; it was right there, buried. In just a couple of hours, she had sent him on an emotional adventure, for better or worse, and he felt like a helpless twenty-two-year-old again, sitting in his hotel room getting emotional about a girl he'd broken up with a million years ago.

He reminded himself that it was just a short and beautiful dream; now, he needed to return to himself and wear his disguise, to wrap up all thoughts of Vivian and place them deep in his heart where they belonged.

He opened the minibar and poured himself a large scotch; looking at his soon-empty glass, he felt even more miserable. Vivian had got under his skin and he knew it. She was the only one who could make him feel so miserable and so loved at the same time. But she did not belong to him and he was to blame for that.

'God, if there was a way to turn back time,' he said.

His eyes still burning, he picked up his phone, brought up a picture of his Vivi and kissed her goodnight.

The following day, when Andre returned to Italy, he tried to focus on his routine, dismissing thoughts of Vivian, which always left him paralysed. But overcoming such powerful memories, engraved on his heart a second time, was much more difficult than he had anticipated.

The next day was difficult for Vivian too. Her emotional state, lack of sleep and the early morning flight wore her down. Back in Barcelona, an eager Sam was waiting for her. She donned her mask of normality and greeted him with a smile as always.

She quietly slipped into her bedroom, closing her eyes and pretending to sleep, while silently debating whether to tell Sam or not. There was no way under the sun that anyone, let alone Sam, would understand what she had shared with Andre.

I just need to be more careful in the future. And once more the feeling of being torn returned – a feeling that had lain dormant within her long enough.

Sam slipped into the bed and, sliding his arms around her slender waist from behind, whispered,

'Missed you, honey.'

'Missed you too,' she said, trying not to choke. 'I'm really tired. Think I'm coming down with something. Would you mind if I sleep?'

'Of course not, take care of yourself, sweetheart.'

He still had his arms around her body, and Andre had his around her soul.

Slowly, painfully, life started to flow into the normal routine. Vivian told herself that she could never hurt Sam. He was one of the most wonderful people she had ever known, and he loved her dearly.

Chapter Thirty-one

Work challenges beyond her control kept Vivian occupied – a welcome diversion from thoughts of Andre. Her travel increased and she was spending much more time in Africa than at home. After one of her trips, when she was back in Barcelona, Sam confronted her again about it.

'What's with you? Why have you been working so much lately? I literally feel we don't get any time together. I feel as if you are drifting away.'

'I can't help it. There is so much that needs to be done, you of all people know that. And there's no "drifting away" … I'm just really busy.' Her tone, she knew, was coloured by thoughts of Andre.

'I do know, but I need some time from you as well.'

There were no answers. All she could do was nod and say that she'd try and balance the two.

Shortly afterwards she was back in Africa, working on a new project to address child malnutrition, a project which she had initiated. Sam had travelled with her and could clearly see that she was working flat out. She seemed to dedicate all her time, energy and more to the project, from meeting with sponsors to working on awareness campaigns, managing every detail of daily operations. She took on everything. Children were close to her heart, he knew that, but so should he be. And then the inevitable happened – she had to extend her trip while Sam was due to go back to Barcelona. He did not say anything, but could not quite come to terms with her current state of frenzy when it came to work.

Back in Barcelona, he missed her terribly. When he rang her number, he heard a distant and preoccupied voice. He could picture her buried in files.

'Hey, what's up?'

'Nothing much, usual stuff. How are you?'

'Missing you big time.'

'Hmm, me too,' she said, her tone flat and dreary. 'Listen, I need to go, need to finish these papers by tonight. Can I call you later?'

Something snapped in him; 'Vivian, you never have any time for me. Why do I always feel like the lowest priority in your life?'

'Sam, you know it's not like that, it's just that this needs to be done tonight. How about—'

'Finish your paper. It's okay. Bye.'

He put the phone down. He was angry at Vivian, and with himself for letting her affect him so much. He knew she would feel bad for him, the way he had disconnected, but he was equally sure, judging by the way she had been acting for weeks, that the moment she looked at the pictures of malnourished children she would go back to work. Anyway, he did not want her pity. He could handle himself without her.

She called up the next day to say sorry but that was not enough for him. They talked a few more times on the phone but she was becoming increasingly distant, and he increasingly aware of it. He decided to work his way through it and not be so dependent on her. He tried to escape, engrossing himself in office work. His hours got longer and he started taking on more responsibilities.

With Sam's looks, attention from the opposite sex was not a problem and he started enjoying it and even, to some extent, encouraging it. A dinner had been long planned with Vivian, Sam, Gloria, and her boyfriend. But Vivian had left a week before for work, and Gloria had broken up with her boyfriend. Not the first choice for either Sam or Gloria, but they decided to meet up anyway because neither had anything else to do. After two bottles of wine and endless talk about their partners and how they were letting them down, Sam began noticing Gloria's curves.

As they walked after dinner, somewhat disoriented, he asked her to come back for coffee. As he was brewing it, Gloria came and stood in the kitchen doorway. By the light above the door frame, Sam, for some reason, found her very attractive. It was not his usual perception of Gloria … The drinks, the absence of Vivian, Gloria's plunging neckline – all these together were playing havoc.

Gloria said, 'So how come you never spoke to Viv about the fact that the work is bothering you?'

'I have, many times, if only she would pay attention. What about you? What went wrong with Robert? I thought you guys were pretty close to getting hitched.'

'I thought so too, but he postponed once too often. I didn't want to be with a guy who keeps stalling; somehow I got the feeling he was only interested in me physically, not emotionally.'

She tensed, as if sensing the word 'physically' was not right. But to Sam it was the final push for his treacherous mind. In one reckless second he made a decision and, leaving his coffee mug on the cold granite slab, he put his arms around her, pressing his mouth to hers. Surprisingly, she returned his kiss with an equal amount of ardour and it took them to heightened levels of passion, which soon translated into torrid lovemaking.

Afterwards, exhausted, they both slept, and when they woke up, Sam felt the guilt but persuaded himself it was a one-off thing, blaming alcohol and Vivian's absence for their steamy encounter. Which, he had to admit, he had thoroughly enjoyed.

Gloria felt the guilt much more keenly. Almost hysterical, she started to blabber sentences through uncontrollable tears.

'Oh God,' she said. 'How will I ever face Viv again? She is like my sister and … and … oh, what did I do?'

Sam consoled her but he found himself on very shaky ground. Gloria and he were complete opposites – indeed he had never really liked her – but today, as he saw her crying for her best friend, he felt wretched to have caused her that pain and had a strong urge to try to fix things for her.

They decided they would never repeat what had happened. Sam felt doubly guilty – first, because he had cheated on Vivian, but also because what he'd shared with Gloria had been so much more physically rewarding.

Vivian came back the following day for a few weeks but Sam, instead of displaying his usual annoyance when she was busy in the week, encouraged her to attend to her office work. His own work hours increased drastically.

On a Saturday afternoon, as they were both sitting on the porch, Vivian said,

'I was thinking of going to my parents' for Sunday lunch. Ma has called so often. And anyway I leave tomorrow – it will be nice to see them before I leave.'

Sam seemed to be preoccupied with his phone. 'Hmm … you go. I don't have the time.'

'Sam, we've cancelled it every weekend. Can't you just take time out over the weekend for a lunch?' Vivian couldn't help sounding a bit irritated.

Sam continued typing something on his phone, and Vivian asked him again,

'Can't you take some time?'

'Do I interfere with your work? Why the hell do I have to listen to you about mine?'

She was not expecting such a drastic reaction to a simple request, but she was unwilling to let it go.

'I didn't mean to interfere, it's just that –'

'It's just what, Vivian? Every time you have work I'm supposed to reschedule. Why should I have to for a damn lunch?'

At a loss to understand his behaviour, she decided to let the whole argument pass and go alone. Her mind was already working on excuses for why Sam was not accompanying her. She walked back inside the house, thinking it must be her travelling that was causing it all; nevertheless, it was her travel which was helping her cope.

When she came out all dressed up and ready to go he was still outside, glued to his phone. After a quick goodbye she drove to her parents' house, a bit confused but determined not to give it too much thought.

Sam went to meet Gloria a few minutes after Vivian left. He drove to her quirky brick-built house, all the while trying to tell himself that it was wrong. The guilt of shouting at Vivian clouded his conscience, but flashes of that passionate night kept dashing through his head, and desire came rushing back into his veins.

The mental tussle still raging, he pressed the door bell, and when Gloria opened the door, dressed in knitted yellow shorts and a beige tank top, all his guilt fell away – but she spoke before he could say anything.

'Look, Sam, it was a mistake. You are my best friend's fiancé and whatever we shared cannot continue.'

Sam's reply made him sound, he knew, like a world class bastard. 'We have a spark, Gloria. We have heat and we have passion and you know it. You saw it in bed the other day. I'm willing not to tell Vivian about this, but I'm not willing to let this slip away. You can call me whatever, but you get one life and I'm going to make the most of it.' With that, he pulled Gloria towards him.

Gloria knew he was right about the heat, about the passion, and she hated it but at the same time found it irresistible. In his beige trousers and plain black t-shirt, which stretched across his broad shoulders, Sam looked incredibly handsome and sexy. She had never felt like this for anyone, it had always been relatively easy for her to come out of relationships, but she was finding the enigmatic Sam hard to resist. Torn between right and passion, she chose passion one more time, and gave herself up to all that Sam wanted.

Vivian returned to Africa the next day, and thereafter the casual one-night drunken affair gradually transformed into something more concrete. There was a slow bond developing between the two of them, and not only was it enticing, it was also physically fulfilling beyond anything they had experienced before.

Lying next to Gloria and gently caressing her bare back, Sam nevertheless felt like the worst kind of human being, and he decided to put a stop to one of the two relationships – which one, he was not sure. Vivian was still the woman he'd fallen in love with, and he still truly cared for her, but Gloria held a different kind of magic. He knew his choice was clear.

Gloria, lying down quietly beside him, said very softly, 'I have never been in this position before. I'm caught between loyalty to my best friend and you. I have to tell the truth to Vivian, I have to - I owe it to her. Although I'm not entirely sure whether the truth will really help anybody or further complicate the situation.'

Sam looked at her. She was right.

'Fine,' he said. 'I agree we need to tell her. I just need to think how.'

Chapter Thirty-two

When Vivian came home after one of her trips, something was troubling her. She couldn't put her finger on it but lately she had been dropping things more than usual. It had been going on for a while but now it had started to catch her attention.

'Sam, I'm not feeling quite right. It's …'

'You need to rest; you've been working too hard. I've gotta go to the office. Lots to catch up on.'

Vivian watched, surprised, as he rocked to and fro on his rocking chair in the porch, looking at his phone. He seemed utterly unconcerned.

'It's okay, honey,' he continued, 'you're worrying too much, just rest and you'll be fine.' He stood up and walked towards the car. 'I'll see you in the evening. Bye.'

Another area where something did not seem right … For one, he had stopped complaining about her overworking, but also he never mentioned marriage now. Once, when Maria had made a hint or two during a family get-together, Sam had comfortably ignored the subject, and today the way he left was odd.

Vivian sat there, trying not to over-think it. She decided that possibly a shower and a hot cup of tea would rescue her from this ... not fatigue exactly, but general malaise. Maybe Sam was right – she needed to rest, she was working too much.

When he comes home we can have a quiet dinner. Another thought crossed her mind. *Does it even make sense marrying him? God, Viv, you've gone through this so many times. Stop it!*

With that, she shook her head and went straight to the shower.

Afterwards she decided to catch up with all the people she couldn't talk to while in Africa. She spoke to her mum for a while and decided to give Gloria a call. Maybe she could discuss Sam's weird behaviour with her. She was an expert on men, after all.

With that thought in mind, she waited for the phone to be answered, but instead of one familiar voice she heard another. Sam's. What followed was a dead silence from both ends. She put the phone down and stood there for a very long time. Then, slowly, she began to come to terms with the fact that her best friend and her fiancé were sleeping together behind her back.

Sam had picked up the phone without thinking as Gloria was brewing coffee – and he knew the mistake was going to cost him. When he told Gloria about it, she became hysterical.

'I told you to stop this! Oh God, what will I do now? How will I ever face her?' The dam of tears was broken and Sam, who until now had been

259

feeling awful for Vivian, now started feeling equally bad for all three of them.

Vivian closed her eyes, and surprisingly a sense of relief flowed through her instead of any sadness or even disdain. Somehow, she blamed herself for this situation, for not giving the required attention to the relationship.

She packed her bags and left a note for Sam:

Enjoy your work, I'm going. I guess this is the end of our journey together and you know why. You are a good guy and you will always have a special place in my heart.

Bye,

Vivian.

She left her ring on top of the note, feeling that a weight had been lifted off her heart. At the very least, no more conversations in her head about whether marriage made sense or not!

She went to see her parents. One look at her and her mother was worried.

'You look terribly pale, what's going on?'

She did not think Sam had affected her enough to go pale, and when her mother said that, her thoughts momentarily drifted to her health. How did her mother know, after taking one look at her, that things were not right?

Vivian sat there sipping coffee, knowing she needed to break the news to her. Taking a deep breath, she told her mother that she was moving out. At first, Maria could not take in the statement and said,

'Moving out? From where? Are you winding up your work in Ghana?'

Vivian knew that even in her wildest dreams her mother could never have imagined Sam would be unfaithful.

Vivian told her, carefully omitting mention of Gloria, as her mother had a soft spot for her. Maria, as expected, was not just angry, she was furious.

'Are you absolutely sure he's cheating on you? I don't … How did this happen? How could he do that?' She came and hugged Vivian before breaking into sobs. 'Oh Vivian, how could he … How will you live all by yourself? It's not easy.'

Vivian felt the pain in her mother's words, and tried to console her by saying,

'Ma, I'm a very strong girl, don't worry. And I have work and I have you guys, and …' *And Andre is there,* she almost said, and stopped – Andre was not there, but he would always be in her heart and the thought put a smile on her face.

Maria was too distraught to take any notice of the change in expression. 'How could he do this to you? If I had my way I would go and beat up the good-for-nothing cheater.'

Vivian made her mother sit next to her and, placing a hand on her shoulder, said,

'Trust me, I'm absolutely fine. We have been quite distant from one another for a while. Look at the silver lining – it all happened before the wedding.'

Maria just nodded and Vivian added,

'Can I get something to eat? I'm starving.' She was anxious to get her mother involved in some sort of activity - anything to distract her from thoughts of Sam.

Maria walked into the kitchen, reaching to put a hand on the worktop as soon as she was through the door, and it occurred to Vivian, not for the first time, that her mother was increasingly shaky on her feet.

'How are you and Dad doing, anyway? Are you still determined to move?' They had informed Vivian on her last visit of their joint decision to move to sheltered accommodation, as taking care of themselves had become increasingly difficult – both suffered from chronic arthritis.

'Possibly next month. There have been a few issues with availability.'

'Well, you know best.'

Vivian was not convinced about their leaving the family home, but her mother was adamant and to an extent she was right. She could not manage the house the way she used to and their social circle was shrinking because both of them struggled with driving. Maria's argument was that it would be nice to meet people of their own age, people with similar problems and similar challenges. Vivian knew her mother had made up her mind and it was impossible to change that. She admired her for it. Vivian knew she got her own headstrong nature from her mother.

Maria looked at her daughter for much longer this time.

'What is it, Ma?'

'I don't know whether my mind is playing tricks on me, but you do look remarkably calm for a woman who has just broken up with her fiancé.'

'Well all the more reason, I guess, that we should go our separate ways. Let's talk about something else.'

'You can't expect me to do that,' Maria said, clearly bewildered. She had been chopping cucumbers and she dropped the knife onto the chopping board. 'You are my only daughter. After years you find someone, and the bastard – excuse my language – cheats on you.'

Vivian was taken aback. Before today, she had never heard her mother swear.

'Ma, we can talk about it as much as you want but will it help anything?'

Maria sighed and whispered, 'I suppose you're right.'

The flame in Maria's emerald eyes died and what was left was the smoke of pain. Vivian assured her that it was for the best and that she was much better off breaking up with Sam. Maria could not respond, but just listened to her, teary-eyed.

After staying with her parents for a couple of days, Vivian left for Africa and dedicated her days and nights to the people there who needed help and support.

She put everything into her work, tending to stay much more frequently in Ghana. She put in the hours more from relief than from grief, and she enjoyed her free time, however little she got, alone with her thoughts and her beautiful memories, without the feelings of guilt, without being torn. Once in a while, she would speak to Andre and that would leave her brimming with happiness. She never mentioned her break-up to him, for she thought it was unfair to disturb his life. He had been with Joanna, his girlfriend, for the past two years now, a relationship clearly going steadily, and she did not want to interfere.

Chapter Thirty-three

There was something else happening too. One day she tripped and fell in a ward while doing the rounds. The nurse who was with her asked,

'Are you okay?'

'Yeah, totally, just my foot slipped.' As much as Vivian wanted to get up immediately, it took her a few minutes before she got her balance back.

On another occasion, while brewing coffee in her hut, her vision became so blurred that she missed the cup when pouring the hot water. As much as she joked about it, saying that it was travelling and the lack of paella in Africa which were causing her problems, she felt increasingly that something was wrong.

A general feeling of weakness made her put in a call to Alex, her fellow doctor and a very dear friend. She wanted to speak to someone about these incidents, someone who would understand and not freak out. She told him about all the falls, the blurred vision. After a brief chat, she put the phone down and tried to get through the day as normally as possible, although her physical condition had started playing on her mind.

Alex had patiently listened and then said, in a light and easy tone,

'Let's try the new MRI machine on you.'

An MRI seemed to Vivian a little drastic but she knew it was needed. It did not strike her as odd that he asked for her to come in the very next day, although it did increase the sense of uneasiness.

Alex greeted her outside the hospital with a worried smile and guided her towards the MRI machine.

As she was manoeuvred around, in readiness for the MRI, once more her thoughts drifted to Andre and their weird situation – connected yet separate. The beeping could not break her chain of thought, nor did the action around her disturb her. It was the raising of Alex's voice, while giving rapid-fire instructions to a new recruit, that finally caught her attention, and when she glanced up she saw the irritation that clouded his greyish-green eyes.

'Damn you, can't you just push a button at a steady speed? It's not bloody rocket science. You've been doing it for months, when the hell do you think you'll learn?' Shock and bewilderment registered on the face of the boy operating the machine.

Vivian looked at the shaken new recruit and said, 'It's just the way it should be – you're doing great, just try and keep it steady,' before shooting a scolding glance at Alex.

After the MRI, Alex asked the nurse to take Vivian for blood and other tests, which he scribbled on his writing pad. As Alex attended another patient, Vivian went with the nurse, wondering about his odd behaviour. The diagnostic room felt very different – normally, she was the one conducting the tests, but with the positions reversed it gave her a completely different perspective.

The fears that some patients might experience in this dreadful room brought pictures unbidden into her mind. Dreadful not because of what the room meant, but what it contained. A clammy treatment table with bits of torn leather hanging from one side. The reflective steel cover of a bright light at the top of the table, like a one-eyed predator coming at you as you lay, looking up. A shelf along one wall crammed with boxes of pills and dressings, test tubes and needles. The smell of disinfectant and the sharp edges of the table that could almost pierce the skin. On the wall, posters about vaccines and what happened if you didn't take them; about AIDS. She lay there wondering why they had never tried to make the room friendlier.

The nurse arrived, carrying a set of syringes and several labelled bottles, and a few minutes later Alex came in like a guided missile, just as the nurse was having trouble finding a vein.

'How long do you think you'll take to find a damn vein? You've been doing blood tests for years – makes me wonder how!'

The nurse, jittery now, stepped aside and he took over, drawing blood from Vivian's arm almost immediately. Vivian gave an apologetic glance to the nurse on Alex's behalf.

'What's with you today?' she said, quietly. 'Why are you overreacting to everything?'

'Nothing, just a bad day.'

They moved through the long list of tests, which went on for a good half-day, during which Alex ran several times from the diagnostics room to his own examination cabin and back.

When the tests were over, Alex said, 'I'll collate the results and let you know. Maybe you just need a good shot of multivitamins.'

Vivian raised her eyebrows and with a slightly amused look replied, 'Alex, you don't need to sugar-coat it for me, I think I know when it's more than multivitamins.'

He flushed a little, and rather too hastily he said goodbye.

Somehow Vivian felt that Alex had recognised the problem the moment she had described dropping things more than usual and her grip getting weaker. She felt he was desperately hoping that his diagnosis was wrong; maybe that was the reason why he was shouting like a madman at everybody today. It was odd alright, Alex was never normally like that.

The fear that had crept over her before started taking a more concrete shape as her initial diagnosis was unconsciously confirmed by Alex. He had undeniably overreacted during the MRI scan, but still … She remembered his expressions changing with each look at the graphs on the screen, dipping more and more towards concern, mixed with traces of sadness. She shook her head. What would be would be, she thought, and she would accept it like many other things she had accepted.

With that thought lingering in her mind she walked outside, trying to find the same spirit in which she came, not unduly worried, taking in the surroundings, the sunshine and the bare earth on which it danced.

Although a bit tired, she climbed into the passenger seat of a jeep at the side of the dusty road and embarked on a two-hour journey. The driver tried to drive as smoothly as he could on the bumpy stretches. Passing tiny villages one after the other, Vivian's exhaustion increased. She tried distracting herself by looking through the dusty window. As with so many others, the road was barely worthy of the name – a muddy stretch with some sort of wild grass growing in patches at the sides. A scattering of mud houses with thatched roofs stood unevenly next to the road. There were few trees, just muddy, rutted tracks and hard earth, dried from the heat, parched and barren, reflecting the atrocity of human neglect.

But still, children, scarcely clad, played on that road, and their faces were in utter contrast to the muddy fields around them, for they were happy even to have the simple sticks they played with. Her head gently rested on the window, inclined towards them as if trying to draw strength from their smiles. Once or twice she raised her hand to wave. As they moved, the country became more scarcely inhabited. Even the few mud houses were left behind and so were the running children – all that remained as far as the eye could see was the barren earth and a hazy sky that merged with it on the shimmering horizon.

The hot, sultry air seemed to flow from one end of the Earth to the other, taking with it a layer of dust and mixing it with the atmosphere. Instead of bright blue, the sky was a dusky blue-grey, reflecting everything else in that place, mute witness to years of hopelessness and poverty. She closed her eyes and instead of the fiery air burning her cheek, she felt the coolness of rain stroking her skin. The gentle breeze running through her hair; his hand on the back of her neck ... The thought did not last long – the driver pulled in and parked on a patch of ground in their base camp. In the far left corner across the road was her tiny house.

Instead of going to the station, she had come straight home. Tired and exhausted from the day, she settled herself on the wooden bed and dozed off.

Chapter Thirty-four

Two days later, Alex walked over when she was about to leave the ward. She looked at him and said,

'You don't need to look so vexed – just tell it the way it is.' She had a quiet word with one of her colleagues, then pointed through the window towards the tents of the adjacent camp. 'Let's go and sit over there.'

The little tent they walked to could barely accommodate a table and a pair of steel side chairs.

She waited patiently for the verdict and Alex shifted uncomfortably.

'I have good news and bad news – take your pick.'

Sensing that he was trying to start the conversation on a lighter note and looking at his pleading face, Vivian said,

'Let's hear good news first.'

'Well, the good news is that even after your extensive travels in Africa, you don't have ebola!'

It was an absurd statement and Vivian was taken aback a little, but tried to keep her expression even as she forced a smile.

'Great! I'm relieved. And the bad news?'

'How the hell are you looking so relaxed?'

'Years of practice, I guess.'

Alex stared at her and said, 'Correct me if I'm wrong. Your hands and legs often go numb, your vision is sometimes blurred, you are dropping things more than you should—'

'I have already told you all this.' She heard a tinge of anxiousness in her own voice as she spoke, but tried to keep her face impassive.

'The tests showed results which … aren't pleasant.'

'I know that, otherwise we wouldn't be here.'

Taking a deep breath he bent forward and held her hand. Lifting his gaze to meet her expectant eyes, his expression a mixture of pity and sadness, he finally told her the truth about her condition.

'I thought so.' She murmured the words.

Lowering her head, she tried to take in as much air as possible and stared through the tiny window for a long moment, as if waiting for the sun to set. She looked up at the sky from the window, which held nothing for her but the scorching heat of the sun. Alex did not intrude, and sat quietly, giving her time to absorb it all.

'How long can I continue to work?' Her words broke the silence, like a porcelain teapot shattered in a quiet room.

'For some time, although I do think you will need care, and that has to be sooner rather than later.' His voice was laden with concern. 'You can work for a while but I cannot say how long. Obviously, I won't recommend that you perform any surgery. Vivian, it is up to you, but you know how fragile the human body can be. In an occupation like yours there is not much you will be allowed to do. If you take my suggestion, you should rest and not do any work.'

Vivian listened, and said, 'I can, I suppose, work with the corporate arm of the organisation instead of the hands on medical team. I'll manage,' she sighed.

'No, you cannot manage, Vivian. It is not easy – you will need treatment and care.' His voice had risen slightly, as if trying to convey the gravity of the situation. 'Let me see what I can do. I know a few care facilities back in Barcelona, in fact one of my friends runs one. I'll see if some arrangement can be made.'

'You don't need to bother.'

'Save that for someone else. I know when I need to bother.'

She smiled. 'Thank you.'

'I'll call you. Meantime start wrapping things up here – and get the ball rolling.'

After he left, she sat still in the tent, closed her eyes and tried to come to terms with her rapidly changing situation.

She opened her eyes to the bleak reality of the scorching sun, got up from the rusted chair and started to walk out of the tent, lifting the green cloth door, breathing the dusty air and feeling the warmth on her skin.

She tried to work as if nothing had happened, as if no one had said anything, but it was difficult. The news played on her mind, along with all the loose ends of her life which she felt needed tying up.

The call from Alex came, and she scribbled down the address and number, listening to his clear instructions.

'Vivian, start making arrangements to leave. That needs to be sooner rather than later.' After a pause he said, 'Do you want me to call Sam?'

'No.' There was no point telling Sam anything, especially after what had happened. Besides, he was scheduled to come tomorrow. She went to her room, picked up the phone and dialled a familiar number. Immediately, she disconnected.

It's not fair to tell Ma and Dad. They will be worried to death. No point troubling them. I can go on talking as usual – tell them when it is absolutely necessary. For now it can be put off.

Satisfied that she had made the right decision, she turned to the next name on her list of people to tell, and her heart felt suddenly heavier. She didn't want to cause him pain, and this news would almost certainly do just that. On the other hand, even if she did not tell him, Andre would be able to make out from the waver in her voice that something was not right and then pester her till he was able to wheedle out every tiny piece of information. She smiled absently at that thought.

Chapter Thirty-five

Sam arrived the next day as scheduled and was working in his office when Alex walked in. He saw immediately that Alex was somewhat agitated, but he was Vivian's friend and after what had happened between them, Alex was bound to be a bit put off. Alex walked towards him with firm steps and a frown. Sam pretended not to see him – he was genuinely busy with paperwork for the construction of the extra wing of the hospital.

'Don't fucking try and act busy with me,' Alex said.

'Mind your language. In fact, get out. I have no time for you.'

'Of course you don't, you ruined my friend's life, and as if that wasn't enough you fucking screwed her best friend. And you, a doctor, couldn't bloody pick up any signs of sclerosis. She would have been struggling with it for months when she was with you but you, asshole, were too busy playing around.'

Sam only heard the word 'sclerosis'. He looked hard at Alex and said,

'What the hell are you talking about? Are you bloody drunk or are you just trying to over-dramatise the situation?'

'Wake up, Sam, for fuck's sake! I'm talking reality and I'm talking about Vivian, your ex-fiancé.'

Sam sat still, as if he had been hit; the world was spinning around him. As the implications started seeping into his mind, his tone lowered considerably.

'Are you absolutely sure, Alex? I mean … it could be a mistake. It has to be a mistake. This can't happen … Not with Vivian, she's too young. Oh God. Oh hell, no …'

'No mistake, Sam.' Alex was no longer shouting, he was absently rubbing his temples. 'I oversaw all the tests myself and I'm sure.' He dropped into the rusted iron chair next to him and closed his eyes, taking in a deep breath.

Sam sat there in silence, breathing in the pain, the guilt, and most of all the dreadful reality.

'What type?' he finally asked, in a voice that sounded like a whisper to his own ears.

'Amyotrophic lateral sclerosis.'

Pangs of guilt started eating through his system like termites. Alex was right – he had screwed up Vivian's life. How the hell could he not pick up the signs? He was a doctor, for God's sake; episodes with Vivian started playing back in his head. Times when she told him she was not feeling well, times when she said she was exhausted – times when he did not pay attention because his mind was on having sex with Gloria.

Covering his face, he sat there as Alex got up and patted his shoulder. Alex did not do any more yelling, he just left without saying a word. The silence that followed was even more dreadful. Sam found himself drowning in a sea of guilt. Even if they were not together she was still a wonderful person – she certainly did not deserve this.

How could this happen to her?

He had to help her, sort things out with her, support her. It was all he could do and it was only right. He got up, full of determination, and went looking for Vivian. One of her colleagues told him that she was in the consulting room, and without thinking he rushed in.

Bent forward with a stethoscope, she was examining an infant in its mother's arms as Sam walked in. She glanced up in surprise.

'I'll see you in a bit,' she suggested.

'I'm sorry, I didn't mean to interrupt.' He was already halfway back through the door before he had finished the sentence.

After ten minutes, Vivian emerged, rubbing her face with one hand, and walked over to him. Despite their differences, despite what had happened, he pulled her close and she rested her head on his chest. Almost immediately she pulled herself away and said, with rather too much cheerfulness,

'So how are you?'

He held on to her hand as he led her out of the little examination centre.

'I'm fine,' he said, 'but what about you – how are you?'

Vivian knew immediately that Alex had told Sam. They quietly walked together towards their regular haunt, Typica Café, just a few hundred yards away, behind the hospital.

The moment they sat down Sam said,

'I'm so sorry, Viv. Please can you forgive me? We can start over again.'

Vivian was shocked – of all the reactions to the news, this was not what she had expected.

'Sam, it doesn't work that way. No, we cannot. Please let's not go there.'

'I'll make it work, Viv, I screwed up, forgive me, please.'

Vivian did not know how to handle this, but he was clearly giving more importance to her happiness than his own, and that thought softened her a little. She didn't want him to feel so guilty over what had happened.

'Sam, it's not just your fault. I was equally to blame. I should—'

'Vivian, I'm not here to apportion blame. I don't want that. What I want is to be with you now when you need it the most.'

'I really don't want any help. I'm perfectly fine. Sam, calm down, it's not that bad. I can manage.'

'No you can't, Viv, I should be there for you. God, how did I miss all the signs? Please, Viv, forgive me.'

'Sam, honey, please … It's got nothing to do with you. Nothing would have been different had you even figured it out. So now can we please drop the guilt trip?' A smile hovered on her face as she added, 'Is the guilt trip compensation for the Miami trip you promised?' And she laughed, desperately trying to infuse some humour into a grim situation. It had worked, too – there was just a flicker of amusement in Sam's eyes.

'When do you leave?' She fired another question before he could pester her about being together again.

'I'll leave when you do.'

'I'm planning to leave in a few days. I need to wind things up. Do you think you'll be okay waiting?'

His eyes started swimming with tears. He slowly lifted her hand and kissed it tenderly before saying,

'I'm so sorry, sweetheart.' He drooped physically, like a stem overburdened with the weight of its own fruit.

She placed her hand on his chin and lifted it gently to reveal the saddened, aquamarine eyes.

'Sam, please don't beat yourself up like this. You'll see – everything will be fine.'

Sam stayed for a couple of days, hovering around, eager to help. On the last day in the camps, he came to help her pack her belongings and take her to the airport.

There was not much. A lot of tiny handmade Get Well Soon cards from the children of the orphanage, flowers, and some eatables were a major chunk of the legacy she was taking with her. She went one last time to the orphanage, and it was an emotional visit. The children loved her, and their love was well reflected in the tears coming from their dark and questioning eyes. She bid them goodbye and told them beautiful things about the future and how they needed always to work hard and be good human beings. She had asked Sam to get gifts for each and every child in the orphanage, and he had duly done so.

Several of the doctors came to the airport to bid them farewell. They boarded the flight to Barcelona and the images of the children waving, tears flowing from their innocent eyes, of the local women standing and blessing her, offering all sorts of local remedies, and of the doctors who worked with her and the sentiment which all of them radiated, gave her a feeling of intense fulfilment.

At the airport in Barcelona, Vivian gave Sam the address of the hospice.

As he stared at the piece of paper with the address, Sam said,

'Vivian, I would be more than happy to be with you.'

'I know that, Sam. It's not you, it's me.'

Before he could probe further, she leaned back into her seat, signalling that she was tired. He did not ask her anything for the forty minute journey and she did not offer anything. The silence between them lived and breathed.

Both were deep in thought when the car pulled up in front of the hospice.

After being shown to her room, Vivian asked Sam a favour.

'Don't tell Ma and Dad about this, please. They would be heartbroken. I'll make excuses for as long as I can.'

He nodded. Vivian had just put her head on the plush white pillow when she heard the question which she was sure must have been hammering around in his mind since the taxi ride.

'What did you mean, Vivian, when you said, "It's not you, it's me"?'

She knew she would have to tell him. But not now. She adjusted the stack of pillows behind her back but the fatigue was getting to her.

'I'll tell you some other time; I need some rest right now.'

Her eyelids slowly dropped, heavy with tiredness. She heard footsteps, then the door closing. She felt sure Sam would be concerned and a bit confused, and even in her drowsy state she felt guilty for making him feel like that.

Chapter Thirty-six

Her room was very basic, just a single bed with a steel frame, a bedside table and a wooden chair next to it. Smelling faintly of medicines and disinfectant, the place was immaculately clean. The most wonderful thing about the hospice was a large rectangular lawn to the rear, with flower beds all around. Leading to the garden from the rooms was a long, narrow gallery.

The staff were lovely and very attentive – they genuinely cared for each and every person who stayed there. They remembered their names, their families, their backgrounds, and made a point of talking about these things to make patients feel at home.

Vivian initially found it difficult to manage a sedentary lifestyle after her usual hectic schedule. But slowly she adjusted to the bed, to the air in the place and the people around her.

Even from her little room she continued to support Providence in whatever way she could. She wrote papers, offered ideas on how to develop campaigns for improving awareness about vaccines, hygiene – anything as long as it was practical.

Sometimes she took trips to Providence's Barcelona office to present her ideas and Sam would generally accompany her. Friends and colleagues continued to send her cards and flowers along with get well messages. She loved receiving them and would pin each card to the wall next to her bed. Sam was in and out all the time – he would bring her favourite food and they would eat together in her room.

On one of his regular visits, she said, 'You need to cut down on these visits and get on with your life.'

'Can you stop being so domineering? I'll do what I feel like, and I feel like coming to see you.'

'Just think of me as gone. You have to move on, look to the future.'

'Stop it, will you?'

'How's Gloria?' It was the logical follow-up.

Sam looked away and said, 'She's fine; we're not talking.'

'Oh? Why?'

'Gloria felt horrible after what happened. She said she couldn't do this to you and that was it – from then on, she refused all my calls and sent me a long text telling me exactly what she wanted. No contact.'

Vivian smiled inwardly, not at Sam's discomfort but at knowing she had a friend who genuinely cared about her – although she felt let down that Gloria had not once come to visit her.

'Sam, can you ask Gloria to come and see me?'

He looked up from the noodle box in his hand and nodded. Vivian lay on her side and looked out the window by her bed. The trees stood in the summer sun and the wind played through their leaves. An image of autumn colour flashed into her mind and she quickly pushed it away.

'I meant it when I said you should come less often; it will be less painful for you.'

As he was leaving, Vivian summoned up all her courage and said,

'Sam, wait.'

He came back, and she pushed herself up and leant back against the bedhead, still gazing out the window.

'Sam, I need to tell you something.'

'Go ahead.'

'It's about …' Her eyes went briefly to Sam, then back to the trees beyond the window. 'It's about … Andre.' She spoke the name very softly.

Sam had heard the name before. He knew the story, he knew she had loved him but he did not know that he still existed in her life or her thoughts.

Vivian was looking at him now. She could see the annoyance, the confusion building up. She felt she saw pangs of jealousy on his face, and he confirmed it by saying sharply,

'What about him?'

She didn't know where to start or how to explain, for who could comprehend that she had loved a man all her life, even after they broke up, even when they had not been together for all these years? Who could comprehend that now, when things were going in the worst possible direction for her, all she could think about was him? She shifted in her bed, trying to adjust the pillows, then finally spoke after a long silence.

'There is no easy way of saying this so I'll say it directly. I still have feelings for him and I cannot help it.'

Sam did not know how to react. His face had lost all colour, the softness had gone and been replaced by frustration.

Still, she continued. 'I have to get it off my chest. Andre has been a thought, a feeling beyond my control and despite my best efforts to forget, he has somehow always been with me. I don't know how to explain ...' The words hung there in the silence of the room.

It took Sam a minute or two to absorb what he had just heard. He said simply,

'What do you want me to do?'

Vivian had no answers; she just looked at him as his irritation grew. Finally he got up and said,

'Vivian, I know I have no right and I cheated on you but still if I had a chance I'd beat the hell out of the guy. Not because you love him or anything but because I am worried about you. Vivian, are you blind by any chance? He left you years ago, never tried to get back together. You tell me he's dating an array of women. And you still feel for him? You're right, I cannot understand this madness. All I can say is it has taken you years to get out of the ditch that bastard pushed you into.'

She flinched when he said 'bastard', and she was sure Sam had seen it.

Regardless, Sam continued, 'It took you years to come to terms with reality. Don't go back to a fictitious world, one which exists only in your imagination. Vivian, I'm a man and I can tell you something: if I genuinely love a woman, I will *not* get out of her life at the first opportunity that comes my way. It's your decision, but don't fall prey to the same absurdity again.'

With that, he walked out of the room and Vivian was left alone in a silence she could almost touch.

Everything Sam had said made sense. The practical part of her brain acknowledged the logic and forced her to think, but some part of her refused all of that – the part that had felt the love in his eyes in London. The love she had seen could not have been a sham. *'A gift from Rodolfo to Mimi ... You are my Mimi, no matter what ...'* Sam was right that he had walked out, but he was young and she had seen the regret in his eyes that day when they had danced together.

'Why can't things be simpler for me?' She closed her eyes, but Sam's voice was in her ears and Andre's face kept appearing in front of her.

Next day, Vivian looked through the open door of her room to see Gloria walking with hesitant steps towards her. She offered inward thanks to Sam for telling her to come, and she knew it must have taken much courage on Gloria's part to do so. She was wiping tears from her already flushed cheeks.

'I'm so sorry, Viv,' she said, standing by the bed and resting her hand on her friend's arm. 'I'm so sorry ... I don't know how it happened, please forgive me.' She was sobbing now.

Vivian could see how distressed she was and, in a very even tone, said,

'Talking to me might help. So you may as well start from the beginning.'

She wanted to hear the truth and at the same time she wanted Gloria to get it out of her system so that she too could feel better and get over whatever guilt she felt. Indeed, Vivian genuinely felt that if Sam and Gloria could hit it off, it would be better for both of them. They were very special people and if together they could be happy, they should not forego that happiness for her. Vivian wanted to make sure that she could convey that feeling eloquently today, and for that she had to ask Gloria to tell her the full story.

Gloria felt sick recounting to Vivian what had happened but she steeled herself to tell her anyway.

'It started as a drunken mistake …' As she continued the story Vivian listened to every detail without any display of emotion.

When she had finished, Vivian said, evenly,

'Gloria, clearly you guys have a physical spark, and I think if you give it time it might develop into something more meaningful as well. He's a nice guy; I know him, he doesn't fall for every other girl. I'm a thing of the past and you guys have your lives in front of you. Don't spoil this magic because of me.'

Gloria would have felt more comfortable if Vivian had slapped her or sworn at her but what she said left her in awe of her friend – so pure, so truthful … so cheated on. The last thought made her feel even more distraught. She came forward and hugged Vivian tight.

'Sorry … I'm so sorry, Viv.' When Gloria finally lifted her flushed and tear-stained face she said, 'Viv, I'm so lucky to have you as my friend and you are so unlucky to have me.'

'Gloria, you know there's only so much drama you can carry, and you're overdoing it right now.'

The pair burst into giggles, like old times. It was as if they were back in school again, fighting over something silly and then making up.

When Gloria left she felt much relieved – and much in debt.

Chapter Thirty-seven

Stepping through the hospice doors out of the mid-morning heat, a visitor signed in and headed for the stairs.

Five minutes later, Vivian opened her eyes to see him sitting next to her, looking at her with deep black, dewy eyes. Her first reaction was that she was dreaming, so she closed her eyes again, but then she felt a light touch on her shoulder. Now, he wore a look of such intensity it could have pierced her all the way to her heart.

And then he spoke.

'You couldn't tell me?'

'Tell you what?' She tried to keep her voice steady and adjusted herself on the bed, but the look he gave her told her that he knew every possible detail. She struggled to sound normal. 'What could you have done? It's my problem. I'll sort it out, but thank you for coming to visit me.' She well knew that that last statement would annoy him. The way Andre could reach her like no one else could – it was an unstated certainty. She knew that treating him this formally, just like anyone else, would surely irritate him.

She was right – Andre was visibly annoyed. In an even more authoritative tone of voice, he said,

'I'm taking you from here, and I'll take care of you.'

'You are what??' Her mouth was half-open; she was completely bewildered. Then, recovering her powers of speech, she said, 'Are you completely nuts? What the hell are you talking about?' She was staring at him in blank amazement.

'You heard what I said. Nuts? Yes, I am. I'm nuts about you … still.' He smiled his bewitching smile.

Going from utter shock to surrender in a matter of seconds, Vivian was momentarily unsure. *Nuts, about me.* The sweet pleasure of his words brought an instant colour to her pale cheeks. In faded jeans and turquoise blue and white check shirt, he did not look the successful businessman. To her, he still looked like the guy she had fallen madly in love with.

Shaking her head to try to think clearly, she decided that under no circumstances could she do what he was asking. She could never give him that pain, and to go with him would be to re-ignite their pent-up emotions all over again. And then what? A sadness came over her face but she said firmly,

'I'm fine here. I'm not going anywhere. It's madness to even think of leaving this place.'

'You might be fine, but I'm not – not with the idea of leaving you in a care home when you should be coming with me. I'm not even going to argue on that.'

Andre had already opened her wardrobe, pulled out a suitcase and started packing her belongings.

Bemused, Vivian said, 'What on earth are you doing? You think you can just walk in after all this time and I'll listen to what you say? Leave everything and come with you?'

All Andre said was a very definitive and authoritative, 'Yes.'

'What do you mean, yes?'

'I mean, you'll come with me, period.'

'I will not!' She tried raising her voice a little as she could see that none of her talking was having any effect on him whatsoever.

'Yes you will. You are coming with me, and I will take care of you and not some random caretakers in the hospice.'

'I. Will. Not – and the people here are lovely.'

He paid no attention and carried on packing.

'Andre, are you listening? I'm not leaving this place, I don't see why I should leave.'

This is when he came over to her bed, sat beside her, gently held her hand. His deep black eyes softened and she saw the authority in them replaced by timeless love.

'There is no woman in my life I have loved the way I have loved you. Every bit of my heart, every breath in my body, every inch of my soul belongs to you. The way you made me feel, nobody has ever done before or since, and I have had my share of women. Baby, the truth is that the love we had was pure, and the more painful truth is that it is still there in our hearts, buried, but alive.'

He stroked her hair and she felt the warmth of his hand on her cold cheeks.

'Don't say no. Don't, Vivi. Please say yes again, one more time for the love we had, for the love we have.'

She could not utter even a word and sat there as if someone had cast a spell. He kissed her cheek and went back to packing; he knew he had won the battle.

'Why the hell do I agree with you?'

'This, sweetheart, only you can tell me, and it would be a very long and interesting conversation.' He winked. 'Let me pack first and then, trust me, we'll come back to this.'

She blushed and sat there looking at him carefully folding every piece of clothing and putting it in a suitcase. All the sternness, the practical thinking were out the window, and she was like a love-struck fool again, agreeing to whatever he said.

Her thoughts were interrupted when Andre said, with a smile lurking at the corner of his mouth,

'There is just one problem.'

'Yes?'

'You'll have to file for divorce.'

She bent her head low, unable to look Andre in the face.

'Actually, Andre …'

'Actually what, my love?'

When she saw the traces of amusement flickering in his eyes, she knew instantly that he knew the truth. She threw a pillow at him, laughing. He came over and raised her chin with the tip of his finger and thumb, looked deep into her eyes and said,

'Liar. Why did you not tell me in London?'

She bit her lip. 'I wanted to put your spying resources to the test.'

He laughed, and hugged her close. 'Oh baby, you can stir such a bundle of emotions in me …'

'But seriously, Andre, this is so weird, me going to stay with you – it doesn't make sense.'

'Have we not settled this already? Besides, most of the things between us do not make sense. You want me to start a list? If it's weird, it's weird. It doesn't matter to me. I'm a weird guy, what can I say.'

Giggling, she said, 'Well, that I can agree to.' Caught somewhere between mirth and disbelief, she didn't quite know what to do besides trying to come up with more logical arguments.

'Andre, you have a girlfriend. She—'

'*Had* a girlfriend. We broke up.'

'Why, what happened?'

'Do you really want to know? Does it really matter? How about you keep quiet, chatterbox, and let me pack?' He leaned over and kissed her cheek. 'I'm not letting you go this time. Can't make the same mistake twice.'

'Why was it a mistake, Andre?'

'Because after all these years, I still love you and you still love me.'

She had imagined this a million times in her head, waited for him to say it for so long, but when Andre actually said it, it was like her last wish come true. Closing her eyes, she leaned back on the headboard, letting this moment fill her empty soul. His words felt like sweet music, slowly enclosing her in a symphony of love and undiluted joy. It was, she imagined, what you felt when you were at one with yourself, when there were no more wishes, because all that you had ever desired or wanted had come true. A feeling of deep contentment.

'You look adorable with that smile on your face and your eyes closed,' he said, and then whispered in an impish tone, 'You can't stop thinking about me, you can't help but imagine me kissing you, you can't help but think about my touch ...'

She almost opened her eyes.

'Dream on. You're not that great.'

'I know. I can't help it if you have bad taste in men.' He leaned even closer. 'You're looking at me the way you looked when we kissed for the first time.'

Her pale cheeks coloured with that statement. Her eyes went dewy and she whispered,

'What took you so long?'

The pure pain in her voice sent shudders down his spine. A poignant sweetness filled his heart at the realisation – she had actually waited for him, loved him all this time, for all these years, and he had never come back. As that thought started settling in his mind, he felt a deep fury with himself. Unknowingly, he had caused her so much pain and now he wanted to make up for all that lost time. He wanted to fill her soul with love, fill her heart with unimagined happiness and fill all her senses with tenderness, care and passion.

'I love you, Vivi. You are mine. I'm so sorry, baby.'

She lifted her head, which had been resting on his chest, and looked at him with a doe-like expression of pure adoration. His eyes, which had been looking straight into hers, dropped down to her lips. He pressed his lips softly on hers. The kiss was meant to be brief, but the touch of her lips on his was so intoxicating that it took him once more to a world far away from reality. Every passing second had an incremental effect on the intensity of the kiss, until he felt his body was on fire. He dug his nose into the cavity around her collarbone as her arms went round his shoulders, and her cold fingers awakened long-dormant sensations in him as they played between his shoulder blades. The tip of his tongue stroked around her ear, all the way to her neck and then back. All the years of longing were turned into ecstatic passion. He was kissing again with the same madness of years before.

Reluctantly dragging his mouth from hers, he whispered, 'It's been a while since I've felt this good after just kissing.' They both laughed, remembering the old sentence. 'I feel I'm twenty-two again,' he said, when he saw her smile.

They were away from the current situation, away from worries of Vivian's health, away from reality, in their very own world. They sat there, Vivian huddled in Andre's arms, living in the silence, breathing in the fragrance, feeling the warmth.

Eventually, though he hated to do it, he had to break the divine silence.

'We have to go. The flight is at eight. We'll have time to get dinner but, if I'm not mistaken, you'll want to meet with your parents as well.'

'You already booked a flight? You knew I would come?'

'Why are you surprised? I know you inside out - much better than you think.'

Her mind racing, she tried one last time: 'Andre, I cannot cause you more pain by going with you. My days are numbered. And us starting all over again will only be more painful when I go away.'

Her eyes looked so sad and worried for him that for a moment he forgot who was sick.

Gently rubbing her hands, he said, 'Vivi, I want to live before I die, and you are my life. Don't take that away from me – even if it is for a few years or months or even days, let me live my life. I have lost most of it and whatever little is left I want to spend with you. And we are not starting all over again, we never stopped!'

Moved by his obvious sincerity, she draped her arms around his neck and whispered after a while,

'Andre, I love you. There is no man I have loved the way I have loved you.'

They were the sweetest words he had ever heard. Stroking her hair and returning to his mischievous self, Andre said,

'You always were my crackpot; you know why? First you argue that you won't come with me, and now you won't let go of me.'

She jerked her arms away.

'You'll pay for this,' she said.

He whispered, 'Anything for you.'

'Before we go,' said Vivian, 'I need to do something – can you pass me a pen and paper?'

He took both from the bedside table and handed them to her. 'I'll go and have a word with your doctor. Write your letter, sweetheart.'

'What are you, psychic?'

'Baby, have you forgotten my hyper-acute sixth sense? Write your letter, my transparent love – don't just sit there looking lost. I'll go have a quick chat with the doctors.' With that, laughing, he left the room, and pulled the door closed behind him.

It all felt like such a sudden change, Vivian was having difficulty deciding whether it was a dream or reality. She pinched herself and laughed like a demented women, staring at her packed bag.

Then she penned a note to Sam.

Dearest Sam,

When you get this letter, I will be very far away but there are a few things I wanted to say before I leave. Things did not work out between us, but that does not change the fact that you are a very special person and a wonderful man. I wish all the happiness in the world for you. Now, on the final leg of the journey, I have to go, with Andre. I would like to spend my final days with him. I know your opinion was different but what I have with him is a love difficult to explain. It has been an unspoken wish and he is here, right now. This was not exactly planned, if that's what you're thinking; I never spoke to him about the disease and we have barely been in touch in all these years. I'm assuming Devyani must have told him.

Whatever time I have left, I want it to be peaceful and with him.

Gloria is a lovely girl, so sort things out with her. From what she told me, it seems you guys had something which looked like a foundation for a lifetime. Don't just let it pass by. I wish you both a wonderful future together.

Bye.

Take care,

Vivian

She folded the note and placed it on her bedside table.

Andre found the duty doctor's office just off reception. He knocked and entered, and was greeted by a young man with a stethoscope round his neck and an air of brisk efficiency. Andre explained the situation and the doctor nodded his approval – care at home, he said, was always the first choice. He gave Andre every detail of how to take care of Vivian, her medicines, her routine, the name of her doctor and most importantly the signs to watch out for.

Armed with files, notes and contact numbers, Andre returned to Vivian's room.

'Ready, my love?'

She nodded, beaming. On the way out, she handed the note to the caretaker to be posted, scribbling Sam's address on a sticky note.

There was one final, all-important thing she had to do. She had to see her parents. Knowing how hard it would be for them, she wanted to reassure

298

them, tell them about Andre – tell them, above all, how much she loved them.

Andre lifted her in his arms and took her to the car.

'What are you doing?'

'I thought it was pretty self-explanatory.'

'I can walk.'

'I know.'

When they arrived at her parents' house, Andre offered his arm but let her walk to the door.

Her parents were in total shock and disbelief when they saw her. Maria's reaction was of complete bewilderment and the tears were already flowing – she could see her daughter was unwell and sensed that it must be serious.

'What happened, Vivian? Why didn't you tell us? What's going on? We spoke so many times, you told me you were busy …' She took Vivian by the hand and led her inside, pausing only to acknowledge Andre with a weak and troubled smile.

Vivian's father rose from his chair with some effort and hugged her, then stepped back and looked at her, his mouth half-open as though to speak. But he said nothing.

She told them the truth about the disease and the way it took its own sweet time, slowly rendering both body and mind dysfunctional.

'I did not want to trouble you guys and cause you pain. I know how difficult it will be for the two of you.'

'Viv ... Trouble? How could you have troubled us?' Her mother breathed the words, covering her face with her hands.

Vivian did not know how to console them. They were the two most important people in her life besides Andre, and both of them looked defeated, suddenly old and helpless.

Andre stood patiently behind Vivian, a mute spectator. She turned her head and looked at him, as though trying to draw strength. His deep eyes were filled with empathy, and he silently rubbed her shoulders and smiled. And strangely, she felt as if she has been infused with new energy.

'Ma, Dad, this is Andre. We ... knew each other in college?'

Maria nodded, tried to smile. 'Of course. Yes I do remember. Nice to see you, Andre. But how—'

'Andre is going to look after me. At his home, in Italy.'

Both parents could barely conceal their surprise. Maria knew of Vivian's affection for Andre but that it would last a lifetime was clearly implausible to her.

After a few seconds of silence, her father, looking intently at Andre, said,

'I'm not sure if I got that.'

'You heard it right, sir. I know it is difficult to understand but it is true. I have to take care of her for whatever time is left, she cannot be left alone. Please understand. Your daughter is precious to me ... I ... well, I love her and I always have.'

All they could do was nod – the situation was beyond their comprehension. Her illness, travelling to Italy with him – it was too much to absorb.

Holding her mother's hand, Vivian said softly, 'I love you both so much, you mean the world to me. But please don't be upset. I have had a very fulfilling life, I have been able to help a lot of people and that is down to your love and inspiration – thank you for making me capable of doing that. I'm very happy and content. And now I'm going with the sweetest man in the whole world, who has loved me to bits for a lifetime. Does anyone deserve to be so lucky?'

For a brief moment, Maria felt genuinely happy for her daughter and the sorrow in her moist sea green eyes faded a little.

Reluctantly, Andre pointed out the time, anxious to get to the airport, but he consoled them by saying that he would make arrangements for them to come to Italy. This took his audience by surprise, and both parents thanked him profusely for the gesture.

Vivian hugged her parents, trying to hold back the tears, and bid them goodbye.

She said again, 'Don't worry about me. I'm the happiest I have ever been, trust me. You two take care, I'm going to miss you so much.'

Maria noticed something in her smile which, despite the disease and all the difficulties that lay ahead, made her look genuinely happy and content as never before.

Maria and Carlos stood at the door and watched as Andre carefully settled Vivian into the passenger seat of the car, and they knew that Vivian was correct – he was the right man to make her happy, though the timing was difficult.

Chapter Thirty-eight

The flight was short and sweet. Andre was very attentive; he had thought through every step of their journey and Vivian could not help but be in awe of his planning – and the sheer fact that she was with him. As they landed at Marco Polo airport, a warm breeze and the distinct smell of the sea welcomed them. Holding tight onto Andre's arm, Vivian felt excited and delighted, as if starting a new life.

A shiny black Rolls Royce was ready at the airport to pick them up. The soft full-grain leather seats had the smell of opulence. Andre helped Vivian into her seat and the first thing she did was call her parents and tell them she had arrived and all was well. After assuring them there would be regular updates, she rested her head on Andre's shoulder, closed her eyes and instantly fell asleep, more tired than she had anticipated.

As he looked at her, a slight fear of the unknown made him ask gently,

'Vivi, are you okay, darling?'

'Yes, I am, just want to cuddle up.' She tried to say it as normally as she could, without showing any signs of fatigue, but her body language gave the lie to her words.

'Rest, baby, rest. I'll wake you up once we're home.'

Holding on to her, he had an overwhelming impulse to pray that she'd enjoy a long and happy life, and that all her troubles and pain should be his. He was surprised at himself. Never in his life had he had any sort of faith or inclination towards the Almighty. To him, life was what you made of it. He always said, you get what you put in – praying was a waste of time; you might as well put that time into work and make something out of it. And yet today in the car, as he felt Vivian's warm breath on his neck and cheek, he wanted to pray, pray to ease her pain. She had always managed to invoke the strongest and the strangest reactions in him and the cycle continued.

They reached home in the late afternoon and Andre's housekeeper Bella came out to greet them, all smiles and outstretched arms. Smiling back, Vivian peeked curiously from her window and saw a great stone pillar outlined against a pair of steel-studded doors.

Andre carried Vivian in his arms straight to her room, and she was acutely aware of the stares of the various members of staff who lined up to greet them. Her room was painted plain white with matching tiles on the floor, emanating peace and serenity. Andre laid her carefully on the bed, removing her shoes and socks and arranging the pillows.

'You don't need to do that, I'll manage,' she said, but he was grinning.

'I know I don't need to, but I like to,' he replied. 'Coffee?'

'Mmm, please.'

He called for Bella and asked her for coffee.

'How would you like your coffee, signorina?' asked Bella, as sweetly as anyone possibly could. Dressed in a cotton dress about two inches below the knee, and with a rounded, caring face, she looked more like a nanny than a housekeeper.

Andre answered for Vivian. 'White and half a sugar please. Does that still hold true, signorina?'

'It does.' She smiled, unaccountably happy that he should remember such details about her.

'Can you also get some chocolate cake with that, Bella? Something with chocolate cream, please?'

'Sure, signore.'

'I'm assuming that still holds true as well?'

'Yes it does! I can't believe you remembered such little things.' Her smile reached all the way up to her eyes. The touch of Andre's warm hand on her cheek was creating an exciting feeling of intimacy.

Andre came close and whispered, 'Can't help it, the devil you were. You were impossible to forget.'

They shared the kind of laughter that had been missing all these years.

So many times he had imagined this situation, when he would bring Vivian home and ask her a simple question like whether she would like coffee, and today, as she sat beside him, there was an inexplicable feeling much greater than happiness. It was contentment.

She put her arms around his neck and whispered, 'Thank you.'

'Pleasure,' he said, and bent down to smell her neck. He took a deep breath and said, 'Your scent is still irresistible. It drove me nuts then and it drives me nuts now.'

He looked deep into her eyes, and his lips glided onto hers, bridging the gap of time. He slid his hands under her t-shirt, forgetting where they were, only stepping back from the gates of this heaven when he heard footsteps. He stood up, straightened himself, and walked to the fireplace. He was amazed at his own audacity – that he should kiss her with such passion, and the strongest desire to continue, while the door was fully open and the servants were spread around the house.

Bella came in with coffee and chocolate cream biscuits, along with some savoury snacks, and left after neatly arranging everything on the table. There was a very strong temptation to complete the unfinished kiss, but the fear of exhausting her after the journey was much more powerful than the desire for her lips.

Over coffee, they whispered about old times to each other, feeling the closeness, a hidden desire for them all these years. Bella came in again to announce dinner, and they realised they had been chatting for three hours.

'We sure can talk,' she said.

'There is a reason I call you chatterbox.' He winked at her and she scrunched her nose. He picked her up to carry her to the dining room.

'You don't intend on carrying me all the time, do you?'

'Yes I do, I'm making up for all the weight training I didn't do in my youth.'

He placed her on a Victorian dining chair with polished armrests and a wide, upholstered seat, then sat right next to her, making sure she was within arm's reach. The dining room was oval and spacious, with paintings distributed around the walls; a Persian carpet graced the shiny mahogany floor. The table, which could have seated twenty, was polished to a high gloss, reflecting the candle light coming from a pair of silver candelabras.

The candles flickered as they ate their food; Vivian felt very tiny in this huge room. The dinner was traditional Italian, minestrone soup followed by ravioli. Knowing Vivian had a sweet tooth, Andre had arranged chocolate tiramisu to finish the meal. Fresh fruit juice was carefully substituted for wine, as Andre thought it would be better for her.

As dinner finished, Vivian was showing signs of fatigue and Andre knew it was time to wrap her up in bed. He picked her up and took her to the bedroom, tucking her under the white duvet. As he was about to leave after kissing her goodnight she said,

'Stay with me. Don't go.'

Looking at her, he could tell she badly needed rest.

He said, 'I'll sit right here next to you on one condition – that you close your eyes.'

She smiled and closed her eyes, and it was not long before she dozed off. He sat there stroking her hair and noticed how pale she had become. When he heard a quiet snoring, he left her sleeping and went quietly out of the room with an aching heart.

The next morning was bright and sunny and, as Vivian awoke, she found a note next to the bed which read, *'Press the buzzer when you wake up or whenever u need.'* Looking at his straight, crisp handwriting, the memories of all those cards he had written came back to her.

There was a small red button next to the note; she pressed it and, almost immediately, Bella appeared at the door.

'Good morning, signorina, how are we doing today?' she asked, opening the curtains to let the sunlight in.

'Great,' Vivian replied, still lying down.

Bella fixed back the curtains with ties and opened the window to let in the fresh air.

'Coffee?' she said.

'Thank you, Bella.'

Vivian was listening to the chatter of birds in a tree right outside the window when her attention was taken by the sound of brisk approaching footsteps. Andre came in, dressed in navy blue shorts and black t-shirt. The morning was getting better and better. Andre came and sat on the edge of the bed, making little circles on her palm with his finger while they talked.

After breakfast of toast and coffee, Vivian managed, with a little help, to carry out the basics, and then Andre took her outside into the garden for some fresh air. The garden was blooming with calla lilies and dahlias. But what caught her attention was the willow tree. She looked at the tree, then at Andre, remembering the words he had written for her.

'Think of the willow tree, under which I can read poetry and when you are bored of me reading, put my lips to better use ... Love you, baby! ;)

He said, 'Want to listen to some poetry?'

They lay together under the willow tree and he read her a poem about the immutable nature of love. Then he came closer and he saw in her big brown eyes another kind of bloom – the bloom of a steadfast and perfect love. Her hand gently stroked his cheek, and he kissed her as they lay under the willow, living each and every moment. She felt alive, as if new energy had been infused into her. His hands on her body, his lips on hers – it was the same feeling, the feeling of being loved beyond this world, of being able to live and breathe every moment, of being lost, the last two souls on Earth, wrapped around each other for eternity. Both of them wanted to go further, but Andre pulled back for fear of putting too much stress on her weakened body. He was conscious, too, of the eyes of others.

She pulled him towards her and whispered, 'Since when have you started thinking so much – or am I losing the magic of driving you nuts?' She nipped his ear and then looked at him with eyes that wanted more. She could not believe herself. With Sam, she'd only participated – sometimes even avoided – and here she was, actually initiating, asking him to make love to her.

Annoyed with himself, Andre picked her up and took her to the bedroom.

'Don't make it any harder for me, Vivi, it's already killing me. Don't torment me further.'

She slid her hands around his waist and said, 'I love tormenting you, it makes me feel special.'

'What a sadist you are!'

'I just want the whole of you, and now – without any worries.'

The look in her eyes, combined with the words she spoke, caused desire to run through him again. Coming close, he slid his hands around the nape of her neck, kissing her with the same, unforgotten passion. Losing the sense of boundaries was not difficult with Vivian; his fingers slipped under her shirt, slowly unbuttoning it and, as more of her body was exposed, he followed his fingers with his lips. Hunger and craving started to build and Andre had to command himself to slow down. As he kissed her stomach, then her breasts, he heard the familiar moans and even in the midst of extreme passion his face softened with a smile. It was something he had so desperately missed.

Making love to Vivian was miles away from any of his other sexual encounters. Her shivers, her moans, every reaction was exquisite to him; sex with her was not merely sex, it was something ethereal, two souls wrapped in love physically as well as spiritually, the delicious culmination of a twelve-year wait.

Years of yearning were put to rest as they lay wrapped in each other's arms.

'Oh Vivi, baby, are you okay?'

'Never better.' She was smiling, and her fatigue was the fatigue of bliss. Wrapped in Andre's arms, as he lay, stroking her hair, she fell asleep. He could not help but see how, in sleep, her long eyelashes served to disguise her sunken eyes.

Dressing, he went to his study and sat with his eyes closed, as if in silent prayer. Flashes of the priest outside the Nani temple in Nainital came to his mind. The words of the priest – *'When you find true love, you will start believing in the Almighty'* – crossed his mind, and it was as if the words glittered in golden magnificence and shone brightly against a black sky. He wondered for the first time whether the words were actually true, and little by little, a belief started to take shape, a belief that there was somebody greater than the forces of nature, beyond human imagination, far beyond the ken of science. Suddenly, he understood what the priest had been trying to tell him: that true love was the closest one could get to God.

Andre tried fitting as much work as he possibly could into the hours Vivian needed to rest. Having been the businessman who worked tirelessly day and night, he was turning into a man whose work was instead just a part of his life, not his whole life. His working hours significantly reduced. He knew that operations at the glass factory suffered when he wasn't there, but for the first time in his life it did not matter. Everything had become secondary next to Vivian; her being there had given a new meaning to his life.

On an idyllic, chilly morning under a cloudless sky, as they were having their customary coffee, Vivian stared at the beautiful princess-cut ring which he had slid onto her finger, and said,

'I would like to see Saint Mark's Basilica.'

'Why is that? Why would you want to stress yourself?' he replied, absently, scanning the pages of a new buyer's contract.

'I'll manage it. I never did get to Venice, because I knew you were here.'

He knew that line was to get his attention, and it was successful, as he stopped what he was doing and looked up.

She continued, 'I couldn't persuade my weak heart to see you again, to feel the pain again. Sam would have sensed it in seconds. Of course, chances of seeing you in a big city were slim, but just the thought of you was entwined with Venice for me.'

A smile playing on his lips from the emotional blackmail being directed at him, he said,

'Vivi, you are such a devil. You know how to get your way.' He squeezed her hand and said, 'I'll see what I can do. Let's plan on next Sunday.'

'That Sunday has to be today, actually. Now, if possible?'

'Now?'

'Yes.'

Before he could argue further, she threw her arms around his neck and hugged him close, whispering,

'Please.'

This one simple gesture took away all rational thinking and put a smile on his face.

'Do I have a choice?'

Putting her face in front of his, she whispered, 'Not really. Unless you want one.'

He did not want a choice. There was an impeccable pleasure in pampering and pleasing this headstrong, impatient girl. Andre asked Bella to pack whatever was necessary for Vivian.

When they alighted from the boat at Piazza San Marco, Vivian was in awe of the symmetry and grandeur of its architecture, and when she saw the basilica itself she knew she had been right to insist on coming.

Easily jumping the queue because of Vivian's condition, they entered the church – the epitome of beauty and sacredness. The golden mosaics gleamed with reflected light as they entered the building. Admiring the sheer magnificence of the structure and its splendid interiors, Vivian was lost in the beauty. Andre, on the other hand, just wanted to make sure that she was safe. They stayed to listen to the service that was in progress, and Andre's hand was constantly in the small of Vivian's back, helping to hold her upright. Afterwards, she insisted on dining in a traditional Venetian restaurant by the canal.

They sat huddled together on a couch-like seat on the balcony of a cosy restaurant overlooking the canal, surrounded by baskets of red flowers. The waiters played "Love is All Around" for them at Andre's request.

When they emerged she said, 'It was a magical time, in Nainital. And now the magic is repeating itself all over again.'

'It was. It is! Because we are together.' He held her close and placed a kiss on her head as it rested comfortably on his chest. The sun was almost setting and the city was slowly beginning to take on an enchanting glitter. They sat by the canal, looking over the water and watching the world go by, living and breathing the moment.

He carried her to the boat, her head almost dropping from the exhaustion of the day.

'I told you it would be too tiring, baby, if only you would listen.' He hurried down the steps, all too aware of her exhausted state.

'It's okay. I enjoyed every moment, it was totally worth the pain,' she said, and closed her eyes.

He almost ran the last few metres to the boat. His heart was heavy with regret as he sat down, cradling her in his arms. His emotions were in turmoil at the sight of her lying weak and feeble on his lap. A man like him, with nerves of steel and the capacity to disguise every emotion, should be strong at such a time, but at that moment he was helpless to control the stream of tears that ran freely down his cheeks.

As the warmth of his tears touched her cheeks, she opened her eyes and tried lifting her frail hand to wipe them for him. Gently bending his face towards her, he held her palm and pressed it to his cheek, sobbing silently. Stroking his hair, she hugged him close and whispered,

'Looks like it's role reversal for a change.' Caught between mirth and emotion, a smile touched his lips as she looked at him so tenderly, and he felt in that instant that he was falling in love with her all over again.

'I'm glad we came by boat, it brings back old memories. Boats have always been good to us.' She smiled as the wind tugged at her hair and sent tangled strands across her face.

The boat glided though the gleaming city of Venice, passing under one marvellous bridge after another. They passed a tiny restaurant lit up with fairy lights and candles and filled with couples who sat listening to the music, giving themselves up to the magic and mystery of the city.

As her eyes started to swim with tears, Vivian whispered, 'I want to live longer with you.'

The pain in their hearts was reflected in the urgency of their embrace as the cool, gentle breeze caressed them.

'I wish, Vivi. I wish. There will come a time, a time for us. If not in this life, then in some other. But it will come – I promise you that, Vivi. You are mine now and forever.'

She closed her eyes, full of hope, despite her wretched situation, and when they disembarked at the house Andre took her upstairs and they slept in each other's arms.

Chapter Thirty-nine

Slowly, winter overtook autumn; the trees outside Vivian's window gave up their leaves and the wind carried an unwelcome chill. With every passing day, Vivian's condition worsened and Andre's heart became heavier with sorrow and dread. She still greeted him with a smile every morning, a smile that made his day. They would have their meals together no matter what – Andre would cancel meetings to be home on time – but they were mainly restricted to the bedroom now. Every Sunday he would take her to church, an activity new to him but important to Vivian. And the more time he spent with her, the stronger was his faith in the Almighty. He would pray with all his heart to ease her pain.

Her parents were with her now; Andre, as promised, had called them last month, when Vivian had indicated. Her time, when Andre was in the office, was spent with Maria and Carlos. To be able to spend time with all her loved ones gave her considerable happiness even now, when her health was constantly deteriorating.

One frosty morning, after their usual breakfast, Andre was leaving the room to go back to his work when she stopped him.

'Andre, can you lie down with me today?'

'Sure, why not.' He quietly came and lay down next to her.

'Hold me close, really close, the way you did when we were in college.'

'Okay, darling.'

As he did what she asked, he began to feel signals of panic.

She spoke with considerable difficulty. 'If you hadn't been here already, I would have given you a call. You know why?'

'No. Tell me.'

'Because my deepest wish – my last wish – is to be in your arms when my soul is set free.'

She wanted only to fill him with her love, to drain away all sadness from his heart.

Placing her hand against his cheek, she said, 'Andre, every moment, every breath, every passing day has brought me to the realisation that you are my life. My love for you has been steady and strong, embedded in my heart, and it will continue to be there no matter where I am.'

He kissed her lips with infinite tenderness, and she closed her eyes. Her final wish was fulfilled – she was resting in the arms of the only man she had ever truly loved.

He lay there holding her, frozen, and then he whispered, 'I know, my Vivi. You will always be there with me. I will see you someday – someday soon. I love you. I will love you forever.'